Highland Storytellers

Teresa MacIsaac

◆ FriesenPress

Suite 300 - 990 Fort St

Victoria, BC, Canada, V8V 3K2

www.friesenpress.com

Copyright © 2015 by Teresa MacIsaac

First Edition — 2015

All rights reserved.

No part of this publication may be reproduced in any form, or by any means, electronic or mechanical, including photocopying, recording, or any information browsing, storage, or retrieval system, without permission in writing from the publisher.

ISBN

978-1-4602-6856-8 (Hardcover)

978-1-4602-6857-5 (Paperback)

978-1-4602-6858-2 (eBook)

1. Fiction, Cultural Heritage

Distributed to the trade by The Ingram Book Company

Dedicated

to

The descendants of the Highland Scots

Acknowledgments

I would like to thank Frances Hurley for her careful review and edit of the manuscript.

I would like to thank Scot and Maureen Williams for help with the wording and the choice of music.

Preface

At the end of each summer day, I look forward to spending some quiet time alone, strolling along the Arisaig shore which borders my home. As I watch the sun go down like a ball of fire over the ocean on this beautiful evening, my thoughts turn to my forebears who travelled these waters en route to a better life in the New World. I smile as I think of my grandmother Mairi, with whom I had walked hand in hand as a child and who introduced me to the beauty and solitude of this landscape. I shall treasure the influence of this remarkable woman for the rest of my life.

My grandmother made it her mission to keep our family history alive and she led me to believe that I was next in line to assume this mantle.

I remember how she would look at me, and with reverence for the past resonating in her voice, say, "Mary, it is so important to remember."

Grandma's powerful memory enabled her to recall events in the life of our family over a span of five generations. She had the advantage of living on both sides of the Atlantic Ocean. Sometimes her stories took us back to her homeland, where she lived the early part of her life in Arisaig on the western coast of the Highlands of Scotland. Sometimes her stories explored the struggles of the settlers and their children to forge a better life here in Nova Scotia. Her stories taught us lessons about the values and aspirations that define the character of our people.

My fascination with the past, no doubt, was forged by my grandmother's storytelling. Storytelling was in her blood. Her soulful narration of the triumphs and tribulations of our kinfolk turned her stories into vivid and compelling dramas, which all members of our family looked forward to hearing. Grandma's dramatic ability to portray the power of the human spirit in the face of adversity made her a hard act to follow. My very special attachment to this gifted woman made me vow to honour her by carrying on this tradition, with one difference. I knew there was no way I could ever be the storyteller she was; so I decided to tell the story of our family, and the larger events in the Highlands and here in Nova Scotia of which it is a part, in writing. My story will span the life of my grandmother.

Grandma traced the events that influenced our family as far back as the 1745 Rebellion, in which the Highlanders rose up with Charlie, the Bonnie Prince, to restore the Stuarts to the throne in Britain. The bard, from whom her kinfolk had learned the history of their forebears, became a legend in his own time. His spellbinding stories so captured the minds and imaginations of his listeners that they gave him the nickname Ossian in honour of the great Celtic bard. Grandma's parents and grandparents grew up listening to him tell tales of the barbaric treatment of the Highlanders after their defeat in the Battle of Culloden in 1746. His tales illustrated how this one-hour battle sealed the fate of the Highland Scots.

Through his oratory and his dramatic ability, he made sure that these tales were burned into the minds of his listeners. The people hung on to his every word. They shuddered at his dark stories of the brutality, murder, rape, theft, and pillage their forebears suffered at the hands of the English soldiers, whom the Scots called redcoats, after the Battle of Culloden.

They cheered when he thundered, "The redcoats called us savages, but they were the real savages."

They listened intently to his stories of the humiliation Highlanders suffered as a result of attacks on their traditional way of life by governing bodies in London and Edinburgh.

"How dare those intruders deny us our bagpipes? How dare they outlaw our kilt? How dare they forbid us to practise our faith?" he was known to ask, in a tone of righteous indignation.

"And worst of all," he would say in a low, slow voice, "for years they have been trying to wipe out our beautiful Gaelic language."

Then in a plaintive tone he would ask, "And what is more natural than to speak in your own tongue? And what is more humiliating than not being allowed to do so?"

After that he would switch to a slow assertive tone to make his closing point, "After those outsiders had outlawed our language, our religion, our music and our kilt, I ask you, what is left of our traditional way of life? No wonder you and I feel like strangers in our own land."

Grandma's parents and grandparents were so moved by such tales that they memorized them word for word, and they repeated them over and over again, in the very voice and pitch and cadence in which they were narrated. Sometimes they repeated these stories in Gaelic, sometimes in English. They figured that in the future it would be important for Highland Scots to be fluent in both tongues.

As a young child, fairy tales did not preoccupy Grandma's mind and imagination so much as gruesome stories of the events that alienated the Highlanders from their homeland. No wonder she was such a serious little girl. Her father lovingly spoke of her as "an old soul." When she grew up, she followed in her parents' footsteps by dramatically telling and retelling these tales, to which she added stories of how these events led her family to decide to leave their homeland, their preparation for their voyage, their departure, their trip across the Atlantic, and their settlement in Nova Scotia—all told with the drama and emotion surrounding these events.

1

Life was never the same for the Highland Scots who fought for the Bonnie Prince in the Battle of Culloden in 1746 and were routed by the redcoats. They paid dearly for supporting his cause. The English were vindictive. As far as they were concerned, it was not enough to defeat the Highlanders; they had to humiliate them. Redcoats marched on the homes of Highland soldiers who were able to flee the field of battle and laughed as they set them on fire, often with the screaming survivors locked inside. Hearing the screams, women and children rushed back from the fields to see what was happening to their men. They too were subjected to horrific attacks. Ruthless redcoats enjoyed hearing their sobs and their pleas for mercy as they roughed them up. Some of the redcoats were so out of control that they raped these women outside the doors of their burning homes and then put their children to the sword. And, as if they had not inflicted enough damage, they then destroyed their crops and marched away with their cattle. And it was these men who called the Highlanders savages!

For years after the violence had subsided, threats to the traditional Highland way of life remained. Even though Grandma's parents, Lewis Lody and Margaret MacDonald, were born decades after the Battle of Culloden, they were concerned about the lingering effects of being on the side of the vanquished rather than the victor. They loved the Highlands; the beauty of its mountains, glens, and seas was a constant source of delight and inspiration. But, at the same time, they were keenly aware of the forces that had turned their homeland into an increasingly hostile environment.

Lewis, with a tinge of anxiety in his voice, repeatedly said, "The bard had it right; I am beginning to feel like a stranger in my own land."

The thought of having to leave his homeland was a nagging worry that preoccupied his mind.

At this stage in her life, Grandma was known affectionately as Mairi Bheag, Little Mairi, and she was only eight years old. She was a very bright little girl, and in spite of her young age, there wasn't too much that escaped her. She listened intently to every word her parents had to say about the possibility of leaving. This conversation heated up every time one of their neighbours or friends decided to emigrate.

As she lay awake in the dark one night, she heard her father whisper to her mother, "Margaret, I'm scared. I would never let on to anyone but you. A man is not supposed to admit he is afraid. To tell the truth, I'm scared to death. Just think, seventy-five years have gone by since the '45 Uprising, and after all that time, life has not returned to normal. I don't think it ever will. Right to the bottom of my soul, I fear we are going to have to get out of here."

To this Margaret replied emphatically, "Lewis, I do not want to go."

Mairi Bheag shuddered at the thought of leaving and all the uncertainty that went with it. Fortunately, her parents usually talked themselves out of this idea, and this was a great relief to her. They were reluctant to take the plunge because they harboured lingering doubts about life in the New World. Stories they had heard about the biting cold, blinding snow storms, deep dark forests, and dangerous wild animals frightened them. They questioned their ability to survive in that harsh environment.

One evening, Mairi Bheag overheard her mother sum up their dilemma in these words, "You know, Lewis, I'm between and betwixt; I don't want to leave, but I'm afraid to stay."

Stories of her parents' fears of the New World played on Mairi Bheag's mind. Her wild imagination spurred horrible nightmares in which she found herself hopelessly lost in a snow storm in a dense dark forest. In response to her screams, her parents would rush from their bed to comfort her. They took turns holding her close and rocking her until she fell back to sleep. The next day they would try to ease her mind by telling her about the good things there were in the New World.

Because religion was so central to their lives, Lewis and Margaret were particularly vexed with the lingering restrictions placed on the practise of their Roman Catholic faith by the dreaded Penal Laws.

"I can't believe that freedom to go to mass is too much to ask," Margaret often exclaimed.

Renewed religious persecution following the defeat of the Highland Scots in the Battle of Culloden resulted from aggressive enforcement of the Penal Laws. In 1746, Lewis and Margaret's grandparents watched in horror and disbelief as the militia set fire to their little church and burn it to the ground. Their parish priest, Father Hugh MacPherson, disappeared, and they never saw him again. The neighbours speculated that he was either deported to the American colonies or imprisoned in Edinburgh. They later learned that he had been hanged.

Even though the people of Arisaig were now at least a couple of generations removed from the Uprising, they were still not allowed to have a parish church or a parish priest. They kept an eye for a tall, thin, dishevelled stranger who appeared occasionally in their community, because they knew that a priest would come disguised as a beggar. When this stranger appeared, they would look at each other and nod their heads to signify that the time for mass had come. Word quickly passed around the community about where and when the priest was to say mass. So under the cover of darkness, Lewis and Margaret would take Mairi Bheag by the hand and with great apprehension make their way to a neighbour's house, designated as a mass house, to attend a celebration of their beloved mass. There their hearts and spirits were uplifted as they joined the priest in worshipping their creator and redeemer. Their continuing sense of outrage at the necessity of holding these services in secret intensified their desire to be free to practise their faith.

On one of these occasions, Lewis turned to Margaret and said, "You know, if we went to Nova Scotia we wouldn't have to skulk around like common criminals in order to get to mass. It is a sad situation when we have to break the law so we can practise our faith."

Her only response was an affirming "Aye."

It did not take long for events to turn the fear that was never far from the minds of Lewis and Margaret into a force compelling them to decide to leave their homeland. Since the laird of the Clanranald MacDonalds had sold Arisaig in 1813, Arisaig had changed hands a number of times, and with each new owner its tenants became more anxious. The people of Arisaig knew that communities to the east of them, Strathglass and Glengarry, had been cleared, and they lived with the nagging fear that they would suffer the same fate. They looked at one another with alarm with each new story they heard about what was happening to the land north of Arisaig. Friends who had travelled to and from Sutherlandshire came back with horror stories about more and more Highlanders being forced off their land to make room for sheep. Lewis and Margaret had been aware of the Sutherland clearances for some time, but now rumours of the extreme violence that accompanied the later clearances were terrifying.

With a glum look on his face, Lewis said to Margaret, "See, things just keep getting worse."

These rumours were confirmed by a childhood friend of Lewis, Duncan Chisholm, who travelled from Sutherlandshire to Arisaig to bid Lewis farewell before leaving for the New World. The grey pallor of Duncan's skin, his furrowed brow, and his watery eyes betrayed his anxiety. Mairi Bheag overheard the frightening conversation between him and her father, who was so preoccupied with Duncan's story that he did not notice that she was lying on her bed listening to them. Even though she was only eight years old, she understood every word they said and she too was terrified by what she heard.

Duncan had the misfortune to be a victim of the clearances not once but twice. Even though he was still in his teens in 1811, he vividly remembered how the proprietor, with a writ of removal in his hand, and his henchmen cleared Strathglass. Most of the Chisholms who were uprooted from the land took a ship from Fort William to Pictou, Nova Scotia and then made their way to Antigonish. However, Duncan's father decided that the family should try their luck in Sutherland, hoping that the large size of the shire and its rocky land would provide some protection against the aspirations of the greedy landlords. There they were safe, but only for a while. The Chisholm family escaped a number of clearances that took place in Sutherland after they arrived because these removals happened to exclude the land on which they lived. However, their luck ran out in 1819, when the proprietor and his henchmen came back to finish the job.

Lewis listened with rapt attention as Duncan told of how these men came to his home in Sutherlandshire to start the final and most violent chapter in their strategy to empty the straths and glens.

"With a menacing look, the sheriff ordered me and my wife, Katie, to get out," Duncan recalled. "'Take what you can carry and go,' he said. He gave us only one-half hour to do so. Then in a stern voice that made clear he meant what he said, he bellowed, 'These are my orders.'"

Lewis interjected, "Oh my God, Duncan, I am so sorry."

With terrible outrage in his voice, Duncan continued, "Lewis, you haven't heard the worst of it. My poor Katie—you should have seen her tremble with fear—she gathered the few household utensils she could carry; I gathered some clothes, and let me tell you, the two of us got out of our cottage as fast as we could. Katie sobbed as she watched the constables—the fellas who did the dirty work for the sheriff—unroof our little home, put the torch to it and burn it to the ground, just as if it was a pile of rubbish. Those miserable creatures got their courage from the bottle. When they downed a few drinks, they got bold and reckless. They had the upper hand and they knew it. With menacing looks, they threatened to beat us if we did not do exactly as we were told. You'd think they were driving cattle. 'You can move faster,' one of those drunken hooligans bellowed at Katie, as he pushed her so hard with his stick that she fell to the ground. Her friend Sarah saw what was happening and raced to try to help her. Another constable, a big burly son-of-a-bitch, then knocked Sarah to the ground and kicked her so hard with his hob-nailed boots that she writhed in pain. Can you imagine anything so cruel? When I tried to help, another constable came forward and glared at me as he held the bayonet on the end of his musket to my chest. Then he laughed. I tell you, I wanted to beat the hell out of him, but there wasn't a damn thing I could do. Those thugs obviously enjoyed humiliating and brutalizing us. They were drunk, drunk with power. Ah laddie, when the day comes when loyal and true Highlanders are considered to be of less value to their homeland than sheep, it's time to get out. 'Improvement.' That's what the landlords call it," Duncan said with disdain.

The grief that came over Duncan caused him to pause.

Lewis said softly, "Duncan, I never imagined it could be that bad."

Then Duncan burst into tears and as he sobbed he muttered, "I know men are not supposed to cry, but I just cannot help it."

Moved by Duncan's grief, Lewis put his arm around his shoulder. When Duncan was able to pull himself together, he resumed his story.

"It was even worse than you imagine," he said. "After our cottage was torched, the burners had a few more drinks and then they went at all the other homes in our beautiful little glen. The scorching heat and, oh God, the smoke everywhere, so thick it darkened the sky. It was choking us. The noise and the confusion were almost unbearable. All we could hear was the sound of barking dogs, bawling cattle, and wailing women and children that filled the glen. Animals and people were running around terrified. I wanted to scream. In the midst of all this consternation, the constables continued to curse at those who did not do what they were told fast enough.

Then the constables ordered us out of our community. After we moved to the surrounding hills with our few belongings, we were so numb with grief that we just sat passively and watched as hundreds of our beautiful little homes continued to burn. Our land, our only means of making a living, and that on which our kinfolk had lived for centuries, was taken from us. What were we to do? What could we do? We felt hopeless and helpless.

Day and night the destruction continued, until there was nothing left but a pile of smoldering rubble. Ah, ha, it wasn't long before we saw the Cheviot sheep being driven up the cattle paths into our glen."

Then, in a broken voice, Duncan concluded, "For as far as I could see, the good people of Sutherlandshire were pushed out and burned out to make sure there was nothing for them to come back to. I tell you, it is a sad day when crimes against the Highland people are committed in the name of the law."

These memories were too much for Duncan and at this point he again broke down and sobbed uncontrollably. Lewis was deeply moved by the emotional state of his good friend, and for a moment, he remained silent to compose himself for fear that he too would cry.

Then he put his hand on Duncan's shoulder as he said, "Ah laddie, what can I say? This news breaks my heart."

After a few moments, Duncan was able to resume his story with a renewed sense of outrage. "Now that I think about it, I can never forgive them, the landlords, those heartless bastards who were our former chiefs. They were quick to forget that we were their loyal servants in time of peace and in time of war. We broke our backs in their fields and we risked our lives in their battles. So what thanks did we get? They turned on us. It just boils my blood to think that they got so greedy that they replaced their loyal clansmen with sheep. Ah yes, their high living in Edinburgh required more and more money. And we paid the price.

"Many of the enforcers who served as their constables were nothing more than riffraff whom the sheriff picked up along the road. For a measly bottle they did the dirty work for the sheriff. That is all the encouragement it took to get them to attack us and destroy our homes—all in the name of the law. As far as I'm concerned, the law is a joke. I'll tell you how far their cruelty went. Would you believe what one of those drunken wild-eyed bastards did? He looked me in the eye and laughed as he threw our beautiful golden collie dog into the fire."

At this point the story was almost too much for Mairi Bheag's young ears. Visions of that helpless animal burning kept flashing before her. She was so upset that she had a hard time hiding it.

She later recalled, "It took all the will power I could muster to keep quiet, for I didn't want Father to know I was listening."

Mairi Bheag managed to regain sufficient composure to listen intently as Duncan finished his story. "A few days after being put out of our homes, the constables ordered us away from our beautiful fertile glen to a piece of barren, rocky land on the shore. Sticks and clubs were used on those who had the spunk to resist. With fury, the wild-eyed constables went after those who tried to escape. They beat the poor souls with clubs and sticks and then left them on the ground. I saw them there—I did—writhing in pain, and with their arms, their knees, or their legs broken. I saw terrified children run into the bushes. Those heartless thugs—the enforcers—they did not give a damn about what happened to us. All that was left for us was some barren craggy shore land that would produce nothing. Some frail old folks who managed to limp to the shore got sick and died from cold and exposure. And that is the sad story I have to tell."

Duncan then looked very seriously at Lewis as he urged, "For God's sake, laddie, get out before the sheriff and his hired riffraff come for Arisaig. Who knows when the current owner will run out of money and decide to sell the land you occupy? You have good grazing land. That is what the sheep farmers want. Take a lesson from what happened to us. The only opportunity left for Highland families who were forced off the land is to make their way to the wharf at Fort William to be sent off to the New World on the next ship that sails. There is nothing here for us; we have no choice but to go."

Lewis intervened to ask when they would be going. Duncan told him that he didn't know the exact time, but it would likely be very soon. Then he added, "I think I know what the transport ships are like. There are rumours, you know, rumours that these vessels had been used by merchants to transport slaves to the colonies. I never thought it would come to this: that we would be sent out of our homeland on a slave ship. It must be awful down in the hold of those ships. Frail women and children and the old folks have been told to stay behind because they would not survive the trip. What can they do to fend for themselves? God help them. I don't care what the ship's captain says; my Katie is coming with me. I can't imagine living without her. I fear we will be herded aboard that boat like cattle. Most of us are now penniless. God help us."

Duncan couldn't bear to say good-bye; so he bolted out the door before Lewis could speak, and Lewis never saw him again.

2

Lewis was deeply troubled by what Duncan had told him. For many hours he sat in silence with his head in his hands and went over and over Duncan's story in his mind. The question foremost in his mind was, "When will they come for us?" The future of his family had become his compelling concern.

Having decided it was time to share the news with Margaret, he sat with her and held her hand as he related the alarming tale Duncan had to tell. Margaret was appalled by what she heard.

With anguish in her voice she exclaimed, "In the name of God, how could the lairds be so cruel? All those greedy creatures want to do is to get their hands on our land. They don't give a damn about us."

Then Lewis turned and looked her straight in the eye as he said, "Margaret, things are bad. It is just a matter of time before the sheriff comes for us. We have good grazing land, just the kind the lairds want for their sheep. We got to get out. I want us to go on our terms, not on the sheriff's terms. I am a proud man; I don't want to give the sheriff the satisfaction of handing us that piece of paper called a writ of removal. That threat hangs over our heads like a dark cloud. What it teaches us is that we need to own our own land, something we just cannot do in this country. Above all, we have to think of the welfare of Mairi Bheag. I would go crazy if one of those drunken hooligans who do the dirty work for the sheriff put a hand on her. From what I heard of the way they handled the people, I don't think I could protect her from them."

"Yes, your parents are dead, but have you thought about my parents?" Margaret asked.

"I have thought of them too," Lewis replied. "They are too old, too frail, and too crippled to travel with us. I know you may not agree, but I think they will be all right here."

Margaret interrupted with a hint of anger in her voice, "Now what makes you think that?"

To which Lewis replied, "Now this is the way I see it. The lairds only want good grazing land. You see, your parents' land is so poor that it would not make a good sheep pasture; so I don't think the sheriff will bother them. And they have enough relatives here to look after them."

Margaret began to weep, but Lewis was determined to continue. Again he emphasized, "Now Margaret, I just don't want to give the sheriff the satisfaction of putting us out and I don't think you do either. After all, a person has to try to retain some dignity. I knew this day would come; I didn't say anything, but I have been planning for it. After I heard what happened in the surrounding townships of Strathglass and Glengarry, I began to save some money from the sale of our black cattle and I know I have enough to buy passage for all of us."

Margaret shook her head in disbelief, but Lewis persisted. "Now Margaret, you have to be sensible," he said in an assertive voice. "There is no doubt that life in Nova Scotia will be hard, but we will have our very own land and we will be free from the cursed landlords. It is plain to see that our loyalty to the lairds, and that of our parents and grandparents before us, counts for nothing. You just can't trust them. You never know when they are going to turn on us. A boat will be leaving from Fort William for Pictou Harbour in Nova Scotia in two weeks. It will dock for a few hours in the sheltered cove just below Arisaig. The ship's captain can pick us up there. We still have time to get that boat." He paused, smiling, and then he said, "By the way, the name of the boat is *The Good Intent*."

Margaret's heart was sore at the thought of leaving her parents and the homeland she loved.

As she looked out to sea, to the magnificent sight of the sun setting over the Inner Hebrides, she paused for a moment and then in a plaintive voice made one more plea to stay, "Ah Lewis, we will miss our beautiful home. Just look over there as the sun sets over the ocean; just watch the islands of Eigg and Rum across the way shine like jewels in the light of the setting sun."

Lewis put his arm around her shoulder and in a gentle voice replied, "Margaret, we will not have much enjoyment of that beauty if the sheriff comes for us."

He had made his point, and Margaret conceded that he was right. "Aye, I guess we really don't have much choice," she said with an air of resignation.

It was with heavy hearts that Lewis and Margaret began to plan to break the news to Mairi Bheag. That night they were awakened by loud sobs and screams emanating from her. They both jumped up and found her trashing about in her bed. Margaret gently awakened her and held her in her arms until she calmed down. Then she sang a lullaby to help her get back to sleep.

As they returned to bed, Lewis commented, "I wonder if she heard us talking. I think we had better talk to her tomorrow."

They had no idea how adept their curious little girl was at keeping abreast of everything that was going on.

So the next day, when Lewis, with Margaret at his side, took her on his knee and gently broke the news to her, she was ready for it, and she simply put her arms around his neck, hugged him, and said bravely, "Daddy, I'll be all right."

Lewis and Margaret smiled and looked at each other with pride as the bravery of their little girl brought tears to their eyes.

Because Mary Bheag took the news so well, Lewis decided that it was a good time to tell her more information about the move. Hesitatingly he said, "Mairi Bheag, I don't want to scare you, but I think you should know it is going to be a long trip."

Mairi Bheag's reaction was to ask, "Will it take more than a day?"

Laughing, Lewis replied, "Yes it will."

Realizing that she had little sense of the length of the trip, Lewis decided it was better to leave it that way.

Later, when he was discussing Mairi Bheag's reaction with Margaret, he concluded, "There is no point in worrying her any more than we have to."

Contrary to what Mairi Bheag had said, she was not all right. Because she was a reserved little girl, she did not want her parents to know how scared she was or how much she was hurting. Likely she was this way because she had no sisters or brothers with whom to share her feelings or to tell her secrets; so she learned to keep them to herself. Her parents' efforts to reassure her were not very comforting.

Over and over again, she asked herself, "What will become of us?"

Mairi Bheag loved her life in the Highlands. Every day, she joyously ran and skipped over its beautiful hills on her way to school. Even though she was forced to speak and study in English, she loved to go to school and she was good at her studies. There she also enjoyed being with her friends and laughing and giggling with them as they played during recess, and before and after school.

There was more to her anxiety than the thought of leaving her home, her grandparents, and her friends. Her heart was breaking at the thought of leaving behind her beautiful pet lamb, Ba. This gentle animal was her constant companion and followed her everywhere. It was only to her lamb that she revealed her innermost thoughts and feelings.

While thinking about her fate, she held her loyal lamb in her arms and she told the lamb the sad story of what was happening to her. "I am so afraid," she repeated over and over again.

As she rocked her lamb, she promised her that she would not be abandoned.

"Don't you worry, little one; I will get you a good home," she promised.

And then she just laid her cheek against her lamb's cheek and she wept, and she wept, and she wept, for the lamb and for herself.

There was a flurry of activity leading up to the departure of the MacDonald family. Lewis and Margaret bickered over what to take and what not to take.

As Margaret kept adding to the pile of things they would need, Louis pointed to the sea chest in which they were to carry their belongings and reminded her, "Remember, woman, I have to carry that thing."

With exasperation in her voice Margaret retorted, "Lewis, Lewis, Lewis, there are times …"

Her voice trailed of as Lewis approached, put his arms around her, and held her close as he said, "Margaret, these are trying times for both of us. We will get through them together."

After Margaret had finished packing, she turned to Lewis and reminded him, "You have to remember that we are going to need every last thing I put in the chest. You will thank me for it later."

Lewis and Margaret then decided it was time to distribute their remaining household goods and their sheep and cows among their family and friends. And most important of all, accompanied by Mairi Bheag, they made one last visit to bid farewell to their relatives. These farewells were not easy. Lewis and Margaret were overcome with emotion. It didn't help that, in no uncertain terms, some relatives cautioned against the move.

"You are damn fools. Do you have any idea of the hardships you are in for?" Uncle Alex asked.

"Do you realize some boats never make it across the water?" warned Aunt Martha.

"What in the name of God do you think you're doing? Do you want my darling Mairi Bheag to die from one of those diseases that ravage the passenger boats? You know that's why they're called coffin ships," asserted Margaret's mother, with an air of grave indignation.

At this point she took Mairi Bheag in her arms, hugged her, and in a loving voice said over and over again, *"M'eudail, M'eudail, M'eudail,"* the Gaelic word for darling'.

Lewis and Margaret were shaken by these warnings and the assertive manner in which they were delivered, but they tried not to show it.

Lewis stuck with his standard reply, "Don't worry; we'll be all right."

When they had finished expressing their misgivings, their relatives looked at them lovingly, and Uncle Alex, in a plaintive voice, said what they were all thinking, "We'll never see you again."

Last and worst of all was their departure from Margaret's parents. No one on either side could speak. Tears streamed down their faces. When their tears were exhausted, Lewis and Margaret broke free from their embrace and walked away. On the long walk home, not a word was spoken. Lewis and Margaret were so overcome with emotion that it was a great relief to get back to their cottage where they sat in silence on their two remaining chairs.

The next morning, before they left, Mairi Bheag had one last chore. With a heavy heart, she carried her beloved lamb to her best friend, Sarah. Holding the lamb close in her arms, she walked as slowly as she could to make their final trip together last as long as possible.

When she arrived at their destination, she hesitated for a moment, and then hugged and kissed her lamb one last time and handed her over to Sarah, with these words: "Take good care of her."

Then she hugged Sarah, and as the lamb bleated and struggled to get back to her, tears began to stream down her cheeks, and she ran from there as fast as she could.

On the many occasions Grandma told this story, she would pause and tears would run down her cheeks. Talking about this very traumatic part of her tale about leaving her homeland took a great deal out of her. On one of these occasions, she turned to me and said, "You know, Mary, that event and those leading up to it have left a scab on my soul that will not heal. Life can be so cruel."

3

In the early morning of a fine sunny day, May 15, 1820, the MacDonald family, with great apprehension, left their home for the last time and walked hand in hand along the Arisaig shore toward a small sheltered cove, where the transport ship awaited them and other passengers from the surrounding area. Their hearts were sore at the thought of leaving the homeland they loved. As they walked southward in silence, they sometimes turned and craned their necks to get one last view of their home. To show their support and their love, some relatives, including Margaret's parents, walked miles to be with them on this, their final journey. Uncle Alex followed, carrying their sea chest on his horse. When they arrived at their point of departure, Lewis, Margaret, and Mairi Bheag stood in silence on the shore and looked pensively out to the ocean they would cross on their way to a new life in the New World. Alongside stood other families who were doing likewise.

Before departing, they once more hugged Margaret's parents and their relatives, whom they would nevermore see, and again they all cried. The pain of this final farewell was like that of an arrow stuck in each of their hearts. The sad strains of a lament, played by a lone piper standing on a hill above the shore, provided an appropriate backdrop for their emotional parting.

When Margaret saw Lewis break free from their embrace, she knew it was time to move on and she strengthened her resolve to do likewise. "This is it," she said to herself. She straightened her shoulders, and with a look of grim determination on her face, she stepped away from her family, took Mairi Bheag by the hand, and hurried her into the small boat that was to take them out to the ship on which they were to sail. By then Lewis was already sitting quietly in the boat waiting for them. Not a word passed between them. Knowing she would never see her loved ones again, Margaret was afraid to look back for fear her heart would break. When the boat began to move out to meet the ship, Margaret finally got the courage to take one last glance back, and there on the shore she saw her father, bent with age, and her frail, wrinkled mother, standing alone, straining to see their last glimpse of them. The sight of her lonely parents almost broke her heart.

With a pained look on her face, she turned to Lewis and said, "Ah Lewis, do you think we should still go through with this?"

In a determined voice, he asserted, "Margaret, we've been through this before." Then he looked her in the eyes as he said, "I ask you once more, do you want to stay to have the sheriff burn us out and then drive us out? Do you want to stay to be persecuted and humiliated by the foreigners who now run our country?"

His authoritative words laid this bone of contention to rest. Margaret breathed a sigh and said no more.

In silence, the MacDonalds boarded the transport ship that was to take them across the Atlantic. Mary Bheag held her parents' hands tightly as the magnitude of what they were doing began to sink in. As the ship sailed out to sea, their souls were sore as they huddled together in silence along the rail and watched their kinfolk and the Highlands until both disappeared from view. Then they began to mingle with their fellow Highlanders who were leaving for the same reasons they were leaving. They basked in the warmth of the sun and the coolness of the breeze that wafted across the deck of the ship, and they made light conversation to try to distract their minds and hearts from the sadness of their departure from the people and homeland they loved.

As the sun sank in the west, its warmth was replaced by the chill of the cool damp evening air. To escape the dampness, the passengers took shelter under the hatch below the deck in the hold of the ship. As they crowded together in the dark, they talked in muffled tones of their hopes, their fears, and their aspirations. They had not talked for long before their conversations were interrupted by the beautiful sound of a mother singing a lullaby to her baby. This helped them all to relax and soon they settled down to sleep. Mairi Bheag laid between her father and her mother and held on to them for dear life.

Her mother put her arm around her and consoled her with these words: "Mairi Bheag, you'll be all right."

As her father held her, he said, "You are a brave little girl."

While Lewis would not say so, he was preoccupied with conflicting feelings of hope and fear—hope for a better life and fear that they might not make it across the Atlantic. They didn't sleep a wink that night. Mairi Bheag felt her parents' every move, as they tossed and turned on the hard, damp wooden floor covered only by a layer of straw. Because of their discomfort, they got up at the first sign of the morning light. This became part of their routine for forty-two long days and nights.

On clear fine days, they were glad to go up on the deck and bask in the warmth of the sun. They washed themselves, and Margaret washed their clothes in the rain water captured in containers provided by the shipping company. To this day, Grandma recalled how on these occasions it felt so good to wash away the stink that permeated the hold of the ship.

4

As the passengers got to know one another, they engaged in lively conversations about their hopes and dreams of a better life in their destination in the New World: Nova Scotia. Each of the men beamed with pride as he talked about the land he would own. The crops he would grow. The animals he would raise. The house he would build. The sons he would have. And on and on they went with a little encouragement from a nip of the malt of the barley.

The women were more expressive than the men. Standing together on the opposite side of the ship, each in a different way exclaimed how grand it would be to be free.

"We will be rid of those greedy landlords, we will."

"And we will no longer live in fear of being forced from our homes and off our land."

"We won't have to look over our shoulders to see if we are being followed as we make our way to mass."

"Our children will be allowed to speak the Gaelic, they will. They won't have to worry about being punished when they forget and go back to their old tongue."

"Ah, and once more our men, in the finest Highland tradition, will be allowed to play their pipes and wear their kilts with pride."

And, just like the men, on and on the women went, expounding their vision of a better life in Nova Scotia. To each of their comments, the response was an affirming "Aye."

Each morning the passengers hustled up to the deck to obtain the rations of food provided by the ship's captain. But they did not look forward to these meals for long. The bread soon got stale, the meal wormy, and before long, some of it was so rotten that they gagged when they tried to eat it. The water developed a rancid taste and a foul smell. It was hard to get it down and it soon became even harder to keep it down.

On one of these mornings when the food and drink did not go down particularly well, Margaret turned to Lewis and Mairi Bheag and said, "I have a little surprise for you."

Lewis, with a look of anticipation, exclaimed, "You do."

Mairi Bheag turned to her mother and asked excitedly, "What is it? What is it?"

Margaret raised her finger to her lips to indicate that she wanted them to be quiet. Then she beckoned them to go to a more private spot in the corner of the deck where she pulled a hunk of her home-made cheese, wrapped tightly in cheesecloth, from the pocket of her apron, and broke a big chunk for each of them.

As they savoured this unexpected treat, Mairi Bheag exclaimed, "That is so good."

Lewis added, "I agree. Right now I think that is the best food I ever ate."

And they laughed as they enjoyed every last crumb.

Adding to their woes was the deterioration of their living conditions. The dampness, the dirt, and the stink in the dark quarters under the deck got worse by the day. Soon they gagged at the repulsive smell of urine that permeated their abode like the odour of rotten fish. With the passage of time, the passengers became quiet, and a pall of gloom descended over them. On most nights, the only sound was that of children whimpering in their sleep—their unconscious reaction to the hardships of the trip. One night when the air was particularly oppressive, the silence was broken, this time by a family who were quarrelling out of sheer frustration with their living conditions. This turn of events upset the children and many of them began to cry. The sound of nasty quarrelling and loud and continuous crying in these tight quarters was more than some of the passengers could bear. The aggravation unnerved them to the breaking point.

Even Margaret, who was normally placid, exclaimed, "I don't think I can stand this much longer."

Fear that the situation might get out of hand moved Lewis to speak up. To the quarrellers he spoke sternly, "Now that's enough. Give it up. The rest of us do not want to have to listen to you."

One of the passengers replied, "Yes Constable," and everyone laughed.

Humour aside, Lewis had made his point, and silence was restored.

As time went on, a never-ending mist and fog engulfed the vessel, until it looked like a phantom ship. As the fog thickened, it enveloped not only the ship but also its passengers as they moved around the deck. An eerie silence set in. The slow listless movement of the passengers through the fog created the mirage of a ghost-like countenance. Many of them did not remain above deck for long in this weather. They soon began to realize that once their clothes got wet, they had no way to dry them, and they shivered as the damp cloth clung to their skin and chilled them to the bone.

Two weeks into this strange, almost other-worldly state, the eerie silence was broken by the shriek of Margaret MacPherson, who awoke to discover that her beloved one-year-old baby boy was dead. As she wept, she held the small, cold body against her breast and rocked backed and forth until her friends, figuring this had gone on long enough, gently took the body from her. Then she got up and insisted on preparing the baby's body for burial. She gently wrapped the golden-haired boy's body in the narrow shroud of the dead. Her husband then took the shroud containing the body to the side of the ship. With his eyes filled with tears, and as he prayed for eternal peace for his baby boy, he slowly and reverently lowered the child's body into the ocean.

The death cast a pall over the ship. No one spoke; some did not eat; the parents all held their children closer and silently prayed for their safety. Margaret thought of her mother's warning about the safety of Mairi Bheag. Lewis worried in silence. The death of the baby left an impression on Mairi Bheag that lasted a lifetime. Grandma still recalls how she cried. Her parents held her close, but even that did not comfort her. She said she had never seen anything like that and she could not help herself. Even though many decades have passed, her memory still returned to that tragic event. At these times she would say, "No little girl should have to go through that ordeal."

The miserable weather took its toll on the passengers' bodies and spirits. The days now seemed endless; the nights were almost unbearable, with the heavy air exaggerating the stink of dirt, urine, flesh, and dampness.

Mairi Bheag once overheard Lewis whisper to Margaret, "I hope to God we make it off this damn ship alive."

At the same time, they were both careful to try to hide their anxiety from Mairi Bheag. They attempted to cheer her up by telling her how wonderful life would be once they got ashore. She was too smart not to sense their fear. She later confided that she had grave doubts about what they were telling her.

Just as the morale of the passengers had reached rock bottom, Lewis alerted them to look to the west, and to their unspeakable delight, they saw land begin to appear. First, they all gazed in awe at this unbelievable sight and then they began to shout and laugh and cheer with joy and excitement. When they quieted down, they watched intently as the ship approached land and sailed for several hours parallel to the shore. The shore was lined by cliffs. Just after Lewis had suggested that they could never land in that terrain, the shoreline flattened and Pictou Harbour came into view.

Then Lewis spoke up again and said joyously, "There it is. At long last we are going to land in Nova Scotia."

A sense of relief swept over the ship. The normally passive crowd of passengers began to buzz around hurriedly. They gathered and packed their meagre belongings and brought them up to the deck where they watched the ship move slowly toward the shore. They were filled with both anticipation and apprehension.

As the ship came closer to the dock, Lewis, with unguarded enthusiasm, exclaimed, "Look, there are people watching our ship arrive."

While the ship was docking, the passengers continued to gaze at the people walking toward the shore. Lewis suggested that that they well might be some of their own kin coming to meet them. He was right. The people who came to meet the ship greeted the newcomers like long lost friends. The passengers had only to look at their reddish-brown hair and their fair skin to know that they too were Highland Scots. The settlers were as delighted to see the newcomers as the newcomers were to see them. They scanned the faces of the newcomers in the hope of recognizing some familiar features. They were in the habit of turning out to meet every transport vessel in anticipation of finding relatives or friends among the passengers. For the passengers this was indeed an unexpected welcome.

5

The MacDonalds were pleasantly surprised to depart the boat to the nostalgic sound of bagpipes playing at a distance by a lone piper.

"Just like home," Lewis remarked with a look of satisfaction on his face.

As they walked ashore, their curiosity was aroused by the sight of an elderly couple who were slowly walking toward them.

Lewis muttered to Margaret, "I wonder who they are?"

He soon had the answer to his question. The couple stopped in front of them with a look of recognition in their eyes.

The man extended his hand, as he said, "I am Hugh Dan Fraser; this is my wife, Catherine."

With a welcoming smile, he looked directly at Lewis as he said, "You have to be one of the Lodys. You look just like them."

Lewis nodded in the affirmative and then said, "I am Lewis, the grandson of Lewis Lody MacDonald, and this is my wife, Margaret, and our daughter, Mairi Bheag."

Mairi Bheag stepped forward and shook their hands, and this adult gesture made them all smile.

Then, in the warm spirit of Highland hospitality, Hugh continued, "You've had a long, hard trip. Indeed, I remember all too well what it was like. It may be many years since we made that trip, but we'll never forget how bad it was. You look as if you could stand a good meal and a warm bed. You must come to our home and let us look after you."

The MacDonalds could not believe their good fortune. No words were ever more welcome, and Mairi Bheag squeezed her father's hand, hoping that he would accept their invitation. And, of course, he was delighted to do so. Hugh helped Lewis to carry their sea chest, one on each side of it, as they walked slowly to the Frasers' home along a footpath through the woods. At the beckoning of their hosts, the MacDonalds made their way into a long log cabin, a humble but inviting dwelling, where they were greeted by the smell and warmth of a crackling fire.

To this day, Grandma retained vivid recollections of their arrival. "Ah, I can still remember how good the warmth of the heat from their fireplace felt. It dried six weeks of dampness out of our bones," she would often recall. "And nothing could equal the smell of stew simmering in a large iron pot hanging from a hook over the open fire. After six weeks of stale and rotten food, you can imagine how we looked forward to having our first fresh meal."

Being embarrassed by how dirty they were, the first thing Lewis did was to ask what they could do to clean up.

"We do not want the condition we are in to offend you," he explained.

Catherine gave them a cake of soap and a towel and suggested they wash in a winding brook flowing through their farm.

"It's over there," she said, as she pointed to where it was.

Because the sun was warm, the MacDonalds adapted quickly to the coolness of the water and found it very refreshing. They washed and splashed water on themselves and on each other and then sat on the bank of the brook to dry.

With considerable satisfaction Margaret sighed as she said, "It's been a long time since I felt this clean."

They basked in the warmth of the sun and inhaled the beautiful smell of the wild strawberry blossoms that grew everywhere around them.

"Quite a change from the smell in the hold of the ship," Lewis remarked. "I think we have arrived in Paradise."

When they were dry, they went back to the Fraser's home for their first meal in Nova Scotia. They feasted on stew made from fresh spring lamb and delicate new vegetables, the first of the season, according to the Frasers. The MacDonalds were so ravenously hungry that not a word passed between them and their hosts until they had finished eating.

The Frasers were eager to hear news from their homeland; so when they finished dinner, Hugh invited their guests to sit around the fire with them and talk.

"You know, this is the only way we have of getting news from home. We feel so cut off from the old country," he pined.

The hours passed very agreeably. The glow of the fire combined with the glow of the candle to create a warm ambiance in the cabin. The Frasers and the MacDonalds sat around like old friends. For the next few days they would wile away many happy hours spinning tales in the finest Highland tradition.

Lewis and Margaret were so engrossed in conversation that they forgot Mairi Bheag was still up, and as she was in the habit of doing, she was listening to every word. Without realizing it, her stock of stories was growing by the day.

Hugh poured a dram of whiskey—*"uisge beatha"* he called it, Gaelic for the water of life—for Lewis and for himself, and of course, the drink helped the conversation. He asked a flood of questions about the relatives and friends they had left behind. Hugh and Catherine listened attentively as their guests filled them in on the news of their kin and friends: their marriages, the lives of their children, the deaths of the old folks, the plight of their schools and churches, the success and failure of the crops, the sale of livestock, and the current political situation.

News of the political situation in their homeland reminded Hugh to ask Lewis and Margaret why they had come to Nova Scotia. He was shocked by what he heard.

With a faraway look in his eyes, Lewis began his reply. "I have a sad tale to tell. When I think of our beautiful homeland, I could cry. You have no idea how bad things are now in the Highlands. Would you believe that some of the lairds, the same fellas who had been our chiefs, the same fellas to whom we had been so loyal, turned on us. Those heartless creatures drove our relatives and friends from the land they held, the very land on which their families had lived for centuries—you'll never believe this—to make room for sheep. That is exactly what they did."

Hugh stopped him to ask, "For sheep. For God's sake, what are you talking about? That doesn't make sense."

Lewis then explained the demand for wool created by the opening of textile mills in the south and how this industry made sheep farming very profitable. To illustrate how bad the situation had become, he repeated a few excerpts from the story of the Sutherland clearances that had been told to him by Duncan Chisholm. This story made his heart sore, and he felt a deep need to share some of its highlights.

"Without warning, the sheriff and his constables arrived at the home of Duncan and Katie Chisholm, and with the threat of force, ordered those good people to gather their belongings and get out," Lewis said. "Can you imagine how the sight of the constables with their clubs, sticks, and muskets struck fear into the hearts of the poor souls. Our good friends, the Chisholms, and their neighbours for miles around, saw their cozy little homes unroofed and burned before their very eyes. With heavy hearts, they took the few belongings they were able to salvage and made their way to the shore, where they were left to shiver in the cold until a boat arrived to take those who were strong enough to travel to the New World. You know, Duncan was so upset that, as he told their sad story, he stopped at times to cry."

This story made Hugh's eyes grow wide with a look of disbelief and he just had to interrupt.

"What in the name of God happened to the sense of loyalty that had been so strong in our homeland?" he asked rhetorically. "I'm so glad we got out while we still had a choice."

Lewis raised his glass as he said, "I'll drink to that. That's why we left when we did. We figured it was just a matter of time before the sheriff and his men came to empty the grazing land in Arisaig."

As the evening waned and as the MacDonalds' first day in Nova Scotia was coming to an end, their eyes narrowed and they were too tired to talk anymore. So Catherine summoned them to the far end of the cabin where she provided fresh woollen bats to put under them and warm woollen blankets to put over them. Here they found themselves on their first night in Nova Scotia with new friends who saw to it that they were well fed, clean, warm, and safe. Grandma often recalled that, as she went to sleep that night, she thought that life could not have been better.

And she sometimes added, "That was the night I began to realize that there is nothing more precious in this world than good friends."

6

The next morning Margaret was awakened by a tap on her shoulder. She opened her eyes to see Catherine put a finger to her lips, to indicate to her to be quiet, and then beckon her to come. Margaret jumped up, put on her clothes, and the two women headed for the barn.

There Catherine pointed to her two fine cows as she said with pride, "Aren't they beautiful?"

Margaret nodded in agreement and then exclaimed, "This is the nicest thing you could do for me. I miss my animals so much. Seeing these beautiful cows makes me feel right at home. You never forgot how much Highland women love their cattle, did you?"

Then Catherine asked Margaret how long it was since she had milked a cow.

"Not since we gave our milk cows away before we left," she replied.

Catherine passed her a bucket as she said, "You milk that one; I'll milk this one."

And then they both sat milking and singing in the Highland tradition. They finished milking at about the same time, got up, looked at each other, and laughed as they headed for the house with full buckets of milk.

On the way in, Margaret thanked Catherine and then said, "That was the best fun I've had in a long time."

When they arrived back in the kitchen, the men and Mairi Bheag were up and ready for breakfast. While they were eating, Lewis asked questions about settling in Nova Scotia. Hugh assured him that while Pictou and the surrounding area were well developed, there was still plenty of land left, and he should not have much trouble in establishing a homestead.

"It will be much easier for you than it was for us; that's for sure," he said.

For Hugh and Catherine these questions brought back a flood of memories of what it was like for them to settle in Nova Scotia, and they felt the need to tell their story.

Hugh described their shock at their first sight of Pictou. "Ah laddie, what a huge disappointment it was," he said. "When Catherine saw the miles of deep dark woods that stood before us, she began to cry. And as she sobbed I heard her mutter, 'So this is *tir nan craobh*, the land of the trees we heard so much about.'"

Hugh then told of how the only thing that kept them from despair was the kind assistance of a small band of American settlers, called the Betsy settlers, who had previously taken up land in the area.

"Because there was nothing around us but woods, we had to build a crude shelter among the trees," he explained. "With the help of these settlers, we cut poles from the logs of small trees to form the structure of our dwelling and then we cut the largest spruce boughs we could find and leaned and layered them over and against the poles. After that, we leaned some thin logs over the boughs to keep them in place. Then we opened a small hole in the roof to let out the smoke and another hole in a wall to serve as a door. When we finished erecting the shelter, we stood back to look at it and we were shocked by how crude it was."

"I remember saying to Catherine, 'We didn't come here to live like wild animals, but I'm afraid that is exactly what we're doing.' And then I laughed as I said, 'I wonder how they feel about sharing the forest with us.'

"Later I told her that this shelter would have to do us until we could cut wood to build a cabin. Because we arrived in September, it was too late to think of planting a crop; so we spent most of our time scrounging for firewood for the winter," he said.

"And how did you get the firewood?" Lewis asked.

Hugh told of the backbreaking work of cutting trees for firewood.

He recalled, "It sure was tough. We were not used to this kind of heavy work, because we did not have trees that large where we lived in the Highlands.

Fortunately, we had saws and axes provided by the American settlers. The sight of the huge size of many of the trees was very discouraging. Then and there we began to realize how hard it was going to be to clear the land. You could tell by the look on our faces that we were near despair. I'm sure the mess we were in would have pleased the redcoats. Our new friends did everything they could to restore our hope. 'With our knowledge and our help you can do it,' they kept assuring us. It was reassuring to find that strangers could care so much."

At the first pause in the conversation, Margaret asked, "If it was too late in the season to plant a crop, how did you manage to get food? I would think that was even harder."

To which Hugh replied, "I'm telling you, food was pretty scarce in that first year. The Betsey settlers gave us as much as they could spare, but that did not add up to much. We also had a small supply of potatoes and meal provided by the shipping company, again not near enough to carry us through the winter. If it wasn't for the help of the Micmacs we would have starved."

Lewis interrupted to ask, "And who are the Micmacs?"

Hugh got up, put another log on the fire, thought for a moment, and then replied, "Now that I think about it, I really don't know that much about them. They are dark-skinned people who live in the woods around us, just like we did when we first moved here. They live on the food they gather and hunt—berries, deer, moose, eels—anything that grows wild. I don't know where they came from. The first time I saw them sneaking along the edge of the woods to see what we were doing, I was terrified. It didn't occur to me that they were afraid of us, just as we were afraid of them. They did not wear our kind of clothes or speak our language. They were different, and that is what scared us.

"Our fears passed when the Americans told us not to be afraid of these people because they would help us. At the time, I thought the idea of getting help from them to be quite odd. 'But,' I objected, 'we cannot talk to them, and they can't talk to us.' 'Don't worry about that,' our American friends said, 'they will not try to tell you how to do things; they will show you.' And show us they did. In the late fall, they took me to hunt for moose and deer so that we would have meat for the winter. Their hunting skills were amazing, and I learned a great deal from them."

Lewis and Margaret were fascinated by Hugh's story of the Micmacs and they listened with rapt attention.

Then Hugh, enjoying his audience, asked, "Would you like to hear the rest of my story?"

And the answer was an enthusiastic "Yes."

"Well then, you are going to find it hard to believe how the Micmacs helped with our clothing," Hugh said as he laughed. "When they saw us starting to shiver from the piercing cold and winds in November, they showed us how to dress ourselves in deer and moose hides to protect us from the harsh winter weather."

At this point we all laughed, and then Hugh, in lighter vein, continued with his story. "As Catherine pulled her deer hide around her body, I looked at her and said, 'You know, you could get shot for a deer.'

"She laughed as she looked at me and replied, 'And you for a moose. We are living more like wild animals every day, aren't we?'

"My only reply was, 'And we are lucky for it. These hides will keep us from freezing our own hides.'

"The Micmacs later showed us how to make nice warm footwear from the hides. The few clothes we brought were not warm enough. We had no idea how to dress for the cold winter in Nova Scotia."

Catherine then added, "Hugh is right. When we left Scotland we had no idea what we were in for."

Hugh then told of the serious problem they had with a poor supply of fuel. He said, "The wood we cut for the fire was wet. The smoke from it damn near choked us. Fortunately, we got smarter in a hurry. We began to look for trees that had been blown down by wind storms, and these trees make good dry firewood. We mixed the dry wood with the wet wood to keep our fire going and to make the dry wood last longer."

When Hugh saw the perplexed look on Margaret's face, he asked what was on her mind.

"Oh, I was just wondering what did you did when the fire went out."

Hugh laughed as he replied, "Ah, yes, that happened quite often. Each time the fire went out, we went to the home of the nearest settler to get some live coals.

I would walk through the woods to their home with a bucket, fill it with hot coals and lug it back to use to start a new fire. If the new fire went out, I had to make the trip all over again. I did that many times. What it comes down to is this: You do what you have to do to stay alive."

Like most Highland Scots, Hugh loved to pass time spinning a tale and he did not often have willing listeners. He found Lewis and Margaret to be delightful company. He sensed that they were a receptive audience for what he had to say about how they survived their first winter, and so he continued with his story.

"It was the hardest winter of our lives," he said. "As I look back, I wonder where we got the courage to go on. It was a good thing we were young and strong. We faced one crisis after another. In the middle of the winter our supply of food ran low. At that time, the moose and deer are too thin to be much good to eat. The Micmacs again came to our aid. To help us out, they took me to Pictou Harbour and showed me how to drill a hole in the ice to fish for eels and smelts. This was a big help, but it was not enough to get us through the winter. We were getting desperate. Our potatoes and grain were nearly gone.

"I said to Catherine, 'We have to do something. We didn't come here to starve.'

"I told her I had to go to Truro to buy supplies with the money we had left. Because she was not over her fear of the woods, she begged me not to go. But I had no choice."

Catherine then intervened to tell how terrified she was to be left alone with the children. "I pleaded, 'I am so scared.' What could I do to save the children if bears come after us?"

"We did not have bears back in the Highlands, and when I saw those huge creatures—the largest wild animals I had ever seen—lumbering around in the woods near our shelter, I was terrified. At that time we did not know that bears hibernate in winter. Hugh assured me that we would be fine, but I was not convinced."

Then Catherine said enthusiastically, "Hugh, you must tell them the story of your trip to Truro."

Hugh obliged. "That was one damn hard trip, I tell you. I had to walk forty miles through deep snow. The American settlers had blazed a trail through the woods by making nicks in the trees with their axes, which were easy to see, and

I was very careful to follow in their footsteps. In the middle of my trip to Truro, a howling snowstorm hit. When the storm became a raging blizzard, I couldn't see a foot ahead of me. I had to stop; I started to panic. I came to my senses when I noticed the low hanging branches of a huge spruce tree and I crawled under them to wait out the storm. As the blizzard continued, I constantly thought of Catherine trying to make out without me—how afraid she would be for me, for the children and for herself. She had never been through a blizzard before and she had no idea how bad it could get. While under the branches, I saw rabbits and deer take shelter just like I did. I thought to myself, 'Good Lord, I have been reduced to living just like them.' Then I began to realize that nature's shelter was pretty comfortable. The branches kept out the wind and the snow, and I did not feel the cold. I actually fell asleep."

Then Hugh laughed as he said, "I woke up just as the snow was letting up, and the rabbits, the deer and I got up and shook off the snow, and they went on their way into the woods, and I continued on my way to Truro."

Lewis interrupted to ask, "Is this story true or are you putting us on?"

Hugh replied, "Yes it is, my friend. And there is more. When I got to Truro, I stopped at the first farm house I could find, and when the owner, a good soul, heard my story and saw the condition I was in, he took me in, fed me, let me dry my clothes, gave me a bed for the night, and the next day, he gave me a few days work in the woods. That was a Godsend. From experienced woodsmen, I learned the best way to cut trees, and for my efforts I received some much needed cash. With the money I earned, and what I had left from our trip, I bought some potatoes and grain, and a hand sled to carry them on, and headed for home."

And Catherine added, "All the time he was away, I was worried that he might get lost in a blizzard or be attacked by wild animals. As each day passed, I got more worried. Every day I got down on my knees and prayed to God for his safe return. What a relief it was for me—and the children—to see him land back home, safe and sound." She shook her head with a slight smile on her face.

Lewis wanted to learn as much as he could about getting settled from the experience of the Fraser family; so he asked them to tell how they went about starting their homestead.

It was Catherine who started the story of the arduous tasks involved in clearing the land and starting to farm. "You talk about back-breaking work," she said. "I watched every muscle in Hugh's arms and back ripple as he swung the axe to bring down each tree and to remove the boughs from its trunk. Then I got the children to help me gather the brush and set it on fire. At night we sat outside and watched the brush fires that burned in the hills all around us—a beautiful sight that reminded us that other pioneers were also clearing the land. From the brush fires, Hugh got the idea that, in the driest part of the summer, he would set fire to the woods so that the the fire would char and dry out the trees and make them easier to cut. 'The fire will speed up the clearing of the land,' he informed me.

"In the meantime, we soon learned that ashes made wonderful fertilizer. The few potatoes we had left from the winter, I used for seed. The children and I planted them around the stumps of the trees. It was amazing to watch them grow. When I saw that the potatoes were growing so well, I decided to plant some grain, and that grew equally well."

Then Catherine got up and poured us another cup of tea, and Hugh picked up the story where she had left off.

"In the middle of August, I set fire to the woods," he said.

Taken by surprise, Lewis interrupted, "You did what?"

Hugh replied, "Yes, I really did set fire to the woods. At first it was awesome to watch the fire tear through the trees. Then I got scared when I began to realize what I had started. The sight of the flames leaping from tree to tree and the roar of the fire as it spread terrified me. It was a bit late to realize I did not know how to put the damn fire out. I was afraid we would lose everything. Fear turned to panic when the pace of the fire quickened and began to spread to our neighbours' property. As a burst of flames sent me reeling backwards, I screamed, 'Catherine, get the children and we will run for our lives.' I took her hand and with the children right behind us, we ran as fast as we could. When we reached a clearing, I exclaimed, 'God forgive me for starting something I can't stop. I fear I am going to burn us out—and all the neighbours with us.' Thank God, within minutes mother nature came to our aid with a heavy downpour that doused the flames and gradually put them out. Needless to say, we both breathed a deep sigh of relief. To this day, I think that setting that fire was the stupidest and the scariest thing I ever did."

These shared memories caused Hugh and Catherine to look at each other and laugh, and then Catherine added, "Believe me, it wasn't funny at the time."

Because the MacDonalds were new to the area, they wanted to hear more about how Hugh and Catherine developed their homestead. Again Hugh was delighted to oblige. He told of how he went about obtaining livestock after clearing enough land to support them.

He said, "I had no money to buy farm animals; so I went to work in the woods during the winter to earn some cash. That was quite an eye-opener. I had no idea what life was like in the lumber woods. You wouldn't believe the way the woodsmen drank. I was shocked to see how quickly they finished a puncheon of rum. Many of them were in no shape to be wielding an axe or a saw, but that did not stop them. I guess this is what they had to do to keep their sanity through the harsh winter in the lumber camps. They were separated from their families. I think the loneliness and isolation got to them. Living and working in these conditions made me anxious. Being sober among a bunch of drunks was scary. I worked just long enough to earn the money needed to buy two longhorn sheep, a male and a female. The female provided the first milk we had in Nova Scotia. Much as I hated to, I went back to the woods the following winter. I worked just long enough to get money to buy a handsome red and white Ayrshire cow. And for the first time since coming to Nova Scotia, we had enough fresh milk to make cream and butter."

"Ah," Catherine interjected, "and the best thing of all, the Micmacs showed Hugh how to draw sap from the maple trees in the spring and make it into syrup and sugar. And then we smothered our porridge in cream and sugar, and what a feast we had. In the summer, I also used the sugar to preserve the beautiful wild berries that grew everywhere. We worked hard, but it wasn't long before we began to live well."

Hugh, realizing that their conversation had taken up most of the morning, got up and announced that he had to do the barn work. He invited Lewis to join him.

On the way to the barn, Hugh asked Lewis, "How bad was the boat trip?"

Lewis breathed a deep sigh and then replied. "At times it was almost more than I could bear. I don't have to tell you how awful the living conditions on the boat were; you already know that. The saddest and most worrisome event was the death of a handsome baby boy. I was scared that the baby's death marked the beginning of an epidemic. I began to think we were on one of those coffin ships the relatives warned us about and I prayed to God for the safety of our beautiful little girl. Let me say that the trip was so bad that I just want to forget it."

And with these words the topic was dropped.

In the course of doing his chores, Hugh showed Lewis the land he had cleared and the livestock he now owned. He pointed to his five pigs, twenty chickens, three cows, ten sheep, and nine spring lambs.

"Quite a collection, isn't it?" he said with pride shining in his eyes.

Lewis replied, "Indeed they are handsome animals. I sure hope the day will come when I will own some just like them."

Then Hugh went on to describe the operation of his farm. He said, "With three cows, we can have two milking while the other is dry, and this way we have fresh milk the year round. It also means that when the three of them are milking, we have extra milk to use to make curds, butter, and cheese. Those cows are the joy of Catherine's life. And not just for the products they provide. They are her pets. She talks and sings to them every day."

The thought of having cows for pets made both of them laugh. Then Hugh continued, "Each fall we fatten a calf for butchering. In December we butcher a pig. By cutting up and freezing most of the pork we are able to have fresh or frozen meat for several months. Believe me, after eating so much salt meat and fish, that is quite a treat."

As Hugh talked, he turned the cattle out to pasture, and Lewis helped him clean the stable.

"The work of looking after the cattle is less in summer," he explained. "The cattle can get their own feed and water as they roam around a clearing in the woods. That is their pasture. This way I can use most of the land I cleared for growing hay."

This point prompted Lewis to suggest that what Hugh was doing reminded him of the way they drove the cattle into the hills in the Highlands to graze for the summer.

"Yes," Hugh replied, "Indeed, I remember doing that."

Then Hugh got back to his story of the operation of his farm. He said, "The sheep aren't much work, but they have been a wonderful resource for us. Before we got a cow, they even provided us with a small supply of milk. And most important of all, they provided the wool Catherine used to make the clothes for our backs."

And in this manner, Hugh and Lewis, who were fast becoming close friends, continued to work together and to talk about farming for most of the day.

Because Hugh and Lewis were doing the barn work and Catherine and Margaret were busy in the kitchen, they had forgotten about Mairi Bheag. Sensing that she had been overlooked, she decided to go outside and explore the farm on her own. The first thing she heard was the grunting and squealing of pigs as they ran around the barnyard looking for food. She became disgusted as she watched them slopping about in the muck, looking greedy and dirty and smelling worse. Then she saw something that made her heart leap with joy. Nine spirited spring lambs rushed from a pen behind the barn and began to play. They ran, kicked their hind legs in the air, and bleated with glee, as only young lambs know how. Mairi Bheag stopped in her tracks. Then she moved slowly toward them, holding out her hand and speaking softly to them, but they did not respond. Obviously they enjoyed their own company more than hers. They were not afraid of her, but to her disappointment, they just ignored her. As she stood for a time watching them, a little lamb stopped and looked at her. Again she held out her hand and spoke softly to it. Then she slowly moved her hand toward the lamb, and it let her pet it on the head. The lamb responded by leaning its head into her hand, and that is how their relationship began. She continued to work on gaining the confidence of the little lamb, and it wasn't long before it let her take it in her arms.

And she said to the lamb as she kissed and hugged it, "You are my new Ba."

And for the next few days she carried the lamb everywhere she went.

7

When Hugh and Lewis returned at the end of the day and settled in front of the fire for the evening, the conversation turned to the question of what the newcomers needed to do to get settled in eastern Nova Scotia. Lewis and Margaret listened intently as Hugh told of how a priest by the name of Father Angus MacEachern from Prince Edward Island sailed across the Northumberland Strait in his canoe to greet the new settlers and to urge Catholics to go east to Antigonish.

And then he thought to ask, "Being one of the Lodys, you are Catholics, aren't you?"

Lewis replied, "Yes, yes we are."

Then Hugh informed them that when the land along the western shore of Antigonish was taken, the priest urged Catholics to go on to Port Hood, Creignish, and Judique in Cape Breton.

Hugh laughed as he said, "The priest must have been afraid the Presbyterians would lead the Catholics astray!"

Lewis was quick to point out that he did not like the idea of going to Cape Breton.

"But," he added, "I think we might know some people in Arisaig and we would really like to go there. You know, some of them may even be our kinfolk."

Hugh cautioned that, because Arisaig was the first community in Antigonish settled by the Highland Scots, starting in 1791, it could well be that all the land was taken.

Lewis insisted, "I still want to go there."

"Well," Hugh replied, "we'll do just that."

The following day, Hugh and Lewis gathered some slim logs, trimmed them, and spiked them together to form a raft, and then they put the vessel in the bay so that the wood could swell to keep out the water.

Then Hugh said with a satisfied look on his face, "This craft should get your family and your supplies to Arisaig safely.

When they finished the task, Hugh pointed to where Arisaig is located as he said, "Look over there. It is not very far."

They both stood and gazed at the shore of Arisaig from the shore of Pictou.

Then Hugh continued, "In the morning we will cross the water in my canoe." As he pointed to the canoe with pride, he boasted, "I made it myself."

Lewis was very impressed with the craftsmanship.

"You did a fine job," he said.

Hugh replied, "Don't give me too much credit. The Micmacs showed me how to do it. As I have said so many times, we do not give those people enough credit for teaching us how to live in this part of the world. I am going to show you how they taught me to make a canoe before you leave. While your raft will be useful to carry more people and supplies, you will need a sleeker vessel for regular travel back and forth between Arisaig and Pictou."

Lewis was so excited about the trip to Arisaig that he tossed and turned all night. His mind was preoccupied with thoughts of owning his own land and of all the things he could do with it. He was up at the crack of dawn, and Hugh and he carried the canoe to the ocean where they put it in the water and headed for Arisaig. The high cliffs soon gave way to a flat shoreline, and it was along the flat shoreline the men decided to land. When the water became too shallow to float the canoe, they both got into the water and hauled it ashore. They wanted to go ashore to get a sense of the layout of the land, to meet some of the settlers, and to find out if any land was available.

An old man who was walking along the shore stopped to talk with them.

When Lewis introduced himself, the man looked at his facial features and exclaimed, "I can tell by the look of you that you are a Lody."

"And who are you," Lewis asked.

"I am William Donald Malcolm Chisholm," he replied.

And he gave Lewis a warm and welcoming handshake as Lewis thought of his friend Duncan and wondered where he might be.

Like Hugh and Catherine, William was very anxious to catch up on the news from the old country. As soon as Lewis got the chance, he turned the conversation to the subject of the availability of land and he was most gratified to learn that a homestead located near the shore had recently been vacated.

"Other than that there is no more vacant land in Arisaig," William said.

Lewis was quick to ask, "Do you think I have a chance of getting it?"

William replied, "A very lucky man you are. So far, I don't think anyone has claimed the homestead. And you don't just get land but land that has been cleared. This homestead is quite a find. It has a cabin made of sturdy logs, and I think it is in pretty good shape. In our community we have our own church and our own school, and you will find the neighbours kind and helpful. Because you are one of us, we will do everything we can to help you get settled."

William assured Lewis that he would make sure that no one took over the homestead before his family arrived. He suggested that Lewis move in right away so that at least he would have squatters' rights.

Lewis, sensing that this offer was too good to be true, asked why the previous owner left. He was somewhat relieved when William told of how the entire family up and left for Upper Canada without making any provision for anyone to take over the homestead.

"I heard that relatives in Hastings County got word to them about a vacant homestead that was at least five times larger than the one they had here," William said. "I guess when they found out about that opportunity, they were in a hurry to take advantage of it."

Lewis' lingering doubts about the ownership of the homestead prompted the next question, "If it is such a fine place, why did no one claim it?"

William thought for a moment and then replied, "Well, the only reason I can think of is that the owners only left a few days ago, and no newcomers have come this way since then."

"Well," Lewis said, "I hope no one else does."

While this information was somewhat reassuring, he continued to harbour a lingering worry about the ownership of the land.

At the same time, Lewis had a hard time containing his excitement. Up to this point, the idea that some day he would own his very own land was only a figment of his imagination. It was part of his dream of a better life—a dream so compelling that it impelled him to uproot his family and make that long journey across the Atlantic to Nova Scotia. Now this dream had become a hope and maybe, just maybe, it was about to become a reality. He could not wait to get back to Pictou to tell Margaret of their good fortune.

On the canoe trip back Hugh filled Lewis in on the procedure for claiming ownership of the land.

"To ease your mind," he said, "I think you should head for Pictou to see the local magistrate as soon as possible. He will figure out if this land has been granted, and that will determine if you can legally claim it. Once the land grant is in your name, no one else can claim it."

Lewis knew this was good advice and he decided that this was the first thing he would do after moving to Arisaig. He understood the urgency of occupying the homestead immediately.

After they docked the boat at Pictou Harbour, Hugh took Lewis to the local general store where he purchased an axe, a saw, a hoe, and some meal and potatoes for their new home. They then headed for home to share the story of their good fortune. You should have seen Margaret's face when Lewis told her the news. She was beaming with pride.

She was so moved that in a slow earnest voice she said, "I didn't dare let myself dream that this day would come."

Lewis added, "Would you believe that, if we get this homestead, we will not have to go through the back-breaking work the pioneers who came before us did in clearing the land and building a home. The hardest work has already been done. I tell you, woman, this is so exciting."

The MacDonalds decided they would sail for Arisaig on the first calm day. They only had to wait two days for the right weather conditions. After the family got ready for take-off, they extended their heart-felt thanks to their hosts.

Lewis said with the deepest sincerity, "You have no idea how much your hospitality means to the scared wretches who left the transport vessel not knowing what to expect. It eased our minds; it restored our spirits. It made our arrival in Nova Scotia so pleasant. Please come and visit us in our new home. It will be a great pleasure to treat you in the manner in which you treated us."

Margaret nodded her head to show that she shared this sentiment.

Catherine was so moved by these words of thanks that, in a gentle voice, she replied, "You are so thoughtful."

Before the MacDonalds left for the shore, Hugh asked Mairi Bheag to come to the barn yard and wait for him. He went into the barn and came out with the beautiful white lamb she had befriended.

"This is a very special gift for you," he said tenderly, as he handed the lamb to her.

As she hugged the lamb tightly and as she smiled at Hugh, she said, "Thank you so much. This is the best gift in the whole world."

The Frasers walked with the MacDonalds to the shore and helped to carry their cache of supplies to the raft Hugh and Lewis had built. The MacDonalds arranged their belongings and themselves on the raft, loosened the rope that tied the raft to the shore, and said their last good-byes as they set sail for their new home.

Mairi Bheag sat upright and held her lamb close as they started their voyage. She later recalled that, in the beginning, the voyage brought back frightening thoughts of bad things that had happened on their boat trip across the Atlantic. But these fears did not last for long. It was a beautiful day, and their craft ran slowly and smoothly over the shimmering water. They had travelled only a short distance before she was able to relax and enjoy the trip.

It was not long before Lewis broke the silence, when he pointed to the shore and said, "There it is."

Margaret fixed her attention on the land to which he had pointed, and then exclaimed, "Oh my God, Lewis! This Arisaig looks just like the Arisaig from which we came."

As she moved close to Lewis and put her arm around his waist, she spoke slowly and reverently, "Lewis, I feel we are going home."

"Isn't that the truth, woman," Lewis replied, with a look of deep satisfaction on his face.

As they approached the Arisaig shore, they saw people gathering on the beach. Word had gone around that one of the Lodys was coming, and the settlers who knew their kinfolk back in the Highlands gathered to greet them. Some of the settlers even waded out to the raft to help the newcomers pull it ashore.

When Margaret started to reach for their belongings, one of them spoke up, "No, no, woman, we will look after them for you."

And before Lewis and Margaret could object, their new neighbours were already carrying their supplies from the beach to the land. Mairi Bheag lagged behind because she was trying to hold her lamb above the water so it would not get wet. When one of the men offered to carry the lamb for her, she would not hear of it. To her carrying this animal was a labour of love.

Lewis' cousin, James, having learned Lewis was coming, came forward to introduce himself and to invite the MacDonalds to his home. "Come stay the night with us, laddie, and we'll get you settled in the morning," he said with a welcoming smile.

James and his wife, Jenny, treated the MacDonalds to a delicious salmon dinner. After dinner, Lewis and James sat and drank a dram of whiskey, while Lewis and Margaret filled James and Jenny in on the news of the relatives back home. Then Lewis shared with James his unease about the ownership of the land. He told him that he wanted to move in immediately—before anyone else might realize that the homestead was vacant—and then go to Pictou to talk to the local magistrate about claiming the homestead.

Before Lewis could get up the nerve to ask for the use of James' canoe, James made the offer. "Laddie, you can have my canoe any time you want," he said. "Now that you made your way here from Pictou, you will have no trouble making your way back on your own. The trip should take less than an hour."

Louis, relieved he did not have to ask, took James up on his offer. As Lewis and Margaret and Mairi Bheag settled in for their first nights sleep in Arisaig, Lewis summed up their good fortune with these simple words: "We are truly blessed."

And in peace and contentment they fell into a deep sleep.

8

On the day the MacDonalds were to move into their new home, they were awakened early by the warbling and chirping of the birds calling the dawn. It wasn't long before the blueness of the sky and the brilliance of the sun as it rose in the east served notice of the beginning of a beautiful summer day, and they got up early in anticipation of their move. After a good breakfast of porridge, hot bannock dripping with butter, washed down with good hot tea, Lewis decided it was time to get started. James went with him to help to check out the cabin. With the exception of a few cracks between the logs that could be filled with clay, the cabin was in good shape. Fortunately, they found that the previous owners, in their hurry to depart, had left their furniture behind: a table, four chairs, a work bench, and two beds. The furniture was crude but useful.

The MacDonalds were hardly in their new home when neighbours arrived with donations of fresh vegetables from their gardens, fresh milk, some butter and cheese and a huge centre-cut of the salmon that populated the waters off Arisaig. Highland hospitality was abundantly evident. This was food that the MacDonald family had little chance of obtaining or growing for some time, and they were deeply appreciative of the thoughtfulness of these good people who did not even know them. Their hospitality was more than Lewis and Margaret had expected, and they again expressed their deep-felt thanks to their new friends.

In the early evening, Margaret prepared boiled salmon with garden-fresh vegetables, and they ate with relish their first dinner in their new home. Then they decided to relax and walk down to the shore to watch the sun go down. As the three of them walked hand in hand, Mairi Bheag's lamb romped along behind them.

Grandma retained vivid memories of that event. "As I think of it now," she said, "we sat silently side by side on the shore, overcome with feelings of contentment and gratitude. We had much to be thankful for. We now lived on our own land—something we could never have in Scotland—and it looked like a land of plenty. We had peace and freedom. We had a good home to live in, a church to nourish our souls, and a school in which I could get an education."

Standing on the shore, Lewis broke the silence with these simple words, "We are truly blessed."

And then he went on to again express his appreciation of their new neighbours. "We are so fortunate to be Highland Scots because our people are so kind and generous," he said. "These people didn't even know us; yet they looked after us from the moment we set foot in Arisaig until we moved into our new home. That kind of hospitality reflects the finest qualities of the Highland Scots."

And Margaret hastened to add these wise words: "We may not have much, but in many ways we are rich."

Then, with tears welling in her eyes, she said fervently, "If only my parents could see us now."

As Lewis put his arm around her shoulder, he responded tenderly, "I know, I know."

The next morning, Lewis walked to the shore, set James' canoe afloat, and headed for Pictou. In just over an hour, he appeared before the magistrate and explained the circumstances that moved him to lay claim to the homestead he described. He told the magistrate he wanted to know if there was anything to prevent him from obtaining the homestead as a land grant.

The magistrate suggested that this was an unusual situation. "Most of the pioneers I know had to clear their land and build their homes," he said.

Then he asked, "And where is this land?"

When Lewis described the location of the land as precisely as he could, the magistrate, pulling his glasses down on his nose, got out his books and his maps of the area and studied both. Lewis waited nervously while the man went about his business.

After what seemed like a long time, the magistrate raised his head, looked at Louis over the top of his glasses, and said, "I have found the land in question on the map, and there is nothing in my records to indicate that it was ever granted. It would seem that the family who left so abruptly were squatters, and that leaves me free and clear to grant that land to you. You are a very lucky man."

Lewis breathed a sigh of relief for now he knew there was no obstacle standing in the way of his land claim.

In an earnest voice he said, "That is more than I ever hoped for."

The magistrate nodded in agreement as he set to work preparing a formal land grant, which he had Lewis sign. He then handed the papers to Lewis and kept a copy for his files. Lewis, feeling elated with the outcome of his inquiry, thanked the magistrate and immediately left for the shore to sail back to Arisaig. All the way home he kept thinking about his father. The thought of how proud his father would be of him on this day filled him with joy. He was the first member of his family to possess his very own land. For his kinfolk who held land in common as clansmen under their chief, and then after the demise of the clan system, as tenants who rented land from a landlord, the thought of owning their own land was a dream they could not fulfil in the Highlands.

Each day the MacDonalds faced new challenges and made new discoveries on their homestead. One of the first things they did was to explore their woodland. Because they did not have woodland where they had lived in the Highlands, this was a real adventure. Together they walked slowly among the tall evergreens and admired their beauty. The green moss that covered the ground was as soft as a carpet. The woods seemed so quiet, but they soon learned that if they listened carefully, it was alive with the sounds of the animals and birds to whom it was home.

As they walked, Lewis began to talk about his plans. "The first thing I want to do is to cut some firewood so it will be dry for the winter," he said. Then he noticed the ferns and other greenery. "Ah," he noted with enthusiasm, "that stuff could feed a pig. You know what, we can get a pig right away, and it will be ready for butchering in the late fall. We can also get a few chickens and then we will soon have some eggs, and an occasional chicken for the stew pot."

As he talked he became more excited, "I never dreamed that we would be lucky enough to obtain cleared land. By the looks of things, I think we have enough cleared land and hay to support a couple of sheep and a cow, and I know we have enough money left to purchase them. James told me that the weather is pretty mild until November; so the animals could live in the pasture until then. I can build a small barn to shelter the livestock during the winter. Heavens knows, these evergreens will provide plenty of logs for the building."

"Now, now," Mother cautioned, "don't get carried away."

"Well why not," he replied. "Can't a man dream a little. You are too serious, woman."

And with those words, he took her in his arms and whirled her around as if they were dancing a reel. Their antics reminded Mairi Bheag of pictures she had seen of fairies dancing in the forest, and she laughed joyously as she clapped her hands. When Lewis heard her clapping, he turned to her, picked her up in his arms and danced around in the clearing in the middle of the woods.

He looked at Margaret and said, "It's been a long time since Mairi Bheag had joy in her life."

Lewis kept twirling her around until he ran out of breath and then he gently put her down and once more returned to the business of planning, which he obviously enjoyed so much.

When they came out of the woods, they stopped and stood in awe at the sight of five handsome white-tailed deer feeding in their fields. The deer turned and looked at them with their heads held high and then leaped away in that graceful flowing motion that is so characteristic of them.

Mairi Bheag's spontaneous reaction was, "Ooooh, just look at them!"

Lewis remarked that they were so beautiful he did not know how anyone could kill them.

Then Margaret put her arm around Lewis as she said, "Lewis, just stop for a moment and look around you, at our hills gently sloping to the sea, at the waves rippling on our beautiful sandy shore, at the ocean water glistening in the light of the sun. Doesn't that just remind you of our home in the Highlands?"

They stood in silence for a moment as these reflections brought tears to their eyes.

Lewis later found an old maple tree that the wind had downed. Because it provided high quality hardwood, he decided that, in his spare time, evenings and rainy days, using tools borrowed from his neighbours, he could craft some dishes from it. With great skill, dexterity and patience he soon began to carve—whittling he called it—bowls of various sizes: some for porridge, some for soup, and some bigger ones for stew.

Margaret felt one of the bowls on which Lewis was working and was amazed by how smooth it was. "Lewis, you have a gift," she marvelled.

Louis smiled in recognition of her approval. It wasn't long before Lewis realized that he did not have much time for this craft; so he decided to discontinue it until he had time on his hands over the long winter months. He also decided that he would then extend this task to fashioning various kinds of spoons: a long-handled spoon that Margaret could use to stir the pot in which she cooked over the fire, another to ladle the food from the pot, and a number of smaller spoons which they could use for cutlery.

The most immediate thing Lewis needed to do was to build a barn. He realized that he could not obtain livestock until he had a shelter for them. While he was busy selecting logs that would provide wood for the structure, Margaret planted some seed potatoes and grain in hope of a late harvest.

"This is what the neighbours call a second crop," she said. "For us it is a first."

It was amazing how much the newcomers accomplished in a short period of time. Their lives were fulfilling. It did not take Lewis long to turn their homestead into a functioning farm.

Each day, he cut a few logs, and when he had enough, he came home and announced, "Margaret, we are going to have a frolic. I need to get the neighbours to help me build a barn."

Margaret spent the day appointed for the task cooking, while she kept an eye on what the men were doing. It was fascinating to watch the men work in unison. Each man seemed to know what every other man was doing. Some peeled the logs; others cut them so that each fitted into the other or others perfectly, and the strongest of the men raised the logs to form the structure of the building. While the men were working, Margaret made a big stew and some bannock. Stew is a good meal for a large number of people, and she soon learned to make stew that was as good as any the neighbouring women made. When the men had finished their work in the evening, they devoured the excellent supper Margaret had prepared, and then their wives and girlfriends came over, and to the music of cousin James' fiddle, they danced in celebration of what they had accomplished. The MacDonalds soon began to realize how much their neighbours enjoyed the Highland custom of working and playing together. According to that tradition, the work the men do together during the day is called a frolic and the fun they have together in the evening, singing and dancing to the music of the fiddle and telling stories, is called a ceilidh. The very special bond that exists among these people made Arisaig a wonderful place in which to live.

After the barn was built, Lewis persuaded his neighbours to sell him a cow, a pig, and a few chickens. Margaret and Mary Bheag treated the animals like family pets. They talked to them every day and treated them to tasty bites of the food that grew wild around them. Lewis laughed as he remarked, "You had better be careful or those animals will follow you into the house."

In late July, Lewis began to make the hay. Again the neighbours came to his aid by providing the scythe, hand rakes, and hay forks needed to do the job. Lewis swung the scythe back and forth with even strokes as he cut a field of hay. Now and then he would stop to rest and to breathe in the smell of the new-mown hay that wafted through the air. After he had finished mowing, he let the hay dry for a couple of days and then, with Margaret's help, he raked it into bundles to be carried into the barn. Even though their backs were sore and their hands blistered, they took great satisfaction in their accomplishments.

At the end of each day, Lewis would pat Margaret on the back and say, "Well done."

That compliment made her glow with pride in her ability to help him on the farm.

On many evenings, Lewis and Margaret, weary but satisfied, sat outside with their nearest neighbours and discussed the progress of their work. These gatherings gave them a chance to be with their new friends and to continue to learn more about how to live on their new homestead. And the neighbours viewed these gatherings to be a great opportunity to reminisce about their homeland. At these times Lewis could not get thoughts of the tragedy of the Sutherland clearances out of his mind. Again and again he though of what happened to his good friend, Duncan. He felt compelled to tell and retell the story of the devastation of the glens and straths that forced out the good people of Sutherlandshire. As he told this story to the people of Arisaig, they listened with rapt attention.

The first time he told the tragic story of the fate of these people, one of his neighbours interrupted to ask, "What did the clergy do to help?"

Lewis stopped to think and then he replied. "The Catholic clergy were no help. They were still on the run because the penalties imposed by the Penal Laws made them outlaws. Most of the ministers did what they could. They were there for their people; they wept with them, and they tried to comfort them. However, there was one heartless cleric—a fellow Duncan said he would never forget—who took the side of the lairds and turned his back on his flock. That fellow had the nerve to tell his parishioners that it was God's will that they get out. 'Eternal damnation awaits those who do not,' he is said to have warned. I just don't know how he could betray his very own people. The poor homeless souls from his congregation who were so loyal to their church found no comfort in it in their time of need. The new landlord bought the support of this cleric by giving him a few acres of choice land and a new manse. The cleric was willing to sell his soul for earthly gain. Judas is not dead yet. There will be a special place in hell waiting for such traitors."

"Hear, hear," was the response of the neighbours.

And in this manner, stories of the past were intermingled with stories of the present to keep the minds of the people occupied.

The people of Arisaig looked forward to Sunday because it was a day of worship and of rest. The MacDonalds made their way to their first Sunday mass in Arisaig's little log church, St. Margaret's, without fear of repercussions.

With deep satisfaction Lewis turned to Margaret and said, "See, at long last we are free to go to church."

While they could not understand the Latin liturgy, they loved to listen to their pastor intone the prayers of the mass, to see the light of the candles on the altar and to smell the incense rising to God, all of which engendered a sense of awe and mysticism that sunk deep into their souls. The aura and sanctity of the ceremony spoke to their inner beings in a way that words by themselves could not. The sermons were in their native tongue, and they appreciated the uplifting message of their pastor, Father James MacDonald. His message constantly reminded them of the mercy and love of God and of their spirituality as a source of inner peace and joy. When times were hard, his words had a way of raising their spirits. And his blessing at the end of mass encouraged them to go forth for the coming week with a renewed sense of optimism. No doubt, their special appreciation of their new church was heightened by the loyalty and devotion of the congregation and the warm welcome they extended to its new members. They were truly a Christian community.

The MacDonalds particularly looked forward to the Sundays on which babies were to be baptized. This was a very special occasion. The whole community came out for this service to participate in welcoming new members into the church. The sight of the beautiful babies filled their hearts with joy. And it was also a great opportunity for a feast in their honour. The lairds may have been in the business of emptying the Highlands, but the settlers would see to it that the Celtic race was well represented in New Scotland.

9

In the late summer, Margaret and Lewis decided it was time to send Mairi Bheag to school.

"If Mairi Bheag is to have a better life, she has to go to school," Margaret argued in her quiet but assertive fashion.

"Margaret, you know you don't have to try to convince me," Lewis replied. "She is obviously very bright, and I'm all for her getting an education. I can hardly wait to find out what her teacher thinks of her."

When they told Mairi Bheag of their decision on the evening before school opened, she was so excited that she could hardly contain herself. She did not sleep a wink that night. It was with great anticipation that she set out on her very first trip to school. On the morning of September 5, Margaret took her by the hand and they walked together to the Arisaig school. After they had exchanged greetings with her teacher, John Ronald MacDonald, Margaret went home. Mairi Bheag smiled shyly at him as he took her by the hand and accompanied her into the classroom, where he assigned her a seat.

"Mairi," he said in a kindly fashion, "I think you are going to like it here."

His reassuring manner and kind words enhanced her confidence. Because she was the only new student in the school that year, he had the other pupils introduce themselves to her.

When they finished, she rose and said in a forthright manner, "I am Mairi Bheag."

Her assertiveness brought a smile to the faces of the other pupils as well as that of her teacher.

From the very beginning, Mairi Bheag was proud to be able to attend school. Young as she was, she knew that going to school was a very special privilege. In the Highlands many girls were not permitted to go to school. Some of their parents refused to allow them to be educated in English. Other parents needed their help at home. Her good experiences in school in the Highlands aroused positive expectations about school in Nova Scotia. She looked forward to each and every day in school, partly because it was a privilege, but most important of all, because she loved to learn. To this day she says she will never forget the first day she learned to read. After their very first reading lesson, she found that she was able to put the sounds together to form words and then the words together to create meaning.

Many times during her adult life, I heard her recall, "The day I leaned to read was one of the most exciting days of my life. It opened up a whole new world to me. It introduced me to new experiences, imaginary and real."

Her teacher, sensing her love for reading, gave her some extra children's books to read at home. The fairy tales had a very special appeal for her over-active imagination because the characters in these stories took on a whole range of activities that were foreign and exciting. Before too many months had passed, she had read every book the teacher gave her. After she became proficient in the basics of reading and writing, she took delight in listening to her teacher introduce the older students to the wonders of language and literature and history.

"A love for these subjects runs deep in the MacDonald family. I believe it has roots in our Highland tradition," Grandma had often told us.

And this is how I remember her story of that tradition. In the Highlands and here in Nova Scotia children grew up listening to storytellers in their communities recite the ancient tales of the mythical heroes of the Highlands and narrate the more recent history of their clans. Every child learned to admire the heroism and great deeds of Finn MacCool and his warriors. They also listened to tragic tales of the efforts of the redcoats to humiliate the Highlanders after routing them in the Battle of Culloden. It was with great sadness that children learned that this battle sealed the fate of the Highland Scots. These stories fuelled the minds, the imaginations, and the spirits of the settlers. Their storytellers were models of fine speech, and listening to these men helped to make people quite articulate. That may be why so many Highland Scots speak so well.

10

For a couple of weeks, Lewis had been noticing a young stranger trespassing on his property without stopping to talk. Lewis thought this behaviour to be strange, but he did not dwell on it. However, Lewis started to be concerned when he saw this man coming closer to the house. When Lewis attempted to approach him, he ran into the woods.

That evening, he shared with Margaret his concern about the young man who was watching the house. "I don't like it," he said. "I think he's a bad egg."

Then for a few days the young man did not return, and Lewis forgot about him. However, about a week later, just as the MacDonalds had finished supper and as Lewis expressed satisfaction with how well things were going, they heard a loud rap on their door. Lewis opened the door to find himself confronted by the young trespasser.

Without even introducing himself, he looked Lewis in the eye and in an angry voice asserted, "You, you crooked bastard, you stole my farm."

Shocked by this allegation, Lewis, in a questioning voice, said "I what?"

"You heard what I said," the angry young man continued. "You stole this farm from me, you rotten son of a bitch. My uncle told me that after he left, this farm would be mine."

"That is not the story I have," Lewis replied. "The people of the community told me that the entire family abandoned the farm and moved to Upper Canada and that no one claimed it."

"Well I have," the angry young man asserted, "and I order you to be out of here in two weeks. I am going to return exactly two weeks from today and you had better be gone."

"Who are you?" Lewis asked.

"I am Ronald Jim Joe," he replied.

Then Lewis said, "I want you to know that I have papers granting the land to me."

"No you do not," was Ronald's reply. "I am the one who has those papers." And with a scowl he turned and walked away.

Lewis and Margaret looked at each other with disbelief.

"I just don't know what to say," Lewis said as he heaved a deep sigh. "Our neighbours assured us that this homestead was abandoned. I have a paper from the magistrate granting me this land. How can he also have that paper? Did the magistrate make a mistake and grant the same land to two people?"

Margaret was beside herself with fear. With a sound of desperation in her voice she asked, "Lewis, what in the name of God are we going to do? There is no more land in Arisaig. Everything we have is here. And you worked so hard to improve the farm."

And these words were no sooner spoken than Mairi Bheag ran to her father crying, "Daddy, Daddy, what will become of us?" As she sobbed, she blurted, "I would rather die than go back to Scotland on that awful boat. I am so scared."

Lewis picked her up and held her close and rocked her as he told her that everything would be all right, even though he did not believe what he was saying. Her tears soon exhausted her and she fell back to sleep. Lewis carried her to her bed and then he and Margaret sat at the table trying to figure out what to do.

Lewis, sounding even more distraught than before, said, "I am so damn discouraged. In our short time here, I have worked my fingers to the bone developing this place. I just don't know how to face starting over again. We left Scotland because we feared the landlords were going to run us out. And now here in Nova Scotia we find ourselves facing the same problem all over again."

Margaret kept shaking her head as she repeated the question Mairi Bheag had asked, "Lewis, what will become of us?"

Lewis sadly muttered, "I don't know."

Their conversation went back and forth like that all night and the only thing it accomplished was to exhaust both of them. The lack of sleep made their problem seem even worse in the morning. Margaret put breakfast in front of Lewis, but he didn't eat a bite. It didn't help that when they looked out the window, they saw Ronald Jim Joe, looking as defiant as ever, walking along the edge of the woods.

Terrified, Margaret exclaimed, "Just look at him; he hung around here all night."

Lewis got up from the table to look out the window as he said, "Margaret, I've had about all I can take. I'm going to leave you here while I go and talk to James. I'll keep an eye on that fellow and I will make sure that he does not come near the house."

So over Lewis went and related the whole distressing tale to James.

"And what did you say the young fella's name is?" James asked.

"Ronald Jim Joe," Lewis replied.

"Ronald Jim Joe, Ronald Jim Joe, I seem to know that name," James mused. "You know what, now I think I remember who that fella is, and I don't think he is a relative of that MacDonald family that left for Upper Canada."

Then James said, "Let's go and talk to Alex Dan and Mary MacLean."

Alex not only confirmed what James had suspected about this young man but he also knew exactly who he was.

Alex said, "He is a young thug just back from working on the fishing boats and in need of a home. Lewis, he knows you don't know him and that is why he is taking advantage of you. When do you expect him back?"

"Two weeks from yesterday. That is how much time he gave us to get out," Lewis replied.

"Good," Alex said. "When he returns, the men of the community will be waiting for him. We'll solve this problem just the way the clansmen used to solve problems."

Lewis breathed a sigh of relief and thanked Alex for his offer to help. He returned home and, as he hugged Margaret and Mairi Bheag, he told them the good news. They too felt that a great burden had been lifted from their shoulders.

Two weeks passed, and true to his word, the young man appeared at the appointed time.

He rapped loudly, and when Lewis opened the door, he boldly asserted, "I ordered you out, didn't I?"

His boldness faded quickly when the men of the neighbourhood emerged from the lower end of the cabin. Taken by surprise, Ronald Jim Joe started to run. When the men bolted after him, he ran faster. James caught up with him and grabbed him by the collar while the rest of the men circled him.

Alex looked at him menacingly as he asserted, "You, you are a no good liar and thief. Don't you ever show your face in this community again."

In an authoritative voice, James added, "We'll be watchin' you. If we ever catch you here again, we'll beat the snot out of you."

And with these words, James let Ronald go with a hard shove, and he ran from them as fast as he could. The men watched him until he disappeared into the woods.

Then James proudly asserted, "That's the last you'll see of that slink."

"Thank God," Lewis exclaimed with a sigh of relief. And he looked at his neighbours as he said appreciatively, "What would I do without you?"

After the men went home, Lewis and Margaret sat at the table, and as Lewis breathed a deep sigh, he said, "Ahhh, what a relief," and Margaret nodded in agreement.

Then, in a thoughtful mood, he mused, "You know, you just can't beat the Highland Scots. There are so many ways in which they are loyal to their kin."

Margaret again nodded in agreement. She was so exhausted after the trauma that she didn't have the energy to talk.

Then Lewis recalled, "I can't help but think of how pleased Father would be with what happened here today. I remember well the story he told about the time the Campbells were coming to steal black cattle from the pasture in our township. When Father heard the rumour, he met with his neighbours to cook up a plan for dealing with the cattle thieves. One MacDonald was overheard saying to the others, 'We'll fix them.' And fix them they did. They sent a spy to a ceilidh in Campbell territory—a fine looking young MacDonald lass. In the course of dancing the night away with the rival Campbell men, she learned that the cattle thieves were coming in the afternoon of the following Wednesday. Back she came with the news. The men smiled as they said to each other, 'We'll be ready for them.' And ready they were. Just before the appointed hour, the men fed the cattle baskets of fermented apples that had fallen to the ground. It didn't take the cattle long to get drunk and riled. When our men saw the Campbells' coming, they set the cattle loose, and they bawled and roared as they ran around the pasture and raced toward the Campbell men. Taken by surprise, the Campbells were scared to death; so they quickly turned their horses around and galloped for home."

This story was a pick-me-up for Margaret, and as they both laughed, she added, "And if I recall correctly, that event gave rise to the ditty, "The Campbells are coming, ho ho, ho ho." Then she said, "From what I heard, the MacDonalds were a tough bunch, weren't they?"

To which Lewis responded, "They had to be."

11

While Mairi Bheag was occupied with her school work, Lewis and Margaret were busy getting ready for their first winter in Nova Scotia. Day after day, they went to the woods to cut more wood to feed the greedy fire in the fireplace. After Lewis had cut down each log and trimmed it, he sawed it into chunks that would fit into their fire box. Margaret gathered the boughs from the trees to put around the base of the house before winter set in to help to keep out the draft. James had told them that the sawdust from the wood he was cutting was even better to keep out the cold. So each day Margaret collected some sawdust and carried it home. It wasn't long before they noticed that the floor of their cabin was warmer.

When Lewis learned that the herring ran in schools in the bay in the fall, he took his boat out to meet them and he returned with more fish than he could handle. From James he had learned how to salt herring and cod to be put away for the winter. He salted what he needed and gave the rest to the neighbours.

"This will help us get through the winter," he informed Margaret.

The potatoes Margaret had planted as a late crop were ready for harvesting. While she was doing the digging, Lewis carried them in to store in the coolest part of their cabin for later use.

With considerable satisfaction, she said, "I think we have enough potatoes to last us until spring."

On dry sunny days, she harvested the grain she had planted, and when she finished, she said, "Now this will provide our porridge for breakfast."

For newcomers the MacDonalds had done a surprisingly good job of getting ready for winter. They took great satisfaction in each task they completed.

As these tasks neared completion, Lewis turned to Margaret and boasted, "We sure make a great team."

They knew they were learning fast how to survive in their tough environment, and this helped them to face their first winter with confidence. Adding to their feeling of security was their realization that they had good neighbours to turn to in time of need.

As they made their way to mass on Thanksgiving Sunday, they realized they had much to be thankful for. On this occasion, Father MacDonald, their pastor, preached a sermon that spoke very personally to each and every person in the community. They listened with rapt attention as he praised them for the strength of their faith. He traced the religious persecution of their forefathers back to the passage of the dreaded Penal Laws in the sixteenth century which outlawed the practise of the Catholic religion. Then he described the impact of these laws on the Highland people.

"After the 1745 Rebellion, the Penal Laws were strictly enforced. Every Catholic house of worship in the Highlands was demolished. Priests were hunted down, and if caught, punished. The persecution virtually reduced the few priests who were not caught by the authorities to beggars who skulked from house to house in search of sustenance. When they saw law-enforcement agents in the area, they hastened to the mountains to hide in caves. Mass could only be celebrated in secret. Some ambitious lairds actually tried to force Roman Catholics to attend the Kirk. One ruthless laird went so far as to tell his tenants that if they did not sign a document renouncing their faith, they would be driven from their land. To a man these people refused to sign. They were not ready to compromise their faith. As a result of their strong stand, they were put off their land and they had no choice but to leave their homeland. They came to Prince Edward Island, but a few years later, some decided to move on to Cape Breton, and a few here to Arisaig. I know there are some of you among us today."

The priest ended his homily with this message, "And so, my good people, I know the price you and your forefathers paid for loyalty to your faith. Your faith and that of your forefathers was so strong that you were willing to leave your homeland and cross the ocean in search of a place where you would be free to worship.

Let us today remember those who suffered and sacrificed for their faith. Let us give thanks for the religious freedom we now enjoy."

At this point, Mairi Bheag looked around and she could see tears trickling down the cheeks of the parishioners for whom this was a very personal story.

When mass was over, the MacDonalds accepted an invitation from Alex Dan and Mary MacLean to join them for Thanksgiving dinner.

"This is a very special day. We want you to celebrate your first Thanksgiving in Nova Scotia with us," was the way Alex put it.

As soon as they entered the house, the inviting smell of turkey cooking on a spit over the fire greeted them. Over dinner they relaxed, and in a nostalgic vein, traded stories about the fortunes of their lives in the past year. For the MacDonalds it was a time to remember the problems they had faced: their fear of being forced off their land, the hardships and dangers of life on the transport ship, the trauma of being ordered to evacuate their homestead. But these stories of hardship were soon followed by stories that celebrated the good things life had brought: their safe arrival in Nova Scotia, the hospitality and kindness extended to them by the Frasers and fellow pioneers in Arisaig, the land grant which brought them ownership of their fine homestead, and the freedom and peace they now enjoyed. It was interesting to note how memories of what was good in their lives had a way of superseding memories of the problems and dangers they had faced.

After their stories were exhausted, Alex expressed these words of wisdom, "It is important for us to stop now and count our blessings. That is the great lesson of Thanksgiving."

And in silence they bowed their heads in a solemn prayer of thanksgiving.

As the days grew shorter, and as the seasonal farm work came to an end, Lewis and Margaret looked forward to joining the people of their community for their favourite Scottish social event, a ceilidh. One or more times a week, they came together in a designated home, where in front of a blazing fire they would wile the nights away telling stories from the old country, singing songs of the Highlands, and dancing to the music of the fiddle. For all the settlers these gatherings were a great source of enjoyment. The men added to the pleasure by downing a few drams of whiskey. The drink seemed to evoke better stories and better singing. The women brought their sewing and knitting and continued to work while enjoying the social pleasure of the evening.

"I can still remember the beautiful glow from the light of the blazing fire and the candles," Grandma often recalled.

The highlight of these events was the music provided by John Ban Gillis, the finest fiddler in the community. He took great satisfaction in the enjoyment his music brought to his neighbours. They danced, clapped, or tapped their feet to the rhythm of the music. Those who were too old or crippled to dance got just as much pleasure from sitting and swaying their bodies to the music.

It was at these events that skilled storytellers perpetuated the folklore that peopled the lives of the Highland Scots with supernatural and preternatural beings. Their powerful ability to spin a tale kept alive the belief in the dark powers of witches and fairies and bocans. The lore surrounding these mythical creatures provided the settlers with another realm of being which took their minds far beyond the concerns of eking out a living in their stubborn environment.

"To these events I owed my overactive imagination as a child," Grandma once told us. "Some of those dark tales scared me to death. I would run to my bed, hide under the blankets, and shiver with fear."

The MacDonalds wondered what winter would be like in the New World and they began to find out sooner than they had anticipated. Winter came early in their first year in Nova Scotia; it arrived in the second week of November. It was cold, colder than anything they had experienced in the Highlands.

This prompted Lewis to turn to Margaret and exclaim, "I hope we're not going to freeze to death in this place."

On November 15, it began to snow and it snowed every night for two weeks. The MacDonalds thought the first few snowfalls were magnificent. Never had they seen anything like it. They often stood together in the doorway to gaze in awe at the beauty of its pure white covering on the trees and the ground. The sunlight played on the the snow-covered landscape to make it sparkle like a jewel. This beautiful sight brightened their days. But as the winds off the water whipped the snow into tall drifts and made it harder and harder to move, their appreciation of its beauty began to wane. The raw wind chilled them to the bone. Heavy squalls made it hard for them to see. Lewis often trudged in from the barn chilled to the bone and with his clothes caked in heavy wet snow.

There were times when the snow was so deep that Mairi Bheag was not able to walk to school. At these times, Margaret, feeling the need to be cautious, would say, "Mairi Bheag, you stay home today. I'm afraid you might get lost in the blizzard, and we would not be able to find you."

There were other times when the blizzard was so fierce that even her parents could not see where they were going. They would step outside only to come back in quickly. "Brrr," Lewis would say as he stepped back inside.

On the days Mary Bheag could not get to school, she would sit by her window and spin fairy tales around the enchanting patterns and colours made by the sunlight on the frost. Missing a day of school was a great disappointment to her because she was so engrossed in her school work. She tried to have a book at home for such occasions. Grandma often told us that a good book made a snow storm pass quickly.

With the passage of time, the temperature kept dropping so that the water in the bay turned to ice. Neighbours told Lewis of how they could walk across the bay on the ice to Pictou and obtain good paying jobs in the lumber woods. According to their reports, big boat loads of lumber left the port of Pictou for Europe every week.

Lewis was excited. He hurried home to tell Margaret about this wonderful opportunity.

"If I go I can make some money to stock our homestead," he said enthusiastically. "We can buy more supplies and livestock for the farm. We may even be able to get a horse. Now wouldn't that be grand?"

Margaret grudgingly gave her approval. To relieve her concern, Lewis said, "Don't worry. I won't be alone; Alex will be with me."

So the next day, off Lewis went with the neighbouring men, and Margaret and Mairi Bheag only saw him on Saturday nights and Sunday mornings.

On one of these trips across the bay, Alex turned to Lewis and said, "I'll bet you never thought you could walk on water!"

They looked at each other and roared out laughing.

After the end of his last week in the woods, Lewis arrived home with a wonderful surprise.

Grandma's face lit up with joy as she recalled, "I could not believe my eyes when I saw him walking across the frozen bay leading a beautiful black horse. Mother and I ran to meet them and we soon found the horse to be as gentle as he was huge. Father took a carrot out of his pocket, and the horse whinnied in anticipation of the treat. He then lifted me up so that I could pet the horse's beautiful white forehead. I cautiously put my hand on his forehead, and it responded by rubbing his head into my hand.

"As I smiled with satisfaction, Father remarked, 'You have a way with animals, little girl.'"

Now Mairi Bheag had a new companion. She visited the horse in his stall every day so she could talk to him. Soon he recognized her footsteps and he would whinny when he heard her coming. She loved the way he looked at her with his big black eyes and the way he nuzzled her shoulder as she told him how beautiful he was.

12

Mairi Bheag continued to love everything about school. School was the centre of her life. This was where she went to be with her friends; this was where they sat and gossipped; this was where she learned to play the games she did not learn at home because she was an only child. Much as she loved the social life, she loved learning even more. Each school year flew by. Even though her academic achievement was excellent, she had no choice but to leave school at the end of the eighth grade because girls were not permitted to attend high school. By that time she had done all of the high-school work on her own by following the high-school lessons. She asked her teacher to let her write some of the high-school exams, which he did. She passed every one of these exams with good grades, but because she was a girl, she was not permitted to get credit for her achievement. Hers was the fate of all girls who went to school in eastern Nova Scotia at that time.

In reflecting back on the end of her school career many years later, she recalled, with an air of resignation, "In my heart of hearts, I was deeply disappointed, but I did not object. This is the way things were. Grammar school was not for the daughters of the pioneers, and it would have done no good to complain."

After she had finished school, she was no longer known as Mairi Bheag. She was now viewed to be a young woman, and this was the time for her to take her place alongside her mother in the home and on the farm, learning to do the work expected of Highland women in rural communities. While she grew up helping her mother with some of her chores, she had never learned how to work independently.

Cleaning and scrubbing did not have much appeal for Mairi, but like most Highland women, she took a great interest in cooking.

As she watched her mother cook and bake the food required for each meal, she came forth with a steady stream of questions. "How do you know how much flour to put in the bread? How much fat? How much salt? How much sugar?"

She asked the same questions when her mother was preparing other baked goods. It soon became clear that Mairi had learned her lessons well as she produced one fluffy crusty loaf of bread after another and pans of light-textured sweet bannock. Good baking is a creative art which was a great source of satisfaction for her.

The preparation of the main dishes brought forth a new round of questions. "Why are you cooking the meat quickly? How do you know when it is done? Why are you cooking the vegetables longer than the meat? How do you know when they are done?"

As the questioning continued, it became too much for Margaret, and in exasperation she said, "For God's sake, Mairi, give it a rest."

Margaret had made her point. Startled, Mairi looked at her, and they both burst out laughing.

One morning while they were in the barn together, Margaret said, "Mairi, now it is time for you to learn to milk a cow. Every farm woman is expected to be a milk maid, you know."

In spite of her love for being around animals, Mairi was hesitant and she looked worried.

"I'm afraid the cows will kick me," she protested.

Her mother replied, "I've been milking for years, and not one of those animals ever tried to kick me."

These words of assurance allayed Mairi's fears and she decided to try. As soon as she sat on the milking stool to the right of the cow's udder, the cow turned her head toward her, and you could see the cow's body grow tense. As Margaret gave instructions, Mairi tried to milk, but the cow would not give a drop.

Then and there Margaret realized that both Mairi and the cow were tense; so she said, "Mairi, she will not let her milk down until you do something to put her at ease."

It didn't take Mairi long to figure out what to do. She began to sing a soothing lullaby and she wasn't very far into the song before she could see the the tension drain from the cow's body. The cow soon let down her milk, and in a short time Mairi came away with a full dish.

Mairi was pretty impressed with her performance. She looked at her mother as she said, "That was easy."

Furthermore, she had learned a skill she could use for the rest of her life. She soon became so good at looking after the cows and milking them that Margaret began to leave these chores entirely to her. Doing more milking and less cleaning was just fine by Mairi—a great trade-off she called it. Her love of animals made her twice daily trips to the barn a continuing source of pleasure.

It wasn't long before Mairi graduated to the next step in learning to be a dairy maid.

Her mother informed her, "Now that you are bringing in so much milk, it is time for you to learn how to turn the milk into dairy products."

First, she showed her how to separate the cream from the milk. "You just lower the container into the well to cool and let the cream rise to the top, and then you use a big spoon to skim it off," she instructed.

The next day her mother showed her how to make cheese. She used sour milk, to which she added some buttermilk and a little rennet. She then slightly heated the milk until it coagulated.

"I add rennet to thicken the mixture," her mother said helpfully, as she continued working.

Then she showed her how to drain off the liquid through a cheese cloth, put some salt in the solids and place them between two presses to form a solid mass of cheese.

As Mairi watched she remarked, "I often wondered how that was done. How did you learn to do all of these things?"

Her mother's reply was, "In the same way you are learning, from my mother. Highland women hand down these skills from generation to generation. That is the most important part of our education."

Margaret let the cheese sit in the presses for a week so it would get good and solid. As Mairi watched her take the cheese out of the presses, Margaret suggested it was time for her to learn to make butter. To do this, she put a large bowl of cream on the table and began to beat it rigorously.

When she tired, she handed the job over to Mairi as she said, "Now it is your turn."

Mairi kept beating the cream until small yellow globs began to form. When the solids became larger, Margaret took over and drained the liquids, salted the solids and pulled them all together to form one golden pat of butter.

As Margaret worked she remarked. "Did you ever wonder where the butter on our table comes from? Now you know. Put all these skills that you learned the last few days together, and you know how we get the cream, cheese, and butter for the table. Milk is a wonderful product. You can do so much with it."

In August, Margaret decided that it was time for Mairi to learn to do the wash. Lewis obligingly hitched their horse to the riding wagon and drove to the front door where the three of them filled the back of the wagon with clothing and bedding. Then Margaret got into the seat, took the reins, and headed for the brook. Margaret started a fire while Mairi hauled buckets of water from the brook to be heated in a boiler placed on large stones over the fire.

When the water had reached the right temperature for washing, Margaret threw some water on the fire to put it out as she exclaimed, "Can't be too careful in this dry weather."

Then she and Mairi each took a wash board and a cake of soap and they sudsed and scrubbed each piece of wash. This was hard physical labour, and it wasn't long before they were both covered with sweat.

As they finished washing each piece, and as Margaret exclaimed, "Thanks be to God," they threw it in the brook to rinse.

With sweat streaming down her face, Mairi remarked, "Thank God we don't have to do this too often."

When they finished the sudsing and scrubbing, they went into the brook in their bare feet, swished the wash around in the cool water to rinse it and then hung each piece of clothing on the bushes and spread the bedding on the grass to dry.

Both of them were now dead tired; so while the wash was drying, they sat on the bank of the brook, dangled their sweaty feet in the cool, soothing water and slowly ate their lunch. Then they both sat in the sun until their bodies were rested and the wash was dry.

Mairi's comment, "There has to be an easier way to do this," made both of them laugh.

They were more than mother and daughter; they were good friends. Margaret enjoyed having Mairi home with her. Their companionship did much to relieve the drudgery of their work.

Next Margaret turned to teaching her daughter how to spin and knit and weave and sew—skills needed to make clothing and bedding for the family. Mairi found learning these intricate skills to be challenging and enjoyable. Each evening after dinner, the two of them sat like old women in front of the fire and did an hour or two of spinning and knitting. They turned out pair after pair of socks and mitts to be worn in the cold winter weather. Margaret also started to knit some sweaters, but Mairi felt she was not yet up to the task.

"I'll stick with socks for now," she said.

When Margaret pieced the loom together and showed Mairi how to turn wool into cloth, she was fascinated by the intricacies of the process. The first time Margaret used colour, extracted from berries, to dye some of the cloth from the loom, and then used the cloth to make a coat for her daughter, Mairi was very impressed with the beauty of the finished product.

"I'll be the best dressed young woman in Arisaig," she exclaimed. "I can't wait to learn how to make some skirts and dresses from the same material, but I'd like a darker colour."

In the summer, Mairi accompanied her mother to the garden daily to help with the weeding and the harvesting. They both loved to watch the vegetables grow.

On one of these trips Mairi astutely remarked, "I think the soil is alive. What happens in the earth is just like magic."

As they observed the changes from day to day, they speculated on when particular vegetables would be ready to eat. Each week, they hoed the soil around the potatoes and the other root vegetables to keep them from burning and to remove the weeds.

At one point Mairi stopped hoeing, turned to her mother, and said, "I had no idea there was so much work involved in keeping our home going. I sure took a lot for granted."

The smile on Margaret's face reflected her deep satisfaction in seeing how much her daughter grew up over the summer.

Mairi came to regard the products of her labour to be a sufficient reward for her efforts in the garden. She never ceased to be amazed at the freshness of the vegetables as they came from the soil or at their fine taste when they were cooked. From the health lessons in school she learned to appreciate the contribution these vegetables made to the family's diet. With these lessons in gardening, Mairi's home schooling in "women's work" was completed. Her mother was a good teacher, and Mairi had learned her lessons well.

13

After Mairi had left school, she joined her parents in participating in the ceilidhs that were held in various homes in the community. Even though she had already heard all the tales of the storytellers, she never tired of listening to them. They always fired up her imagination. And, most of all, she loved to dance. Her feet were as nimble as her brain. Then one night, a handsome young man by the name of Ronald Black Donald MacDonald, with dark hair and even darker eyes, asked her to dance, and according to Mairi, it was love at first sight.

"That was the best night of my life," she often recalled.

They had a common heritage. They had both been born in Arisaig, Scotland, and even though they were only children when they left, they retained the fondest memories of their homeland. Their personalities complemented each other. While Mairi tended to be serious, Ronald was high spirited. He would call for her with his fast trotter and riding wagon, and when she climbed in, they would race off together. They quickly became inseparable. At that time, Mairi was eighteen and Ronald was twenty-four. They had only known each other for three months before they decided to marry.

After Lewis had approved Ronald's request for Mairi's hand in marriage, he said to Margaret, "Our little girl is going to have the best wedding ever held in Arisaig."

And a grand wedding it was. By that time, Lewis owned a handsome trotter and an eye-catching riding wagon, a two seater, and this was the vehicle in which he, with Margaret seated beside him, proudly drove Mairi to the church for the wedding ceremony. During the ceremony, tears ran down the cheeks of Lewis and

Margaret as they realized that their beautiful little girl, their only child, would be gone from them for good. After the church service, Margaret put on a fine spread for all the neighbours. And everyone in the community came and feasted, and drank, and danced well into the night.

While the guests were dancing and merry-making, Ronald said to Mairi, "Let's get out of here."

Then they quietly slipped away to the home Ronald had inherited from his father, where for a few years they had a wonderful life together. Between 1832 and 1851, Ronald and Mairi had five children—four sons, John, Alex, Ronald, and Hugh, and one daughter, Margaret.

Just as there are gaps in history's coverage of the past, there are gaps in Mairi's story of her past. Beyond the details of her courtship and marriage to Ronald, she said very little about their life together. And there was a good reason for that. The story of their relationship was a sad one, for love can go so wrong. Mother, who was their daughter Margaret, filled me in on the details. Unfortunately, Ronald developed a problem that afflicted many Highland men. He was only married five years before he began to drink and dark, handsome Ronald Black Donald MacDonald gradually became Ronald the drunk. He remained charming and personable, but he was not dependable. Margaret clearly remembered the first time she realized he had a drinking problem. She overheard her mother talking to him.

Mairi came in from the barn one evening, exhausted, and looking at him with disgust, she said, "Ronald, I worked outside all day, and you did not raise a hand to help me. Have you been drinking?"

To which he replied in that state of denial which is characteristic of the alcoholic, "I never touched a drop. Woman, that is the God honest truth."

In spite of Ronald's weakness for the bottle, according to his daughter, Margaret, he was wonderful with his children. He was warm and affectionate and loved to spend time playing with them.

Margaret fondly remembered how he would pick her up in his arms and dance around the kitchen floor.

"He had his failings, but he loved us dearly," she often said.

In the midst of all this fun, Mairi was usually working out of doors. As Ronald's drinking worsened, he further neglected his work, and according to Margaret, her mother then found herself having to do all the farm work, as well as the house work, in addition to carrying out her responsibility for looking after the children. She would ask Ronald to do some chores and he would agree, but being the weak man he was, he never showed up. Mairi soon realized that she might as well cut her losses and she quit asking. Their relationship was over; she had been replaced by the bottle.

When the burden of hard work and heavy responsibility were too much for Mairi, with tears in her eyes, she would say, "I don't know how much longer I can go on. Oh how I miss my parents. If they were here, I wouldn't have to carry this burden alone."

Their premature deaths in an accident in which both of them were thrown from their riding wagon deprived her of their support. Kind neighbours did what they could to help, but their efforts were not nearly enough to look after the continuing work the homestead required. The wear and tear of hard work on Mairi's body showed in her thin, peaked, weather-beaten face. Her sons began to help her with the farm work as soon as they were big enough to do so. They were inducted into child labour at a very young age.

Margaret remembered that, even as young as the age of eight, the boys had some sense of the burden their mother carried, and she heard more than one of them say, "Mama, we can help you."

In response, Mairi would hug each thoughtful child and then take him by the hand to work with her. She had no choice; she could not continue to carry the burden alone.

When she returned from working out of doors in the evening, she would cook supper, spend a little time with the children, and then settle down to her weaving, spinning, and knitting. She had learned her lessons well from her mother. She made all of the clothes for her family. Even though she was tired, she would work well into the night. While she stayed up late working her fingers to the bone, Ronald was usually in bed sleeping off a hang-over. On many occasions, Margaret found her mother asleep from exhaustion in front of the fire late at night, with the knitting needles still in her hands.

She would slowly and gently take the needles from her and say, "Mama, come with me," and then take her by the arm to help her up to her bed.

On some of these occasions, Margaret again heard her mother softly say, with anxiety in her voice, "I just don't know how much longer I can go on. I am worn out—old beyond my years."

In spite of her misgivings, Mairi continued to work like that for many years. With each passing year she looked more thin and frail, and her body was wearing down prematurely from overwork.

Just as fifteen years of hard work had taken its toll on Mairi's strength, fifteen years of hard drinking took its toll on Ronald's health. His body demanded more and more liquor. When he was without it, his hands shook and he was unsteady afoot. The only cure was even more liquor, which he drank compulsively. His long body became thin and then emaciated, his complexion pasty and sallow; black circles developed around his eyes and made them look even darker than they were. He looked wasted. At the age of forty-four, he passed away in a drunken stupor. This was a story too painful for Mairi to tell.

Shortly after Ronald's death, Margaret remembered hearing one of the neighbouring women say to her mother, with some lack of discretion, "Mairi Dear, I know how hard it has been for you, and God forgive me for saying it, Ronald's death must have been a relief."

Taken back by her directness, Mairi replied, "No, no, Mary, don't say that. I know Ronald had a weakness for the drink, and yes, there were times I was so angry I wanted to hit him, but in spite of it all, I still loved him."

After Ronald died, Mairi packed up their belongings and she and the children moved back to the old homestead because her father left his farm in much better condition than Ronald left his estate. Following Ronald's death, Margaret said that she seldom heard her mother speak of him.

And this painful story was also the story of my mother's upbringing. If Mairi worked hard, Margaret worked equally hard beside her in the kitchen and alongside her brothers in the fields. Because she could only do light labour in the fields, she took over the chores involved in milking and looking after the cattle. Between and among them, Mairi and her children were able to eke out a living. Margaret recalled how Alex would show her the blisters on his hands after driving the horse and plough through the fields for many long hours. After the ploughing was done, John would hitch the double team of horses to the harrows and guide them through the rough furrows made by the plow. Ronald and Hugh loaded and unloaded cartloads of manure to fertilize the newly cultivated ground. While they did not complain, you could see them wince when some of the tougher callouses on their hands broke open and bled. During the planting and harvesting seasons, their bodies were caked with a mixture of sweat and dust, the by-product of their hard labour.

In the frosty winter weather, the boys went to the woods with their saws and axes to fell and limb trees for firewood. The frost in the trees made them harder to cut, but the lowering of the sap in the cold weather made them easier to dry. Being the least robust of the boys, Hugh was the one appointed to lead the mare from the woods to snig the limbed logs into the clearing. He learned to coax the mare to move the particularly heavy logs by offering her an apple saved from the fall harvest.

During these periods of heavy winter labour, the boys' hands and feet and backs were sore. Like old men they sometimes complained that they were sore all over. They came back from the woods dead tired, ate some supper, and fell into bed.

14

By the time Mairi's older sons, Alex and John, had reached their late teens, they became restless. They were torn between the urge to get away and make a living on their own and their guilt about leaving their mother. They grew tired of working their fingers to the bone with no hope of release from the drudgery of farm work. Their restlessness turned to impatience; they wanted something more and they wanted it fast. They longed for adventure. Like other young men from their community, they were excited by stories they had heard of good job opportunities in the United States. Margaret had vivid memories of how, when they were alone working in the garden, out of earshot of their mother, they would often tell her how much they wanted to leave.

"We want to get out of here and earn some money. We're going to 'the Boston States' and we're gonna get rich," Alex often boasted. And then he would warn, "Whatever you do, don't tell Mama. We'll tell her ourselves when the time is right."

And while Margaret obediently kept their secret, she asked, "Have you thought about who is going to help Mama with the heavy farm work?"

To which John replied, "Don't worry, we'll look after Mama. We know what to do. As soon as we make money, we'll send some home for her to hire help. And don't forget, she will still have Ronald and Hugh with her on the farm."

Alex and John kept an eye on the shore to get a glimpse of the the fishing boats that plied the waters between Nova Scotia and Massachusetts. It wasn't long before their efforts paid off. When they saw one of these boats stop at Arisaig, they rushed down to the wharf to ask its captain for a job, and he agreed to hire both of them.

Margaret pleaded with them to stay. She could tell that they felt guilty, but, as she soon found out, not guilty enough to change their minds.

Their response to her plea was, "We can't take it any longer. We've gotta get out of here."

Margaret had vivid recollections of the moment Alex and John told their mother of their plans. Even though Mairi knew this day would come, its arrival left her speechless. For a moment she was shocked, and then she was gripped with fear—fear that she could not get along on the farm without their help.

Her first response was, "Lord have mercy, I can't go on without you." And then she started to cry.

Mairi quickly began to realize how selfish her concerns were. So she pulled herself together and told the boys she understood.

"I know you have to live your own lives. Go and do what you have to do; the rest of the family will carry on," she said, as she hugged each of them.

Her eyes again filled with tears as she watched them run to the shore to board *The Mariner,* where they were put to work helping to haul the fishing nets.

As the boat sailed down the east coast, the captain had an opportunity to observe John and Alex for several days. He admired their positive attitude and their capacity for work. As they neared their destination, he told them that their work habits could help them to get jobs–good jobs—on the docks at Boston harbour. This was the first information they got about specific jobs, and it raised their hopes. When the boat reached its destination, John and Alex worked for hours carrying the heavy landing of fish onto the dock. Their backs were bent from the weight of the containers. When they finished, the captain gave them their pay, and they left and walked to the residential area surrounding the docks.

The boys were shocked by what they saw. Before them stood a range of large, dark, grungy-looking houses built close together and bordering almost directly on the street. To them all the houses looked equally bad; so they decided to look for a room in the one closest to the docks. They took the first available room in a three-storey tenement building occupied mostly by immigrants, particularly the Irish. They were amazed at the number of people who were crammed into this residence.

It wasn't long before both came to enjoy listening to their fellow tenants talk in their Irish Gaelic, which was similar enough to the Scottish Gaelic to enable them to understand some of it. Occasionally one of the Irish brought out a fiddle, and Alex and John tapped their feet to the familiar beat of the Celtic music. Even though they had been so anxious to get away, they were lonely. Listening to Irish Gaelic and Irish music was the closest they came to a touch of home, and it helped to raise their spirits.

The Irish tenants were friendly, and it wasn't long before Alex and John got to know some of them. They soon learned that these men felt a pressing need to tell their story of the horrors of the potato famine that drove hundreds of thousands of men and women from the shores of Ireland. To a man, they said that their last lingering memory of Ireland was of the tragedy of its starving people, young and old, weakened and emaciated, and in many cases, dead or dying around them. The sight and smell of death were everywhere.

According to Rory, their best storyteller, "Few of us were strong enough to walk to the boat. It was heart-wrenching to hear the plaintive cries of hungry children with bloated bodies, not knowing why no one would feed them. The weakest of them would hold out a hand while lying on the ground, and sadly, we had no food to put in it. The birth of a child, which used to bring joy to our hearts, was greeted with fear and regret. One more mouth our people could not feed. On the side of a hill in Kerry, outside the sacred grounds of the local cemetery, was a mound of dirt that covered a mass grave of hundreds of babies who starved to death before they were baptized. What did those dear little souls do to deserve such a fate? Those visions will haunt us for the rest of our lives. This is a sad way to remember our homeland," Rory concluded, as tears filled his eyes and rendered him unable to continue speaking.

To this horrendous tale we had no response. We had no idea of the extreme suffering the Irish endured. We just shook our heads in disbelief.

At the first opportunity, Alex asked Rory how to get work on the docks.

"Boy," he said, "you do just like the rest of us. You line up in the morning over there," as he pointed to where they were to go. "Some mornings you get work. Some mornings you don't. That's the way it works for all of us."

So, following his directions, at five o'clock the next morning, Alex and John made their way to the line-up, and to their surprise and disgust, they stood in line for hours in the blazing sun only to find that they were not called. And that was only the beginning of their long frustrating wait. They returned day after day to the same line-up with the same result. They recalled that the ship's captain had said nothing about how tough the competition for work was going to be.

After waiting in line for ten long days, Alex looked seriously at John as he said, "We should never have come here. We only have enough money left for our rent and no money for food. We could starve and nobody would even notice."

Both of them were out of sorts. Hunger was gnawing on their stomachs like a dog on a bone. It moved them to recall fond memories of the delicious food their mother always managed to put on the table. But just as they were about to give up hope, the foreman called their names.

"You Alex, you John, step right up," he barked and then he gave them their first assignment.

They were to work with a crew—a tough-looking bunch—who were loading a ship. They worked beside these men without saying a word. They had already seen enough of life on the docks to make them wary of their fellow workers. They soon learned that the hard work on the farm was nothing compared to the hard work of loading huge boxes and bails onto the ships. But hard as it was, they stayed in hope of better days to come.

Their foreman was a tyrant. He cursed at them as he barked orders, and then in a growl like that of an angry attack dog, he would say, "Can't you move your sorry asses a little faster."

Rory, who happened to get work with the same crew just after John and Alex did, muttered under his breath, "That guy is a mean son-of-a-bitch."

After a twelve hour shift at this back-breaking work, every bone in their bodies ached. Tired as they were, the brothers took their pay from the foreman and rushed to the the grocery store before it closed to buy bread, cheese, baloney, and milk. Then they returned to their room where they ate greedily to make up for the meals they had missed when they had no money for food. Relief from hunger helped them to relax enough to fall into a deep sleep. This became their routine when they were lucky enough to get work.

As Alex and John walked the streets of Boston on their way to and from work, they were particularly alarmed at the sight of homeless drunks lying in the streets. They never got used to watching these miserable souls who had no one to turn to.

Alex would often say, "That sort of thing would never happen in Arisaig. Someone would take them in."

Their rooming house was dirty and dingy. The room they shared was small, dark, hot, and poorly furnished, containing but one bed, one chair, and a wash basin. The walls were paper thin. They heard everything that went on around them. Life at best was uncomfortable and at worst frightening. The discomfort bred frustration.

Some of the young Irish men had hot tempers; they had one way of resolving their differences, and that was with their fists. After they got their pay, they would head for the liquor store, and the beer only seemed to rile them more. On the street in front of their building they would pound each other, often with little thought to their health or well-being. The on-lookers often enjoyed baiting the more hot-tempered fighters by collecting a purse for the winner. You would think they were at a boxing match. They reacted to every thrust, as the fighters punched and kicked and screamed. Bloodied faces and broken noses did not halt the fights. No matter how bloodied and maimed, the fighters did not stop until one of them went down and stayed down. The one who won the purse acted like the heavyweight champion of America. That is what poverty did to these people. The fighters never learned; injuries took their toll on them. Bones were broken; organs were damaged. After the fighters returned to their rooms, you could hear them moaning in pain for hours. Some of them incurred injuries that would last for life.

One evening, while Alex and John were sitting on the step in front of their rooming house, Rory came by, feeling his oats after having had too many beers.

He approached them with a sly grin and asked, "Wanna fight?"

The question struck fear into their hearts and in unison they replied, "Noooo," as they got up and walked away, laughing.

Alex turned to John and said, "I'm sure glad he gave us a choice. He would have beaten the hell out of us."

In summer, the heat, the flies and the cockroaches were so unbearable that they drove the tenants outside. Alex and John sat passively on the steps or benches that surrounded the front and sides of the building and watched what was going on. Sweat rolled down their faces and backs. Rotten food and scraps carelessly thrown out on the street drew flies, mice, and rats. As the flies pestered the residents and the mice and rats darted in and out, in sheer exasperation some men went in and came back with their guns to shoot the rats. The heat, the humidity, the stink, the vermin, and the occasional gunfire strained even the most patient of the tenants. Alex and John worried that the sheer frustration of life in their neighbourhood might drive some hot-blooded young men to turn their guns on the residents.

When they left, they never thought they would miss Arisaig, but already they found themselves longing for the cool breezes from the Arisaig shore and the peace and quiet and safety of their country home. But they were too proud to admit that they were failures and return home. Their sense of failure was compounded by feelings of guilt about leaving their mother.

On a day when they were feeling particularly down, John asked Alex, "Do you still feel guilty about leaving Mama?"

Alex replied, "Not a day goes by that I don't think of it."

Alex and John felt they had no choice but to hunker down and continue to vie for work. Each day they returned to the line-up at the docks with the hope they would get enough work to keep them alive. The people in the line-up were not passive; it was every man for himself. Frequently men jumped ahead of them in the queue. Sometimes these men pushed Alex and John out of line as the foreman neared. Nobody seemed to notice—or for that matter care—when they objected. Even though they were very discouraged, they had no choice but to hunker down and continue their efforts to obtain work.

Eventually their persistence paid off. After John and Alex had worked on and off for a few weeks, the foreman began to treat them better and to give them more shifts. Coming from a farm where they were well fed and in excellent physical condition, they had quite an advantage over the Irish who were malnourished and in poor physical shape from hunger compounded by weeks of inactivity on the boats from Ireland. It did not take the foreman long to notice their excellent capacity for work.

After one month of part-time work, the foreman was so impressed that he came to them and said, "Boys, I have some good news for you. You are hired. Your jobs are now full time."

And Alex and John worked on the Boston docks from that day forward. They eventually got used to the heavy work and the strange things that happened on the waterfront. It was a rough place to work.

In one of his letters to his mother Alex described how rough it was.

> *We saw men fighting, sometimes even knocking each other out. We saw men pilfering containers, but as far as they were concerned, we saw nothing. We knew what would happen if we squealed on them. We kept clear of the men who were trouble. We wanted to stay alive.*

After a few years, life on the docks got much better. Over time, the foreman came to appreciate their dependability, and they were rewarded by being appointed foremen. In this position, they began to earn good wages and had much better working conditions. As soon as they got promoted, they started to walk the streets in good neighbourhoods in search of better accommodations. It did not take them long to find a room in a nice boarding house, which was clean and quiet and where the landlady provided good meals.

Alex summed up their success in these words, "We are beginning to achieve what newcomers here call 'the American dream.'"

15

For five years, Ronald and Hugh remained home to help their mother, but they too became restless and longed to follow in their brothers' footsteps.

Margaret overheard Ronald say to Hugh, after the older boys left, "John and Alex knew what they were doing. They knew they would never get ahead if they stayed here. We won't either."

Mairi sensed that they were eager to go. She was greatly distressed at the thought of not having any men to help on the farm. There was only so much that a little woman could do. Who would butcher the animals? Who would do the ploughing and harrowing? Who would plant and harvest the crops? Who would cut the logs for firewood? These questions played on her mind. While Alex and John sent her money to hire help, it was not nearly enough to cover the cost of farm labour and supplies.

Mairi soon learned that no amount of coaxing would persuade Ronald and Hugh to stay home. Her offer to let them take over the farm did not change their minds. Neither did their sense of guilt about leaving their mother alone. Like their brothers before them, they'd had enough of farming. And just like their brothers, they were able to obtain work on the fishing boats that plied the waters along the eastern seaboard.

As the boys prepared to depart, they said to their mother, as their brothers did before them, "Don't worry, when we make money, we'll send some home."

With tears in their eyes, each of them hugged his mother and left for the boat. While the boys loved their mother, they never had any desire to return to the farm. The drudgery of farm work made them turn against it.

Ronald and Hugh were good letter writers, and from their letters Margaret was able to piece together the story of their lives in "the Boston States." When the boys arrived in Boston, they had their brothers to look out for them. Their brothers made sure that they got good jobs on the docks. This made their induction into working on the docks much easier than it was for other new arrivals. The brothers enjoyed their time together, but after a few years, Ronald and Hugh again became restless. They talked about moving on, but they did not know where to go.

Their restlessness moved Alex to comment to John, "We spoiled those fellas. If they had to go through what we did when we first came here, they would of had all the challenge they needed."

And John added, "And then some."

Ronald and Hugh worked on the docks for six years, but this work was never enough to satisfy their desire for adventure. They kept watching for an opportunity to make a move, and it finally came in 1883. They were excited when they heard about the railway that was being built from the east coast to the west coast of Canada. So they made their way back to New Brunswick to go west as part of the work crew building the Canadian Pacific Railway.

Conditions in the work camps in which they lived in the West, which in many cases were nothing more than tents lined with buffalo hides, were tough. In the heart of winter, the temperature sometimes dropped as low as forty degrees below zero. The biting cold took its toll on them; frost bite was common; their diet of hard tack and beans was hardly sufficient to sustain them. Their jobs were hard, but not near so hard as the jobs assigned to immigrants, particularly the Chinese. The Chinese were so agreeable and eager to please that they did not turn down dangerous work. Our prime minister's National Dream had become their personal nightmare. Ronald and Hugh noticed that it was usually the Chinese who were assigned to place and ignite the fuses to blow out the rock. They got sick at the sight of so many of these men being blown to bits with the rocks they were sent to blast. They felt it wasn't fair to treat them that way.

Ronald would look at Hugh and mutter, "They didn't come this far to have that happen to them. Just because they are so agreeable and anxious to work doesn't mean that they have to be assigned the most dangerous jobs. The bosses are ruthless bastards; they have no respect for the lives of the Chinese. Thank God we don't have yellow skin."

But Ronald and Hugh would not speak too loudly for fear they would get in trouble. Other men who spoke up were given dangerous jobs, and like the Chinese, some paid with their lives. As far as Ronald and Hugh were concerned, that was too high a price.

Ronald remarked, "We may be cowards, but at least we are live cowards."

They had learned to keep their mouths shut and continued to put up with a great deal of adversity in order to make good money. They were there at Craigellachie when the last spike was driven in 1885. During the celebrations, their thoughts were with the men whose lives were sacrificed doing dangerous work for the cause. After the celebrities and workers had left, the two of them stayed behind to pour part of a dram of whiskey on the last spike and to say a few words to honour these men.

As the end of their work approached, Ronald and Hugh listened intently to stories told by other workers of the the great money to be made in the gold mines on the other side of the border. They were excited.

"Could this be the land of opportunity?" Ronald asked, as he looked at Hugh.

In an upbeat tone, Hugh replied, "Well, let's go and find out."

Then and there they decided to made their way down to Butte, Montana to join the influx of young men pouring into town to make their fortune working in the gold mines. Among these men were a number from eastern Nova Scotia, some of whom they knew. So from the very beginning, they were among friends.

They wrote home frequently. They found mining and life in a boom town exciting. Ronald was a better writer than Hugh; so it was he who wrote to their mother. He made sure he incorporated Hugh's thoughts into his letters. Their mother put their letters away for safe keeping. Many years later, she showed me one of these letters and she asked me to read it out loud. And this is how it read.

Dear Mama,

Hugh and I are enjoying life here in Butte, Montana. You will be happy to learn that we both have good jobs in a gold mine in what is called the richest hill in the world. For twelve hours a day, six day a week, we mine for gold. We both stay at the same boarding house where we only have time to go to eat and sleep, except on Sunday. During the week we are so tired that we don't do much other than work. However, life is not dull. Many of the other miners are also from Nova Scotia. There are MacDonalds, MacIsaacs, and Walshes here from Antigonish. These guys are very friendly, and we enjoy being together. After work, we all go to the saloon to have a beer and to share the latest news from home. Saturday night is our big night out. Because we do not have to work the next day, we stay at the saloon most of the night, where we drink and play cards and talk. More than once some of our friends have gone too far. When the MacIsaacs get drunk, they get rambunctious and fight. It is not unusual for us to have to help one or more of them home. Fighting has landed some of the MacDonalds in jail more than once. Sometimes we have to go to the local jail to bail them out, so that they would not miss work. This is what drinking does to them.

I realize that this description of life in our boom town may worry you. Do not be concerned. We learned our lesson from living with Father. Our memories of his drinking have made us cautious, and I want to assure you that while we like to drink, we do not get drunk.

Our landlady is very good to us. She cleans our clothes, and on Sunday, she cooks us a special chicken dinner. In some ways she reminds us of you. When we get colds, she fusses over us. She even brings hot soup and lots of water to our room.

She keeps saying, "Keep warm. Wear dry socks. Look after yourselves."

She is not nagging. We can tell she really cares.

Mama, there is something we have to say that we could not bring ourselves to say earlier—and we are saying it for John and Alex too. We want you to know that as we got more mature, we felt so guilty about leaving you. It was very selfish of us. There is no other explanation for why we would leave a frail woman alone on the farm. We are very sorry and we hope you can find it in your heart to forgive us. To try to make up for what we did, we are going to send you thirty dollars a month to hire help to do the heavy farm work. Combined with what you already get from Alex and John, you should have enough to cover the cost of labour for all the outside work. We make good money and save a good amount of it; so we are now in a position to help you. We hope this contribution will make your life easier. You sure deserve it.

We miss you so much.

Your loving sons,

Ronald

Hugh

As I read these words, Grandma's eyes filled with tears. Sobbing she said, "It breaks my heart to think of what I did to my boys. I worked them too hard; I robbed them of their childhood; I drove them away."

I put my arm around her and tried to console her with these words, "Grandma, you only did what you had to do to survive. You could not do all the work on your own; you know that. You must also remember that child labour was part of the life of every farm family."

With a sad look on her face, she replied, "But that did not make it right." And then she added, "Because of our circumstances, their child labour was heavier than that of most other children. I cannot deny that."

Grandma's sons grew used to being away and they became permanent residents of the United States where they found it easy to get work and to make money. They kept in touch, but they did not come home. Time did not allay Grandma's sense of guilt or her desire to see her sons. She continued to regret the wedge that hard work had driven between them. Even though the boys had no desire to ever see the farm again, they remained loyal to their mother. They continued to write to her regularly and with every letter they sent money. In fact, I was able to reconstruct the story of their lives in the United Stated from information Grandma provided from their letters. Because Grandma used the money they sent to hire help to do the farm work, she and her daughter Margaret were able to get along by themselves on the farm.

16

When Margaret had finished school, she and her mother Mairi worked side by side for seven years, in the same way Mairi had worked with her mother, but for a longer time. Then one night, at a neighbourhood ceilidh, Laughlin Angus Mor MacDonald asked Margaret to dance. While she liked many other young men from the community, she felt particularly drawn to him. She sensed there was something special about him. It wasn't long before they began to spend as much time together as their work permitted. In the evening, they often walked hand in hand along the shore or through the woods—anywhere that was peaceful and quiet and where they could be alone.

Laughlin was a tall young man with a powerful build generated by years of hard work on the farm. He had straight black hair, large brown eyes, and an angular face. He was striking looking; Margaret thought he was handsome. Theirs was not a hurried affair; they saw each other for over a year before Laughlin asked her to marry him. Margaret was anxious to say yes, but she was worried about leaving her mother alone. She was not going to abandon her mother the way the boys did. The dilemma weighed heavily on her mind. Silence did not allay her anxiety, nor did it solve her problem. Mulling the matter over and over in her mind got her nowhere. With great reluctance she decided that she had better talk with her mother.

While they were washing the dishes one evening, Mairi, noticing how nervous Margaret was, turned to her and said, "Ah lass, there is something bothering you; I can tell. Now you know you can tell me what it is."

Because of her anxiety, Margaret could not think of a delicate way to say what was foremost on her mind; so she blurted, "I want to marry Laughlin."

While this news did not surprise Mairi, she did not respond immediately. She had a perplexed look on her face. Her quietness worried Margaret.

So Margaret turned to her mother and said, "I'm sorry. That did not come out right."

Her mother replied, "Dear, you have no reason to be sorry. I was quiet because I was thinking. I know you are feeling guilty about leaving me alone on the farm, but you cannot put your life on hold for me. The boys taught me that lesson a long time ago. I think I may have a solution to the problem that will be good for both of us."

In her own thoughtful way Mairi proposed this solution. She said, "Look Margaret, we have no man with us here on the farm. Now Laughlin is the youngest of five brothers. Their father's farm isn't big enough to provide a living for all of them. And, being the youngest, Laughlin is not likely to inherit the homestead. Why not invite him to move in with us and he can take over the farm. I think I have reached the stage in my life where it is time for me to give up managing the farm. You know, if it wasn't for the hired help, we couldn't carry on. Look at me; I am old beyond my years."

Margaret threw her arms around her mother, and said, "Thank you; thank you."

She then raced to see Laughlin to tell him the good news.

He was surprised by the offer, and after deliberating for a moment, he replied, "It sounds wonderful, but I had better take some time to think about it."

And think about it he did. After a couple of days, he got up the courage to discuss the offer with his father. He need not have been hesitant about making his request, for his father was relieved by his proposal to move out.

"Good," he said. "Now we will have one less fellow trying to live off this land."

His mother, who was sitting near his father, nodded her head in approval.

His father's answer hit Laughlin like the blow of a hammer to the head. He was offended by the thought that his father was glad to get rid of him. Even after the sting of his father's answer had subsided, Laughlin felt "put out" by his bluntness, and it made him angry. His parents' lack of appreciation of his efforts to help them increased his desire to make the move. It also heightened his awareness of the limitations involved in trying to eke out a living on his father's farm. He quickly came to the realization that getting out was not just the right thing to do but, under the circumstances, the only thing to do.

He raced back to tell Margaret the news. Still feeling vexed. he finished the story of his meeting with his parents with these words: "It was obvious that they will be glad to get rid of me."

Margaret laughed as she replied, "Well, I think their loss is our gain."

Then and there Margaret and Laughlin decided to get married as soon as possible. After the time period required by the reading of the banns, they were married in the Arisaig church, and Laughlin immediately moved into Mairi's home. And that is how Mairi and Margaret came to be together for the rest of Mairi's life.

Mairi quickly grew fond of Laughlin and soon came to admire him. Being very perceptive, she was quick to notice a marked contrast between him and her late husband, Ronald—differences she now and again shared with Margaret.

As her first point of comparison she noted, "I marvel at how reliable Laughlin is. You know exactly what to expect of him."

On another occasion, she said, "Laughlin is so industrious. God forgive me for saying it; he is quite a contrast with my late husband."

One day after Laughlin had finished helping Mairi with some work, she paid him a fine complement, "Laughlin is quite a change from Ronald, whose behaviour was so erratic. He is as solid as a rock."

Of course, these differences had a great deal to do with the fact that Ronald was an alcoholic and Laughlin was not. I learned about these comparisons, not from Grandma but from Mother. Because Grandma had put up with so much uncertainty in her life, she was particularly appreciative of the stability Laughlin brought to their home. And another thing that endeared him to her was how much he reminded her of her beloved father. They had the same physical build, the same easy temperament, the same sense of responsibility. She often smiled when he reacted in the same way as her father. She wondered if it was these characteristics that attracted Margaret to him.

One day Margaret overheard her mother say, "My father will never die as long as Laughlin is alive.

In a few years, Laughlin had turned the old homestead into a prosperous farm. He broke more land, raised more calves and lambs, and generated the extra produce and income needed to make their home more comfortable. He also built a new house. Margaret was so proud of him and she loved him dearly.

Between 1872 and 1880, Margaret gave birth to three daughters: Mary, Catherine, and Anne. Each of us grew up to follow very different paths in life.

17

I had been in school since 1877, and like my grandmother before me, I loved every minute of it. For me academic work had a special appeal. No doubt, my grandmother's love of history, and the love of learning that went with it, developed in me an appreciation of my studies. From her I had learned a lesson that I don't think any other girl in our community had the privilege of learning—the importance of the life of the mind. That is a precious gift.

Even though I knew it was inevitable, it was with deep disappointment that I saw my schooling come to an end when I had completed grade eight. My academic achievement was excellent. But it was only boys who were allowed to go on to the higher grades. However, I was not as accepting of that situation as my grandmother and mother before me. I thought it to be terribly unfair, but what could I say. Sadly, this is the way things were, and nothing was going to change it. This realization did not relieve the emptiness I felt. I moped around home in poor cheer. Working full time in the house and on the farm had little appeal for me.

While I was sitting outside on the step one evening, I overheard my parents discussing my education. Father was more broad minded than I realized.

My spirits picked up when I heard him say to Mother, "Mary has not been herself ever since she finished school. You know, it is so unfair that she cannot go on to high school. This is how your education ended and that of your mother before you."

Then he stopped for a moment to think before continuing. "It is time to put a stop to it," he said. "I talked to Mary's teacher who told me she had the highest achievement in her class and is a very promising student. He said we should try to do something to help her to continue her education."

As Father continued to mull over the situation, he realized he needed to talk to someone who could give him advice. And so he decided to discuss it with our parish priest.

"Father MacDonald will know what to do," he said.

This decision further raised my hopes, and I had a hard time containing my excitement. Father MacDonald was very helpful. He told Father that a new school for girls, called St. Bernard's Convent, run by the Sisters of Notre Dame, had recently opened in Antigonish, and this was the place where his daughter could get a high-school education.

"The sisters and the clergy now realize that girls should have the same educational opportunities as boys," the priest said. "This is your chance to help your daughter get an education. I encourage you to send her to the convent."

Father thanked him for his help. He hurried home to tell Mother the news, and they immediately decided they should find out more about this school.

"Before we do that," Father advised, "we had better talk with Mary."

When I overheard what he said, I thought that he was the best father in the whole world.

So that evening, my parents called me into the kitchen, and Father put the question to me, "Mary, would you like to go to high school?"

Of course, there was nothing I wanted more and I began to smile from ear to ear as I gave my one-word answer, an emphatic "Yes." Then Father said that he would see what he could do.

Grandma was listening to all of these deliberations while she knitted, and I could see that she too had a big smile of approval on her face. The next day she told me that, when she had finished junior high school, she longed to go to high school, but back then there was no such opportunity for girls.

"It gives me great joy to think that you may have the opportunity to achieve the goal I could not," she said.

Mother expressed concern about how they were going to pay for both my education and my board at this private school.

"We do not have much money," she said.

Father too admitted that money could be a problem.

"At the same time," he said, "we are not poor. We have lots of meat and fish and eggs and cream and cheese and butter. That has to count for something."

They both thought about this problem for a few days, and then Mother came up with an idea.

"I think I know how we can do it," she said. "Maybe, just maybe, we can use the farm produce you talked about to cover the cost. Cash may be scarce in our house, but these goods are not."

Father laughed as he said, "I never thought of trading farm produce for an education, but I think it's a good idea. Let's go to town and talk with the sister in charge of the convent. First things first, we had better find out if the sisters will accept Mary into their school and then we can discuss the matter of payment."

And Father, with a twinkle in his eye, added, "We'll take Mary with us to meet the sisters. I'm sure they'll be impressed."

So on the following Sunday, all three of us climbed into the riding wagon and headed over Brown's mountain into town. I was so excited I could hardly contain myself. And I was so appreciative of my parents' sensitivity to my desire for an education. Most parents were not interested in sending their daughters to school beyond grade eight. I was so very, very lucky to have such progressive parents.

When we arrived at the door of the convent, we were warmly greeted by the superior, Sister Andrew. The first thing I noticed was her clothing, and it took me by surprise. I had never before seen a woman dressed in a full-length flowing black robe with the headdress culminating in a starched white peak. Her dress made her appear more aloof than our lay teacher. While I was preoccupied with her dress, she brought us into the parlour and sat us down to discuss our business. My parents immediately proceeded to make their case for my admission to her school.

Father proudly stated, "Sister, my daughter was the best student in her class."

To confirm what he said, he showed her my final academic report.

Sister Andrew looked over the document and then, to my delight, looked at me and smiled approvingly as she said, "I am impressed. We would be pleased to have this fine young lady attend our school."

She then proceeded to describe the life of a boarding student and to outline the cost of her education.

After Sister Andrew had described the arrangements for me to enter the school, Mother, feeling somewhat embarrassed, raised the question that was bothering her.

"Sister," she said with some hesitation, "like most farm families, we do not have much cash. Do you think there is any chance that we could use our farm produce to pay for Mary's education?"

Sister Andrew looked at her and asked, "What did you have in mind?"

Mother, still feeling embarrassed, looked at the floor as she said slowly, "We have lots of butter and cheese and cream."

Sister Andrew stopped and thought for a moment and then she replied, "Well, I don't think that should be a problem. We need all those kinds of food to feed our boarders, and therefore, they are just as good as cash. You will have to come to town at least four times a year to transport Mary, and we could take delivery of a load of produce each time you come. Give me a few moments to figure out how much produce will be needed to cover the cost of Mary's tuition and board."

She did some quick calculations and then suggested amounts that were more than acceptable to my parents. Father and Mother were very relieved to hear this. Sister Andrew ended our meeting by informing me that I was to enrol in September and that over a four-year period I could complete my high-school education, and if I wished, I could also complete the requirements for teacher certification. This was a bargain, a good one in the minds of my parents, and each of them shook hands with the sister as they thanked her profusely and sincerely. On the way out, I too thanked her, for young as I was, I sensed that in some way her offer marked a turning point in my life.

Thanks to the thoughtful action of my parents, the high-school education that only a few weeks before had seemed out of the question had now become a reality. I felt so pleased and so privileged. No other girl in our community had ever gone to high school. They left school and worked at home until they got married or else they went to "the Boston States" to work as domestics.

More than one of my friends asked, "Why don't you come to Boston to work like the rest of us?"

That was the last thing I wanted to do at this stage in my life. Grandma had broadened my horizons.

Over the summer months, Mother was busy sewing little black dresses with white collars and cuffs—the uniform for students attending St. Bernard's Convent.

One evening, while she was having me try on one of these dresses for fit, Father teased, "I see you are going to be a little nun."

We all laughed, and I made a face at him. I later found out that there was some truth in his humour. Indeed, I was soon to learn that the sisters looked upon their student body as a source of new candidates for their novitiate. Each year, on the feast of the founder of their order, Marguerite Bourgeois, the sisters talked to the student body about the importance of vocations to religious life.

The summer passed very quickly, and on September 1, Father and Mother, keeping the bargain they had made with the sister, loaded the back of the riding wagon with produce, and then the three of us squeezed into the front seat and headed for the convent. Believe it or not, for all my desire to continue in school, I found that as my dream was about to become a reality, I was very, very scared. The realization that I would be away from home for the first time and that I would be among strangers was beginning to sink in. As we drove along, questions raced through my mind. Will the other boarders like me? Will they be stuck up? Will I be lonely? Will I be able to make friends? What will it be like to be taught by sisters? Will I be able to do the school work they require? In the end, my desire for an education proved to be stronger than any of these nagging fears.

When we arrived at the convent, we were again met by the superior, Sister Andrew, and several of the teaching sisters, and they all greeted us warmly. I began to think that the sisters were not as stiff as their garb made them look.

Sister Joseph accompanied me to my room and then took me to a common room and asked me to introduce myself to the other boarders. I approached the other students hesitatingly. To my great relief, I soon found that they were friendly.

The first student to whom I introduced myself burst out laughing as she replied, "Hi, I'm Mary MacDonald."

I reacted by saying, "And that makes two of us."

Then with a twinkle in her eye she said, "But there are more."

Before I finished introducing myself, I found out that there were two more Mary MacDonalds in our class.

Laughing I said, "Maybe we are going to have to use our Scottish nicknames to distinguish us from one another."

As we talked, the other new students started to confess their fears about coming to the new school. It was reassuring to find that we were all in the same boat.

The next morning, I began my new life as a high-school student and with it the routine I was to follow for the next four years. At six-thirty every morning, a bell rang and we dragged ourselves out of bed to go to mass. Then we had breakfast in the dining room and we had to be in class by nine.

All of us relished the relief from household chores brought by life in the convent.

On the way to class, one of my classmates joyously remarked, "No more lugging buckets of water."

Another said enthusiastically, "No more washing clothes in the brook."

And still another, in an exuberant voice, said, "No more scrubbing floors. We are now ladies of leisure."

Well, we were in for a surprise. The school program was heavy—heavier than any of our previous studies. I found myself studying so much grammar in English, Latin, and French that in my head these languages began to run into one another. The course I liked the most was literature, particularly English literature. Our English teacher, Sister Genevive, played the role of every character in the plays and novels we studied, and this highlighted the drama of these literary works. I looked forward to each class to hear the next episode. This course was so much fun that I sometimes wondered what educative value it had. When I was more mature, I began to appreciate how much the study of literature broadened my understanding of human nature and human experience. I felt very comfortable in my history, mathematics, and religion courses because these subjects seemed to pick up where my previous studies had left off. Domestic science was no problem because it seemed I was learning to do household activities I had already learned at home.

Now science was a different matter. Most of the science classes were taught in the lab, and being used to learning from books, I found this situation to be very uncomfortable. Never before had I worked with biological specimens and lab equipment. I enjoyed my music class because we spent most of our time singing, and for most of us this was a form of recreation.

Our course load kept us in class from nine in the morning until three-thirty in the afternoon. For relief from this routine we had three breaks: one for recess between ten-fifteen and ten-thirty, a second for lunch between twelve and one, and a third between two and two-thirty for something called meditation.

When we were told about this meditation requirement, we turned to one another with questioning looks on our faces. This business of meditation was a new one for me, as it was for the other girls. "What is this about," I wondered.

I soon found out. On the very first day of class, our English teacher, Sister Genevive, took us to the chapel, gave each of us a little book of spiritual readings, counselled us to read for five minutes and then sit quietly to give our souls a chance to talk. I had misgivings about this exercise. I certainly had never before done anything like it in school. In fact, I thought to myself, "What does this activity have to do with school?"

These misgivings were soon allayed when, young as I was, I began to find this spiritual exercise comforting. There, every day in the stillness of the chapel, I emptied my mind of everything that was going on in the world and I found myself at peace. Contemplating what was in my heart and in my soul turned out to be an invaluable spiritual activity.

A fellow student reflected my sentiment when she remarked, "Believe it or not, meditation is a pleasant surprise."

Meditation turned out to be a coping mechanism that served us well in times of distress. It was a refuge from the pressure associated with major assignments and exams. I didn't realize it then, but I was later to realize that attaining peace in my soul would serve as a refuge from the stresses of adult life. It wasn't long before I felt at home in the convent school and in the chapel.

Many of the high-school students were boarders, and the sisters decided that our everyday activities outside of class could be used to add some refinement to our lives. Cultivation they called it. In fact, Sister Andrew told us that an education meant little unless it produced cultivated individuals. This was a joke among those of us who came from rural communities where on the farm cultivate has quite a different meaning.

Our first lessons in refinement took place at the supper table. First, we were reminded to say please and thank you when passing or receiving food. This aspect of etiquette was something most of us had already learned at home. Then we were shown how to use our cutlery properly—which spoon, which knife, and which fork to use on different kinds of food.

I thought to myself, "Most of us would be lucky to have one knife, one fork, and one spoon to ourselves at home."

We were also instructed in how to use our napkins—again something we never had at home—when to begin eating, and how to pass dishes around the table. Then we were required to practise this etiquette in the course of eating our meals. I always enjoyed our conversations around the table, and this added touch of refinement did not detract from it one bit.

From table manners, we graduated to lessons in the fine arts. The sisters viewed knowledge of the fine arts to be another important part of the education of a cultivated woman. One evening, Sister Paula took us to the music room where we saw a fine piano for the first time. The only musical instruments we were familiar with were the fiddle and the bagpipes, and so we were fascinated by this new instrument. Without saying a word, Sister sat at the piano and began playing some of our familiar Scottish music. When she knew she had caught our attention, she then eased us into the classics by playing popular excerpts from Strauss, Mozart, Verdi, Tchaikovsky, and Brahms. We had never heard anything like this, and it was fascinating. We intuitively sensed that this music had its own special beauty. We sat there in awe as Sister introduced us to a whole new realm of music. When she finished, she asked if we would like to spend more time on music, and we all agreed enthusiastically. So each evening we would gather around the piano to listen to her play.

Sister did not want us to be just passive recipients of the beauty of this music. She told us that she wanted us to feel the music, to capture something of its expressiveness.

"I want you to respond joyously to the music," she exclaimed. "You can sway your bodies, hum, clap, tap the beat with your hands or feet, or make up a dance appropriate for the music."

We laughed as she gracefully illustrated each of these gestures while she hummed the music, and we so looked forward to getting into the act of mimicking her motions. It wasn't long before we were galloping our fingers and our toes to the *Radetsky March*, humming *The Chorus of the Hebrew Slaves*, and swinging, and swaying, and sometimes whirling around the room to the Strauss waltzes. She always ended these sessions by playing Brahms Lullaby. This was the signal for us to return to our rooms, not to rest but to study.

This active response to the music enhanced our appreciation of it, and we continued to look forward to our time around the piano. We were having so much fun that we forgot that these musical interludes were also part of our education. I later realized that this broad-based approach to education grew out of the sisters' desire to have a formative influence on us. This delightful reprieve succeeded in sensitizing us to the beauty of classical music. No doubt, we'll cherish this music for the rest of our lives.

Our induction into classical music aroused in us a very special warmth for Sister Paula, more than for the other sisters who taught the straight academic subjects in a structured setting. Even though they were strict, they too were caring and kind, but they did not have the opportunity to get to know us in the informal way Sister Paula did.

My course work went really well until I hit a bump in the road in grade eleven. Our science courses, chemistry and physics, both required lab work, and I soon discovered that I was not very good at its mechanical aspects. With each passing class, I became more worried. The manipulation of lab instruments and materials required manual dexterity. I think my hands were made of lead. I simply could not get the hang of the precise measurement of materials and the exact manipulation of instruments. Furthermore, I could not get my hands and my head to work together, and this clumsiness could ruin my chances of passing science.

With a look of grave concern, I turned to my lab partner and said, "I can't do this."

"You can't do what?" she asked.

"I can't do lab work. My hands and head just won't work together," I replied.

She quickly came up with a generous proposal. "I tell you what. I'll gladly do all the work that requires hands if you agree to do the work that requires a head," she offered. And she laughed as she added, "That should bring the combat between your hands and your head to an end."

Her proposal suited me just fine, and we soon found this partnership worked to the benefit of us both. It also served to teach me that I would never be much good at science. I understood science; I just couldn't do it.

At the end of each academic year, we had a two-month break. Even though I was busy helping my parents with the farm work, I found the summers long and I yearned to get back to school. Sadly, I began to realize that my time away from home made me grow apart from my friends. We were following different paths in life. When we were together, they talked enthusiastically about their work at home and their boyfriends, and I quickly found I no longer had much in common with them.

Noticing how quiet I was, my friend Catherine turned to me one evening and asked, "Did the cat get your tongue?"

My only reaction was to smile as I shrugged my shoulders. Because they did not share my experiences, there was no reason for them to have any interest in discussing my life in school or the new friends I had made. Furthermore, because the convent was an all-girls' school, I was cut off from contact with boys and thus I did not have a boyfriend to discuss. I had to face the harsh reality that the bond of commonality that used to bind us together had been rent asunder and I felt a keen sense of loss. I doubt if my friends had any sense of what I was feeling. It is not easy to find yourself cut off from the people with whom you had previously shared your life. I was beginning to realize the price I was to pay for following a different path in life.

My years in high school passed so quickly. My parents made four trips a year to and from the convent to transport me and the food supplies that paid my way.

"Honouring our part of the bargain," Mother called it.

In my last two years in high school, I made sure that I enrolled in the subjects leading to teacher certification. As I matured, my dream of becoming a teacher was something that occupied my mind more and more. You see, teaching was the only career I knew anything about because it was the only profession to which I had been exposed. I could visualize myself teaching in front of a class, because I had seen others do it. It was also something that I thought I would really like to do. The only other professional option for girls was nursing, and about that I knew little and had no interest in learning more. So it was with great satisfaction that in June, 1889, I completed high school and with it the requirements for teacher certification.

Our principal had told us that there would be graduating exercises to which we could invite our parents. I was excited; young as I was, I sensed that this was an important milestone in my life. In the days before graduation, I went home to help my parents with the spring planting. On those days I luxuriated in that very special freedom that comes with the period between completing one chapter of ones life and starting another. Great anticipation marked my return to the convent for the closing exercises, accompanied by my parents and my grandmother. When my name was called as the top student in my class, I made them very proud. This was a momentous event in the life of my family, for over the generations, I was the very first member to complete high school. Furthermore, I had achieved this goal in the days when girls had few opportunities to go to high school.

After the ceremony was over, I spent my last moments with my classmates. As our conversations came to an end, our sense of loss began to set in. The strong bond that had been forged from shared experience was being shattered. We found it painful to part. We looked longingly at each other one last time as we said our good-byes and as memories of our good times together flashed through our minds. It was hard to hold back the tears.

Before I left for home, Sister Genevive, who knew how much I wanted to be a teacher, took me aside and helped me to complete an application for teacher certification, which she then forwarded to the Department of Education in Halifax for me. I am sure she had no idea how much her support and helpfulness meant to me. I was on the way to realizing my dream.

Mine was a summer filled with anticipation. On July 15, the arrival of my precious teaching certificate made my heart leap with joy. Fortunately for me, the teaching position in the Arisaig school had just come open. There had never been a female teacher in Arisaig, and I decided I wanted to be the first. My academic success had filled me with considerable confidence, and I did not hesitate to write a formal letter of application to the chairman of the local school trustees. My anticipation soon turned to anxiety. Days passed and I heard nothing; weeks passed and still I heard nothing. I was worried. If I didn't get this job, what would I do? Where else could I look for a teaching position?

The idea that I would not get this position because I was a woman began to play on my mind. Until fifty years ago, it was not even legal for a woman to teach in this province; so what could I expect. Knowing that all the teachers in Arisaig up to this time had been men, I feared the trustees were looking for another man. This was the first time in my life that I was confronted by the reality of the inequality of men and women and the feeling of injustice that accompanies it. Just as I had become angry at the thought of the unfairness of our trustees, they proved me wrong, or so I thought. The Chairman of the Board of Trustees for our school district came to our home to see me. To my great relief, he told me that when the trustees reviewed my academic record, they viewed me to be an excellent candidate for the teaching vacancy in Arisaig and they agreed to hire me for the job.

He smiled as he said, "I don't often get to deliver good news and that is why I came. Congratulations."

After I had thanked him, he accepted my father's invitation to share dinner in celebration of the good news. I made sure to let him know how appreciative I was of his gesture. After he left, I went to my room, and the magnitude of his message began to sink in. My dream had come true. I was going to work at a job for which I had longed. Life could not have been better.

At that time, I did not realize that the pursuit of a male candidate for the position was the reason it took so long for the trustees to offer me the job. I was their last resort, and it was just as well that I didn't know. By the time I found out this information, several years had passed; my career was off to a good start; so I did not dwell on it.

A few days after I had received my teaching position, Grandma took me aside, and to my surprise, told me that she too once dreamed of being a teacher.

"Circumstances kept me from doing that," she confided, "and it does my heart good to see that you are able to do what I could not. I was born seventy years too soon. I can now realize my dream through you." And then she gave me a warm hug.

It is a shame that social conventions kept a woman who had such a marvellous mind from using it to good advantage in the classroom.

Grandma continued to reflect on my teaching career. As we were walking one day, I noticed she was lost in thought and so I asked, "Grandma, what's on your mind?"

"Well," she said, "things have sure changed since I came here in 1820. You are so fortunate to be able to get a paying job outside the home. And, even better, you will be paid to do something you love."

She was right. I looked forward to the challenge of trying to open young minds to the wonders of learning. And, at that time, I once more thought of the tremendous influence Grandma had on my education. Her compelling stories and her exhortations about the importance of remembering our past did much to enhance my appreciation of learning. Grandma never had the chance I had to get an education, but this did not keep her from being a woman of vision. That is so much a part of the special bond that exists between us.

18

The day was September 3, 1889, a day I shall remember for the rest of my life. It was my long anticipated very first day of teaching. I was not nervous; in fact I was naive enough to face that day with considerable confidence. More than anything else, I was excited. Maybe it was a Godsend that I had no idea of the complexity of the challenges I faced. At nine o'clock, I found myself standing in front of twenty-five boys and girls between the ages of six and eighteen. So here in my very first class I found myself faced by students who were twelve years apart in age. The oldest was almost as old as I was—and a foot taller. The youngest was just an innocent little boy, Johnny, six years old, who was away from his mother for the first time and was very scared. No matter how hard I tried to comfort him, he continued to cry.

As a last resort, I picked him up in my arms and whispered words of reassurance in his ear, "You are very special because you are the youngest student. I will look after you. Everyone else in the class will look after you. Do not be afraid."

This message seemed to reassure him and he stopped crying. And I breathed a sigh of relief.

Those who had been in school previously were excited about being together again. School is a good place to socialize, and they knew it. I welcomed them and I asked them to be seated. It is important for students to feel comfortable; so I introduced myself, and then we spent some time getting to know one another. This was more for my benefit than theirs because most of the students had been in this class before and knew each other well. I asked each of them to rise and state his or her name. After the first six students identified themselves as MacDonalds, they began to giggle, and I could not help but laugh. I decided to do a different take on this exercise. I suggested we would know more about each other if we resorted to using the traditional Highland Scottish names by which they were known in the community, which involved the use of the student's first name, then the name of the head of the house, followed by his father's name or nickname. This change elicited the names by which the MacDonalds and the Gillises and those with other clan names were differentiated from one another, including William John Ban, Mary John Ban, Angus Laughie Mor, William Donald Malcolm, and I was Mary Laughie Lody. The students obviously were used to and liked this way of identifying themselves, and it seemed to help them to accept me. After all, I was one of them.

Then I decided to address the behaviour expected of them in the classroom. Over the summer, I had thought a great deal about this matter. Some adults suggested the use of corporal punishment. They often repeated the old adage, "Spare the rod and spoil the child." But when asked, it became clear that they did not want corporal punishment used on their children.

"Just on other bad kids," they would often say when questioned about their view.

So if the parents whom I questioned did not want me to use corporal punishment on their kids, why should I think that other parents would? To me the idea of corporal punishment was distasteful. My parents never used it on me, and I could not see myself using it on these children. Furthermore, I knew enough about the children of this community to know that they were not spoiled. Realizing that parental advice was not helpful, I decided that I was on my own to come up with an idea of what might work.

As I reflected on this matter, I asked myself, "If I were a student, how would I like my teacher to treat me?"

And it is from this perspective that I decided how to approach student behaviour.

I explained my approach to my students like this. "When we come together as a group in class, it is important for us to respect one another. You come from good homes where you are taught how to behave. I expect the good behaviour you learned at home to carry over into the classroom. School should be a good place. It is up to us to see that it is. You treat me well, and I'll treat you well, and we should get along just fine."

At this point, I decided I had said enough to create a sense of the atmosphere I wanted in the classroom. For openers, I wanted to create a positive image of our classroom environment. For these students, the first day of school was not the time to lay down rules and penalties for non-compliance. Because they were unspoiled, I was hoping that there would be little need to spell out these restrictions. I was willing to give them the benefit of the doubt.

After I had passed out the textbooks that had been left behind by the previous teacher, it was time to settle into the classroom routine. I had no idea what I was in for. I soon realized that I needed to be something of a magician to come up with school work appropriate for each and every one of these students. For the first time, the complexity of the task I faced began to sink in. I was getting nervous.

"How do I do this?" I asked myself.

As doubts arose in my mind, the next question was, "Can I do this?"

Young as I was, I knew I had to rise to the occasion. I could not afford to panic.

"Pull yourself together," I said to myself. "You are just going to have to figure this out on your own. You can do it."

Because of the many grades represented in my class, I decided that the only way I could teach this diverse student body was by grouping them for instruction. While I was teaching one group, the rest of the students would either be working in pairs on subjects that require a great deal of seat work or they would be working on their own. Because of its complexity, I was hesitant to use this approach, but I really did not have a choice. I was relieved to find that my students had already learned good study habits. This allayed my fear that they would be wasting time when I was not teaching them directly. And that was very important to my survival as a first-year teacher. Most of the time my students were kind and thoughtful and did everything they could to help one another and to help me. Their co-operation even exceeded my expectations. I was also relieved to find that they decided that they liked me.

When I was not working with an instructional group, I went around from student to student to help each with his or her work. Students frequently raised their hands for help. Regardless of the limitations of these procedures, it enabled me to teach nine grades in one room, and that is quite a feat for any teacher, much less an inexperienced one who was still a teenager. After a few weeks, I realized that this approach worked reasonably well, in no small part thanks to the continuing co-operation of my students.

Each day, I left school dead tired but feeling good about what I had done. I got a great deal of satisfaction from my teaching. I had heard many people say that teachers are born, not made. Would that it were so. School teaching requires a great deal of knowledge, thinking, and planning, as well as the ability to relate to young people. This knowledge-base has to be learned.

My students took their work seriously. It was amazing to stand back from the student body and see every one of them working. I suppose I could have given myself credit for being some kind of an organizational genius. But the credit really belonged to the students' appreciation of the opportunity to be in school. Not every child got the chance to go to school, and they knew it. They were the fortunate few.

Out of the earshot of their peers, more than one of them said to me, "I love to go to school."

And to each of them I would reply, "You know what? So do I."

Furthermore, my students had learned to be industrious at home where child labour was a fact of life. They were little men and women. On a busy homestead all hands are needed. They had learned their work ethic and their discipline from doing hard manual labour.

These children took their place alongside their parents working on the farm and in the home. I listened to them share stories of their work. No one was exempt. Even little Johny carried kindling for the fire. Brothers Jackie and Jimmy, only nine and ten years of age, carried bucket after bucket of water from the brook, a quarter of a mile from their house. From hearing them describe this task, I learned that one walked on each side of the bucket, knees bent, each lifting with one hand on the handle, because neither was strong enough to carry the bucket alone. When their arms became sore from the heavy load, they would stop, put the bucket down and and rest for a while, and then switch sides. In winter they carried an axe to break the ice so they could reach the water. In the late afternoon, the horses followed them to drink from the hole they had made in the ice. On most days they made four or five trips to the brook for water.

The older boys all talked of how they sawed logs into lengths to be used for firewood and then split them into smaller pieces so they would burn better. On the weekends, some went to the woods with their fathers to cut logs with either a bucksaw or a cross-cut saw, trim the branches with axes, and lead the horses that snigged the logs from the woods. They then cut the logs into pieces that were small enough for them to load onto the bob-sleds to be carried home. Days away from this work while they were in school made them soft and they paid the price. As they worked together, moving the cross-cut saw back and forth, they winced in pain from the blisters forming on their hands. After a particularly hard weekend working in the woods, William Donald Malcolm announced that he wished we had school seven days a week.

Angus Laughie Mor showed him the blisters on his hands, as he said, "Boy, do I agree with you."

In the late fall, the boys talked excitedly about going hunting with their fathers. They viewed this activity to be part of their initiation into manhood. In a grown-up way, William John Ban talked of the rush he felt as his rifle shot brought down a deer and then of how he ran with his father to bleed and gut and skin the animal and divide it into quarters to be carried home. The younger boys who were listening to this conversation looked very impressed.

The girls were less taken with their obligations at home. There they helped their mothers with the barn work and the house work. While their mothers milked the cows, the girls cleaned the stables, forked hay from the mow onto the barn floor and then carried the hay to the stalls to feed the animals. Each and every day they also helped their mothers with the routine household tasks of washing dishes, scrubbing floors, making beds, and looking after the younger children. They longed for the escape from housework that school provided.

With my ability to organize and their ability to work, we made a good team. Not that my students were unduly serious. At recess the usual teasing, jostling, and horseplay that one expects from children were abundant. I was delighted to see that most of them had a lively sense of humour.

Some students came early in the morning to start the fire in our pot-bellied stove. Others swept the floor and neatened the desks. Two of them were designated the responsibility for taking fresh water from the well each day. At noon the older girls took turns heating soup so that everyone could have something hot to drink. To them this work was fun because it gave them a chance to socialize. While childhood for them was short, they were normal healthy children who, given the opportunity, knew how to play as well as how to work.

I only faced one serious discipline problem, and thank God, it did not happen until the new year. Fortunately, by that time, I had enough experience under my belt to keep me from being unnerved by it. In January, the snow storms, the bone-chilling cold, the biting wind, and the high drifts made outdoor activity impossible. Because my pupils spent their free time indoors, they did not have the usual outlets for their energy. Conditions were trying and it showed in their behaviour. I was worried; I never had problems with discipline before and I did not want these problems to get out of hand. Discipline is one aspect of teaching that most teachers fear. Losing control of a class could cost a teacher her job. The trustees might not know the difference between good teaching and poor teaching, but they could tell when a teacher let the kids get out of hand.

Being confined to the classroom, my students became restless and fidgety. They took their frustrations out on one another. Pulling hair and making faces and talking loudly were one thing, but pushing and shoving, and making rude and hurtful remarks, and, in one case, fighting, went too far. They did respond to my requests to behave, but their good behaviour did not last for long. My regular exhortations about goodness and kindness did not appeal to them very much in these trying times.

What could I do to restore civility to their behaviour? That question occupied my mind and it made me anxious. This was the time it would have been nice to have a colleague with whom to compare notes, but I did not have that luxury.

While I was in church the following Sunday, I read the epistle for that date, and as I read, I thought, "Wait a minute, there are passages here that may be just what I need."

The epistle I am referring to is taken from the passage in The Bible that contains the eloquent statement of Paul to the Corinthians which elaborates the meaning of love. I normally use the Baltimore Catechism to teach religion, but this passage speaks to people in a way in which the catechism does not. So before the next religion class, I wrote this excerpt from the epistle on the board so that we could look at it together.

And if I have prophecy and know all mysteries and all knowledge,

and if I have all faith so as to remove mountains, yet do not have love, I am nothing.

Love is patient, is kind; love does not envy, is not pretentious, is not puffed up, is not ambitious, is not self seeking, is not provoked, thinks no evil,

does not rejoice over wickedness, but rejoices with the truth.

So there abide faith, hope, and love, these three; and the greatest of these is love.

When I started class, Laughie Angus Mor asked why I was taking the church to school.

I laughed as I replied, "You'll see."

Then I asked my students to read this passage. I pointed out to them that it not only tells us to love one another but, more importantly for us, how to love one another. Now that I had their full attention, I asked them to pull the passage apart to see what it told them about how to do this. On this matter the passage is pretty straight forward. It was to reinforce its message that I asked them to describe the ways in which students can show their love.

Some of the senior students had sheepish looks on their faces. It was not hard to get the point of the exercise. They came forth with a flurry of answers which paraphrased the message of this passage.

"It tells us to be patient."

"To be kind."

"Not to envy others."

"Not to act as if we were superior to others."

"Not to put oneself ahead of others."

"Not to think evil of others."

"Not to take joy in wrong-doing."

To reinforce further the powerful message of Saint Paul's epistle, I then asked them to think about the lessons they could learn from it about their behaviour in school. The students obviously understood the message of the passage very well, but I wanted even more. I wanted to enhance their consciousness of its message for them. So I decided to conclude the class by asking them to continue to dwell on the meaning of this passage for their behaviour.

I said, "To help you to do this, I want you to take your ideas about how this passage applies to your behaviour and turn them into a written code of conduct for the classroom. By a code of conduct I mean expectations or guidelines for your classroom behaviour. I shall put your ideas on the side blackboard and leave them there so that you can turn to them for guidance when the situation demands."

The students quietly went to work on their assignment. When they finished this exercise, I accepted one answer from each one who volunteered a response and I wrote it on the board. And to my surprise, it was paradoxical that the student who seemed to have a problem relating to a particular principle asserted a guideline arising from that principle.

First, Jack William Malcolm, who was foremost in taking out his frustration on other students, stated, "We should be kind to one another."

His response elicited a few smirks, but I pretended not to notice.

Then John William Ban, a very bright boy who did not have much patience with the relative slowness of some of his peers, said, "We should be patient with one another, particularly when one of us is slow in answering."

Again some of the students looked at one another, for they knew exactly where he was coming from.

Next John Hugh Martin, a gentle lad who was not very bright, responded, "We should try not to envy others who are smarter than we are."

This response elicited sympathetic looks from many students.

Then Mary Laughie Mor, who learned with ease and tended to do excellent work, said, "When we do things better than other students, we should not act as if we are superior to them."

There were a lot of bright students in the class, and I noticed many nods of approval.

Next James John Joe, who tended to get easily frustrated, blurted, "We should learn to hold our anger."

Most of the students laughed, as one of them remarked, "The rest of us would like that."

Impatient as always, John Jimmy Red, the most aggressive student in my class, asserted, "We should quit pushing and shoving one another."

Again the students laughed as one of them said, "He got that one right."

Next, Lisa Red Rory, a very quiet student and one who felt ashamed of her inability to keep up with the others, meekly said, "We should not be jealous of other students."

This response elicited looks of sympathy from all the students, and no one commented on her answer.

Then Mary Ann Donald Malcolm, without a doubt the pushiest girl in the class, asserted, "We should be considerate of others."

The students just gave her a look that said, "You should know."

And finally, Duncan Laughie Mor, who had a pronounced mischievous streak, in an assertive fashion said, "We should learn not to take pleasure in misbehaving."

All his fellow students laughed.

I was still perplexed. Why a student who had a problem with a particular principle enunciated its guideline was curious. Were they trying to sabotage this exercise?

"No, they wouldn't do that," I thought to myself.

Was this a deliberate attempt to poke a little fun at themselves? Or just as I was trying to manipulate them, were they trying to pull a little prank on me? Most of them had sly grins on their faces, but I didn't take the bait. I thought it prudent not to ask. When I finished putting their ideas on the board, I again spent some time talking about the point of the exercise. I emphasized that its purpose was to reinforce the ideas underlying good behaviour in the classroom. Again, a pensive look came over their faces. It was quite clear that they got the message. They behaved well for the rest of the day. And I hoped that my assignment would serve as a reminder to behave for days to come.

This seemed like a lot of work to get across a simple yet profound message—to love one another and behave accordingly. But then, when you think about it, clergy have been promulgating this principle for centuries, and yet human behaviour still falls far short of the mark.

As days passed, I had evidence that the exercise worked. The behaviour of the students improved. While I had to deal with the usual day to day misbehaviour, mostly involving mischief and restlessness, which I did not regard to be of much consequence, I did not have a serious behaviour problem for the rest of the term. Then I knew that, whatever wrinkles the students were trying to work into the exercise, they were doing so in good fun and good faith. The fact they had a mischievous streak made them even more interesting and likable.

When I discussed this assignment with Grandma, she was very impressed.

Dipping into her well of wisdom, she said, "You know Mary, your assignment gets to the heart of our faith. Above all else, the passage from St. Paul asks us to love one another. Ah yes, it sounds so simple until it comes to following it."

I shared these ideas with Grandma, because when I come home from school, she is in the habit of asking, "How are things going in the classroom?"

And I soon learned that the answer required a detailed description of what I was doing. As I filled her in on my exploits, she would stand or sit with her eyes closed and a thoughtful look on her face. My details of life in the classroom likely gave her fuel to think about what she would do as a teacher, something she never got the chance to do. In her own way she was trying to relive my experiences. With her advancing age, the adventurous part of her life was over, and no doubt, this was one of the reasons why she was so interested in my adventures. For her, vicarious experience had become a rewarding substitute for real experience.

19

At last the summer break had come, and after a gruelling first year of teaching, I was looking forward to more time at home, working on the farm with my hands, a welcome change from working with my head. The smell of apple and strawberry blossoms permeated the air, and this would soon be overpowered by the smell of new-mown hay. I glorified in experiencing the annual renewal these smells signified, and for that reason I loved to spent time out of doors.

In mid-July, Father put the whet stone to the blade of the scythe and then he began to mow the hay. He was a big powerful man, and with strong even swings of the scythe, he quickly mowed a good-sized patch of hay. When the hay was dry, my mother, sisters and I raked it into piles and then forked it into a cart to be carried into the barn. Making hay was hard work, but seeing the results of our efforts made it very satisfying. I revelled in the warmth of the sun on my face, the cool ocean breeze on my body, and the smell of new-mown hay in my nostrils. I was one with nature.

Each day, Grandma came to the field with a basket of delicious food to provide an opportunity for a break from our work.

And each day, she made the same comment: "Ah, there is nothing like hard work to whet the appetite."

We proved her right as we gorged ourselves on salmon sandwiches, hot biscuits, cookies, and tea.

Hay making coincided with the beginning of the run of salmon in the bay. Father took great pride in walking into the house with a forty-pound salmon under his arm and plunking it down on the kitchen table for us all to admire.

He would then ask, "Margaret, what cut do you want today." And invariable, the first cut she would ask for was the centre-cut. And oh, how we enjoyed our summer dinners of hot poached salmon drizzled with butter, and served with fresh peas and the first small, delicate new potatoes from the garden.

On days when we were waiting for the hay to dry, we went to the hills to pick berries. Mother planned to sustain us by preparing a big picnic lunch. Father would hitch our reliable Clydesdale mare to the riding wagon, and we would pile the back of the wagon with baskets for gathering berries. Mother and Anne would climb into the seat, and Catherine and I would ride on the back with our legs dangling over the edge of the wagon, and with Father laughing and waving goodbye, we would head for the hills. Grandma remained at home because she found berry picking too hard on her back. She cooked and baked while we picked berries.

The hills yielded a supply of the largest, plumpest, wild strawberries, ripe for the picking. The smell of the berries permeated the air like a delicate perfume. We picked and stemmed the berries in one operation. It was so satisfying to see the pile of shimmering red berries rise in each basket. From time to time we would pop a few of these delicacies into our mouths. The red rims around our lips betrayed our self indulgence. After several hours of picking, we grew tired. We would then retire to the shade of a tree by the brook, sit on the river bank, dangle our bare feet in the cool water and enjoy our picnic lunch. Revived by the food and rest, we resumed our berry picking until all our containers were full. We then put the containers of berries into the back of the wagon, and those that didn't fit, we carried on our laps. In the days before people cultivated the soil, they were food gatherers, and I think that stage of social development still lingered in our psyches. And so it was that, with that deep feeling of satisfaction that comes from our deep-seated need to be food gatherers, we headed for home. At supper we received our reward for our work, a big bowl of delicious red berries smothered in cream and sugar, accompanied by hot biscuits, country cheese, and hot strong tea.

After I had devoured every morsel, I thought to myself, "That was food fit for the gods."

The strawberry crop was followed by the raspberry crop, and the raspberry crop by the blueberry and blackberry crops. We repeated the same ritual for harvesting each of these crops. Mother and Grandma kept busy in the kitchen making jams and jellies for the winter months. And from the blueberries they made the finest treat of all, fresh blueberry pie. We drooled at the sight and smell of these beautiful confections cooling on the kitchen table. There is no finer dessert than a piece of warm blueberry pie accompanied by a glass of cold milk. I'm sure the finest restaurants could not match the food produced in our kitchen from nature's bounty.

By the middle of August, the barn was full of hay and the pantry cupboard was full of preserves. Our harvesting was done, and Father found he had time on his hands. And so he was casting about to find something to do. At supper one evening, he suggested that because we enjoy salmon so much, he should try to catch a few more to salt for the winter.

"I think I'll head for the bay in the morning to make one last run," he announced.

That night Grandma woke from a sound sleep in a cold sweat. It was as if she were in a trance. Her eyes were fixed on a coffin moving around the altar in St. Margaret's church. From stories she had heard as a young girl in the Highlands, she knew the meaning of forerunners and she was alarmed. Strains of the influence of the supernatural and preternatural forces that permeate the spirits of the Highland Scots ran deep in that woman.

The next morning conditions on the water seemed to be just right. The water was as smooth as glass; there was not a breath of wind; sailing conditions were perfect; so Father decided he was going to head out. This was not the news Grandma wanted to hear after the night she had and she tried to dissuade him.

Repeatedly she pleaded, "Please Laughlin, don't go."

He didn't listen to her. When she found she was unable to influence him, she decided to tell him about her vision of the coffin.

He dismissed her tale with these words, "Ah woman, that is nothing but a superstition that people in the Highlands believed in the old days."

In another effort to convince him, she then related the story of the meaning people attributed to forerunners back in the Highlands. Again he dismissed her misgivings, and with a spring in his step and his faithful collie dog by his side, he headed for the shore.

As he was leaving the yard, Grandma made one last plea, "Laughlin, please don't go."

And once more he ignored her plea and kept going.

She stamped her foot in vexation as she said, "That man is stubborn as an ox."

The day was quiet and overcast and the sea was calm. Father's boat was anchored near the shore. After he released the boat from its anchor, he pushed it into deeper water, and with his trusting collie dog occupying her place of honour in the prow of the boat, he set out with smooth even stokes on the calm sea. As they moved out, the dog sat tall with her nose pointing in the direction in which the boat was moving. Father always enjoyed her company when he was fishing. She had been accompanying him ever since she was a pup. She had learned to anticipate his every move.

Alas, after noon there was an abrupt change in the weather. By the mid-afternoon, the sky had darkened and ominous thunder clouds gathered in the west. The story of Grandma's vision was foremost in our minds. It was a bad omen that cast a dark spell over our home. The stillness of the air evoked an eerie feeling of foreboding. Our eyes were peeled on the water and we silently prayed to God for Father's safe return. In the late afternoon the storm hit in all its fury. The rain poured; the thunder roared; flashes of chain lightening cracked down around us like long whips, and heavy waves crashed on the shore. Then the wind came up and blew the storm out to sea, and once again the sea was calm. Evening came. Father did not return. We exchanged worried glances. It began to get dark, and still no sign of Father. I could see the fear in Mother's eyes as she went to alert our neighbour, John, to the failure of Father to return. John in turn alerted several other neighbours, and we saw them rushing from their homes to the Arisaig shore to put out in separate boats.

As we watched and listened, we heard them yelling to one another, "Do you see any sign of him?"

They did not go very far before they spotted Father's overturned boat, but there was no sign of Father. They knew what that likely meant.

John decided to go back to the shore, but the others continued the search. He waited and watched anxiously as his companions continued to look for Father. An hour passed, and his companions still did not find him. Then John decided he had to do what he did not want to do, and that was to go to see Mother.

He put his arm around her shoulder in a consoling fashion. "Margaret," he said, "I'm afraid I have some bad news."

As tears streamed down her cheeks she said, "Stop right there, John. Don't tell me. I know what you are going to say." Then she asked, "Did you see Laughlin's boat?"

John nodded in the affirmative.

Then Margaret continued, "And what about our dog? She could swim to shore. Maybe, just maybe, Laughlin went across to Prince Edward Island to wait out the storm. It is not that far from here, you know."

John interjected, "Ah Margaret, dear, stop right there. Don't get your hopes up. We looked everywhere and found no sign of Laughlin or his dog."

Later in the evening, Grandma noticed that our faithful collie dog still had not returned home, which she normally did every night. She knew this was another bad omen.

Then her mind drifted back to the warning she had received in her dream and she mused, "My, my, my … why wouldn't that man listen to me? Was he driven to pursue his fate? Are we nothing more than pawns in the hands of the gods? There is so much about life that we do not know."

Word that Father was missing passed quickly through the community, and the women gathered at the house. They made tea and chatted through the night to try to distract us from our worries. While all this was going on, Mother just sat and grieved in silence.

At the first light of dawn, the men got back into their boats and headed up the coast. They did not go very far before they spotted our faithful collie dog lying on the shore close to the water, and as they moved closer, they heard her whimpering. This led them to investigate further, and there in the shallow water a few yards from the dog, they found what they feared they would find. The waves had washed Father's body up close to the shore during the night. With heavy hearts they pulled his body from the water and carried him home, with his ever faithful dog following close behind. John was so overcome with grief at the sight of the lifeless body of his good friend that he cried all the way home. Mother and Grandma too were overcome with grief at the sight of Father's body. My sisters and I put our arms around them, and the tears welled up from the bottom of our souls. I was beginning to understand what is meant by a broken heart.

The people of our community did everything they could to console and to help us. The men crafted pine boards into a casket for Father. Two of his closest friends respectfully and carefully prepared his body for the wake. Women came with baskets of food. For two days and two nights Father's body was laid out in his casket in our parlour. Our loyal collie dog laid beside the coffin and refused to move. Helpful neighbours tried to coax her away with food. In response to these overtures, she turned her head away from them. She refused to eat.

This situation moved Grandma to say, "Leave the poor animal alone. She is mourning just like we are. Dogs are every bit as sensitive as human beings."

People came from miles around to pay their last respects and to commiserate with us. The men who were Father's closest friends sat up all night with his remains. This was a custom originating in the Highland belief that the soul remains around the body until it is buried, and out of respect, friends kept the soul company. These men expressed their solidarity with Father by occasionally raising a glass in his name.

More than once I heard one of them say, "Aye, a good man you were, Laughlin."

On the morning of Father's funeral, his best friends carried his casket to the Arisaig church, and his family and neighbours followed in a funeral procession. The melancholy sound of *Lord Lovat's Lament* came from the bagpipes of a lone piper playing on a nearby hill. From the shore we could hear the seagulls cry. The sounds of sadness were all around us. Grandma took Mother's right arm and I her left; Catherine and Anne walked behind us, and stoically we did that slow, painful walk behind the casket to the church. It took all the discipline I had to hold back the tears, for this ceremonial procession heightened my sense that this good man, who loved me so dearly and whom I loved in turn, was with us no more.

The prayers for everlasting life and eternal peace, which are central to the funeral liturgy, helped to sooth our souls. At the end of the funeral mass, the priest left us with the consoling thought that life is changed, not ended. On our walk to the graveyard, the funeral procession was led by a piper playing a slow air, *The Mist Covered Mountains,* a haunting reminder of the homeland our people left behind when they came to these shores. When Father's body was lowered into the grave, our hearts went down with him.

"Ashes to ashes, dust to dust ..." These words of the priest, which reflect the fate of the body, not the soul, made Father's death so final. A darkness again invaded our souls. After a few minutes of quiet prayer and reflection, punctuated with tears, we walked slowly back home without a word passing between us. There we found the people of the community waiting for our arrival. The feeling of solidarity with our neighbours continued to be a great comfort. It was a poignant reminder of how good people are; Highland funerals have a way of doing that.

Grandma, at her philosophical best, made this observation, "The central message of Christianity is to love one another. The Highland Scots go to great lengths to heed that message."

The women consoled Mother with words of hope. They spread the food they had brought on the table and poured tea. The men had a few drinks and exchanged stories about Father. They had the right idea; they were celebrating a good life well lived. Exhausted by the emotion of the day, they all went home in the early evening.

With the return of quiet, tears welled in Mother's eyes as she said, "Being left alone is my cross to bear."

Grandma went over and lovingly put her arm around her and helped her to her room. Release from the whirlwind of events surrounding Father's death, wake, and funeral, and the emotions that accompanied them, brought exhaustion, and we all headed for bed.

The next morning, we were not up to much more than sitting around. The harsh reality of our situation, exaggerated by continued exhaustion, really struck home.

The question foremost in our minds was, "How are we going to carry on without Father?"

His abrupt death meant that we were totally unprepared for the situation in which we found ourselves. Grandma took this opportunity to remind us that this was not the first crisis she had faced on this homestead. And then she told the story from her childhood of the man who appeared at their door shortly after they had settled and claimed their homestead was his.

"That was one of the worst days of my young life," she said. "I was terrified that my parents would have to go back to Scotland. The thought of another long horrible boat trip across the ocean was more than I could bear, and I cried my heart out. My life as a little girl was hard, harder than you'll ever know. The hardships I faced then prepared me to cope with the hardships I had to face as an adult. Dealing with hardship made me strong. And when you dig deep into your souls, I think you will find that you too have the strength to carry on."

The issue of survival without Father was on our minds all day. That evening found us still sitting around, still too sad and too exhausted to do anything else. Grandma decided that the occasion called for a better job of putting things in perspective, and to help us do that, she came to the fore with a stirring narrative on survival, drawn from stories of the Highlands perpetuated by the bards. And in telling an epic tale, she was as articulate as any bard from whom she had heard these stories. This is the story she told:

"At this time, it is important to remember that our line of MacDonald women, who were descendants of the MacDonalds of Glencoe, were survivors. And their ability to survive has a long tradition, as far as we know, dating back to the Massacre of Glencoe in the late 1600s in which our MacDonalds were brutally attacked in the midst of a howling blizzard. I have nothing but contempt for the trickery and deceit of the Campbells who came to the MacDonalds of Glencoe, claiming to be their friends, while their real mission was to destroy them.

"The chief of the Campbells—and a slippery fellow he was—hated the MacDonalds with a passion. Soldiers under his command marched on Glencoe. That deceitful Campbell chief told the chief of the MacDonalds that he came as a friend, and he made excuses for the presence of his soldiers. Then he had the gall to ask to impose on the chief's hospitality for himself and his men.

"In the finest spirit of Highland hospitality the MacDonald chief took the two-faced Campbell chief at his word and welcomed him and his men into his home, as well as the other homes in the glen.

"Little did he know that he had let the fox into the hen house. The MacDonalds shared with the soldiers their best food and their finest drink and they made sure they had comfortable bedding. The soldiers befriended the MacDonalds and together they wiled away many a happy hour, singing the songs of the Highlands and drinking the finest whiskey from the malt of the barley.

"One of our kinfolk, Mary Alexander Martin MacDonald, waited on these men hand and foot. She had her husband, Sandy, kill a fine sheep to feed them. She baked hot bannock for them to have with the meat. In a spirit of generosity, she shared with them the family's best cheese and butter, which were scarce during the winter because the shortage of feed kept the cows from producing enough milk to make a good supply of these products.

"While the soldiers were basking in this fine hospitality, the men in charge were busy planning the execution of their hosts. They sent soldiers to block the passes from Glencoe. Chief Campbell gave orders stating when the execution was to begin and that none were to be spared. The appointed day and the appointed hour had arrived. The reward poor dear Mary received for her hospitality was to have her guests shoot her husband, Sandy, in the back before her very eyes. Speechless and in shock, she next saw those turncoats, those devils, turn their guns on her innocent children, who were also shot in the back as they ran to escape. There was nothing she could do to stop them. Her youngest son, her dear little six-year-old boy, Angus, was gunned down as he clung to a soldier's legs pleading for mercy.

"In the midst of all the noise and confusion, she had the presence of mind to grab a shawl and sneak out the back door unnoticed.

"Fortunately, the weather was in her favour. It would seem that even the gods were upset with the Campbells' treachery, for the night winds had brought a howling blizzard down on Glencoe. The visibility was so poor that when the soldiers noticed Mary was gone and went to look for her, and others who had fled, they couldn't see a hand in front of them. As she stood some distance from her home, she was numb with shock and fear as she listened to the cries of the men, women, and children who were being hacked and shot to death.

"After the soldiers set the homes of their hosts on fire, the blaze of the burning cottages lit up the surrounding landscape. Even through the blizzard, Mary was able to see the snow around the burning cottages red with blood. She was shaken to the core when, from one of the cottages, she heard the desperate screams of those who were being burned alive.

"'I must not think about these things or I will go mad,' she told herself.

"Here she was, pregnant, alone, outside in a raging blizzard, with no safe shelter in sight. With this stark realization, her determination to keep herself and her unborn child alive became a driving force within her.

"With no one else to turn to, she took to talking to her unborn child. 'Do not be afraid, little one,' she would say in a gentle voice. 'I will do everything I can to keep you alive. We'll get through this together.'

"She had the courage to scramble up the side of the nearest mountain. She stopped on a ledge that jutted out from the slope to rest and to view what was happening, but the blizzard prevented her from seeing any more than a few feet in front of her. There it was safe for her to rest for a while. Fortunately, she knew every inch of the terrain, and after resting, she was able to resume her climb in spite of the storm. She did not climb very far before she encountered other men, women, and children who had also escaped. They were resting on another ledge on the mountain.

"There were a few decent men in the Campbell regiment. Some of them were unwilling to kill fellow Scots; others were reluctant to kill people who had been so kind to them. These men warned their hosts of their impending doom and let them slip away under the cover of darkness. The Highlanders who had escaped trembled with cold and fear. Together they helped one another climb up the mountain until they came across a cave, which was big enough for all of them and which provided welcome relief from the weather. They were cagey enough not to try to escape through the mountain passes, for they suspected they were guarded by the enemy.

"When the weather cleared, the survivors watched Campbell's soldiers looting the cottages that had not been burned. They were particularly vexed when they saw the turncoats march away with their cattle, sheep, and goats, and with them went their sole source of livelihood. In the cave where they took refuge, they were forced to survive on the fare of the animals that normally occupied it.

"'If we are going to stay alive we will have to hunt for our food like wild animals,' said Hugh Ranald Mor MacDonald.

"'Things may be bad, but they are not that bad,' replied John Hugh Gussie MacDonald with a cunning smile, as he pulled a gun from under his coat.

"Later in the day, John used his gun to shoot a deer and some rabbits, hopefully out of the range of hearing of the soldiers. Knowing that a fire would attract the attention of the enemy, the survivors had no choice but to eat the meat raw. Ravenously hungry, they tore the meat apart with their bare hands and ate greedily.

"During the next few nights, Mary was pained to see some of her neighbours die of exposure because they were unable to get their cloaks before they left their cottages. Under the cover of darkness, the escapees put the dead bodies in deep snow banks so that they would not have to watch them deteriorate. In spite of all this adversity and heartbreak, Mary's determination to survive did not waiver.

"At the end of each day, she would lovingly say these words of reassurance to her unborn child, 'We are still alive, little one. We are going to make it.'

"Each morning, the men went out to check on the enemy and came back with reports of their location. On the fourteenth day, they found that the soldiers had departed from one pass, but the others remained guarded. They interpreted this as a sign that security was lessening. Mary decided that for the good of her unborn child, she had better try to move on. Her companions urged her not to go. They warned that it was too dangerous for her to head out on her own. But she was headstrong, and so on the first sunny day, she pulled her shawl around her and started her journey. She made her way down the mountain slope through the unguarded pass to seek refuge with the MacDonalds of Keppock, who occupied land to the north of Glencoe. Throughout this ordeal her determination continued to be spurred by her unborn child.

"As she walked she talked to the wee one within her. 'Don't be afraid, little one. You are the source of my strength, and no matter what, I will go on,' she repeated over and over again.

"When she was within a mile of the cottage of a relative, Allan Laughie Mor MacDonald, her heart leaped with fear as she was unexpectedly accosted by a member of the Campbell regiment.

"'Madame, what is your name?' he asked.

"She was quick witted enough to realize that she could not use her real name. So she did her best to remain calm, and without any hesitation, she replied, 'Mary, Mary Gillis.'

"The terror in her heart abated when the soldier waved his musket and said, 'Move on.'

"For her protection she decided to adopt the name 'Mary Ban Gillis' in place of Mary Alexander Martin MacDonald, and her son, born three months later, was named John Alexander Gillis. According to our local bard, to whom this story had been passed by a bard in the Highlands, it was from her line that the first permanent settler in Arisaig, John Ban Gillis, was descended, and it is from his line that we are descended."

And Grandma concluded, "Surely if Mary Gillis was able to survive that terrible ordeal, then we too can survive our ordeal."

Grandma's story made us pause to reflect. Her story was a parable, the moral of which was meant to address our uncertainty about our ability to get along without Father.

After a moment of silence, I turned to Anne and whispered, "That was an amazing story. I think we got the message."

Anne nodded in agreement.

I decided this was a good time to reassure Mother; so I went to her and took both of her hands while I made this promise, "Look, Mother, things may look bleak now, but everything is going to be all right. I'll continue to teach here in Arisaig, and my salary will cover most of the expenses of running our household. We've had a good life and we will continue to have a good life."

As Mother looked at me, I could see that her pale face was creased with lines of worry, and she looked as if she carried the weight of the world on her shoulders. Even though the burden of responsibility weighed heavily on her, Mother was resilient, and so it took only a few days for her to begin showing signs of resignation to her fate.

I knew this when I heard her muse, "I have been doing a great deal of thinking and I have finally come to accept Laughlin's death as the will of God."

I nodded in the affirmative, while at the same time thinking, "The will of God sure operates in strange ways."

Enough of this introspection. It was time for us to get on with our lives. There is nothing better to distance a person from pain and grief that the distraction of good hard work. Daily, Catherine and Anne and I put on our barn clothes and went out to do the barn work. While I didn't much care for barn work, the physical labour was good for me, for it helped me to forget my problems. We milked the cows, let them out to graze, and then cleaned the barn. Milk production was heavy during the summer. The milk we brought from the barn day after day kept Mother busy making butter and curds and cheese. Just like the barn work was good for us, making dairy products was good for her. It wasn't long before she was singing again to the rhythm of the click clack of the plunger moving up and down in the churn. She would smile with satisfaction as she turned out one beautiful pat of butter after another. While Grandma was watching this operation, she laughed as she recalled how her mother would blame the fairies for souring the cream when she discovered that the cream was not fit for churning.

On one particularly long day of work producing dairy products, Mother turned to me and said, "Mary, my kitchen is as busy as a factory."

After a couple of weeks of churning cream and pressing curds, Mother had a supply of cheese and butter ready for market. While all this productive activity was going on, Grandma was busy attending to the cooking, while she told stories about food in the Highlands.

One night while we were extolling the merits of her fluffy mashed potatoes, she looked up from her meal and said, "My mother told me they did not always have potatoes in the Highlands."

Then she went on to tell how her grandparents remembered when potatoes were first introduced from Ireland and what a great addition they were to the Highland diet.

"They kept a lot of Highlanders from starving," she informed us.

However, she was quick to add that the potato was not so important to the Highlanders' diet as their beloved oatmeal. On many mornings, she warned that we did not have sufficient appreciation of our oatmeal porridge.

"Over the centuries, oatmeal was the staple of the Highland diet and it helped to make the Highlanders big and strong," she kept reminding us. "This was the diet of our men when they went into battle. This was the diet of the people who had to flee to the mountains to hide in caves. They licked it raw from their hands. In many ways it was the lifeline of our forebears."

Since Father died, Grandma was full of these stories. Maybe thinking about the adversity Highlanders faced in their homeland helped her to come to terms with the problems we currently faced.

After all this productive work was finished, Mother asked if one of us would go to town with her, and I volunteered. I hitched our reliable mare, Nellie, to the riding wagon, and we piled our supply of cheese and butter into the back.

Grandma was again in a very talkative mood, and as she watched me hitch the mare to the wagon, she recalled that her father's horses were not always so patient and gentle.

"I remember one time when our horse was very rambunctious, I heard him complain that he could not do a thing with him after the impish fairies pestered him in his stall. Back in the Highlands fairies had a reputation for playing nasty tricks like that," she said.

Mother and I no longer believed in these superstitions; so we just looked at Grandma incredulously as we climbed into the seat of the wagon and headed over Browns mountain into town.

Mother then looked at me and said, "I bet those impish fairies were horse flies."

We both burst out laughing.

John, the owner of the general store to whom Mother sold her goods, came out to greet her when he saw her coming, and being a thoughtful man, he took time to communicate his deepest sympathy. More than once, I heard him say, "Margaret, I am so very sorry."

He was soon joined by other store owners who did likewise. I could tell by the look on Mother's face that she was deeply touched by their compassion.

When the conversation ended, John very obligingly carried her supply of dairy products into the store and asked, "Do you want to be paid in kind or in cash, Margaret?"

"Both, please, half in kind and half in cash," was her reply.

As he gave her the money, she said, "Thank you, thank you. Now I can get supplies for the kitchen and have some money to put aside for a rainy day."

Mother bartered some of her dairy products for goods we could not produce on our homestead. She got enough sugar, tea, molasses, baking powder, spices, dried fruit, and flour to last for several months. Then we had a good chat with the other customers before we headed for home. On the way back, we talked optimistically about how well we were getting along on our own.

And Mother, again showing signs that she was coming to terms with her fate, added, "I was brought up with the idea that God will provide, and sure enough, here we find ourselves getting along just fine."

Just when we thought that mother was adjusting to life without Father, we noticed that she began to look worried. As this condition persisted, we became concerned.

"Mother, is there something wrong?" I asked one morning during breakfast.

She just shook her head in the negative and said nothing. What she was not willing to tell us was that she had noticed some Micmacs, who lived in the woods surrounding our farm, walking beyond the edge of the woods, each day moving closer and closer to our home. When she opened the door, they would quickly disappear into the wilderness. She could not speak to them because she did not know their language nor could they speak to her. As this situation persisted, her anxiety grew and she became paranoid. We could see by her pale face and her tired eyes that she was not able to sleep. She would lie awake at night, worrying that they might try to attack us now that there was no man in the house. She also feared that they might steal the one precious horse we owned. Deep down, she knew they were not like that, but the fact that they persisted in hanging around near her home gave rise to these fears. She did not discuss her concerns with us because she did not want us to worry. And just as her distress had reached its peak, she opened the door one morning to find a large chunk of fresh moose meat.

We heard her say, "I had no idea what they were trying to do. Those good people wanted to bring me a gift, but they did not know how to approach me. All the time I was afraid of them, they were trying to help me."

It was only then that she was able to open up and tell us what had happened.

After she had finished her story, she concluded, "I feel so guilty. Here I was thinking the worst of those kind and generous people. That just goes to show what a hard time we have understanding people who are not like us. After all the Micmacs have done for our people, we still do not trust them. I am so ashamed."

To show her appreciation, the next day, Mother went to the edge of the woods, called for the Micmacs to come, and gave a large round of her finest cheese to the one who appeared.

This incident moved Grandma to again remind us that the Frasers, with whom she and her parents had stayed in Pictou when they first came to these shores, and the other pioneers who had arrived on the Hector would not have made it through their first winter if it were not for the help of the Micmacs.

She said, "They showed our people how to hunt for deer and moose, how to fish through the ice, and how to use the hides of the deer and moose as clothing to keep out the cold. They also showed the men how to make canoes, which became their only means of transportation. The Micmacs knew how to live in the New World and we did not. We owe them a great debt of gratitude."

20

It had been a harrowing summer, more harrowing than I could ever have imagined, and I was glad to escape to the classroom in September. The exuberant youngsters with their fresh faces and their impish smiles were just the antidote I needed to offset the gloom that penetrated my soul. My first year of teaching had been my baptism of fire. Even though I was only beginning my second year of teaching, I felt like a seasoned veteran. I felt comfortable in my position, because by this time, I knew the routine of the classroom, and I also had a better idea of which teaching practises worked and which ones did not. This is called learning from experience, and every teacher will vouch for its value. While the routine for the school year was established early, and while I realized how important it is, I also realized more than ever how important it is to depart from this routine to celebrate festive occasions. Children need more joy in their lives. The ache in my heart brought on by Father's death made me more conscious of their need, as well as my own. This was especially true of the children who worked hard at home, where they were overburdened with the responsibilities of adults. I wanted those for whom school was an escape from this burden to have a chance to be children again. They needed to have some fun, and it was my job to made sure that they had the opportunity.

Halloween and Christmas provided special occasions for digressions from the routine of school work. On Halloween, I distributed some candy and apples and told my students ghoulish tales about mysterious creatures and superstitious happenings. Scottish lore is full of stories about fairies, witches, bocans, second sight, and the evil eye, and this was just the occasion to share some of those dark tales that are deeply embedded in the Highland folk culture. Even though my stories sometimes made my students shudder with fear, they loved every minute of it. They shivered when I told stories of the dark power of witches and related tales of the power of those possessing "the evil eye" to bring misfortune to those to whom it is directed.

"If put upon you, it could destroy your health, your home, your animals, or even your family," I said in a serious voice.

When I stopped, they pleaded, "Tell us more; tell us more."

Then I resumed with a tale of the ghostly bocans that roam our homes and land at night trying to finish something they had left undone on earth.

"When you hear the wind sighing through the trees or when you hear the floorboards creaking at night, you will know where they are," I told them in a scary voice.

At this point, all my students laughed when one of the girls exclaimed, "I will never go to the outhouse again after dark."

The occasion for the most enjoyable digression from the routine of school work was preparation for the annual Christmas concert. The students eagerly anticipated every aspect of this event, as did the whole community. Because Anne had an artistic bent, she volunteered to help. She started to come to school with me in early December to assist with the preparation of the Christmas pageant and to teach the students to sing the traditional Christmas songs. These unspoiled young people were very impressed with the opportunity to play roles in one of the greatest stories ever told. The girl with the warmest personality was an appropriate choice for the role of Mary. I am sure that the original Mary was no more reverent that the Mary chosen for this pageant. Joseph was played by the oldest son of the largest family in our community, a young man who in many ways served as a father to his younger brothers; so he had the kind of experience that would help him to understand his role. The boys who agreed to serve as shepherds did their best to be humbly attentive. Most of the girls in the class agreed to assume the role of angels, which they wanted to exaggerate.

When Anne asked them to tone it down, one of them remarked, "We are just being ourselves," which prompted a great laugh from her classmates.

The students revelled in the opportunity that acting gave them to express themselves. Acting is something most of them had never done, and they were so taken with it that they gave it their full attention.

Anne made a perceptive comment about the educative value of this activity. "Putting themselves in the place of others may well help them to understand their fellow human beings better. That is an important part of growing up," she said.

The concert was scheduled for December 18, and because it was one of the main social events in our community, people came from miles around. On this night, the school yard was filled with horses and sleighs. Before the concert the men stood around outside chewing tobacco, smoking their pipes and gossipping. A few of them enjoyed a nip of the malt of the barley, but in deference to the children, most decided to abstain. The women went inside immediately to find space to lay out biscuits, cheese, cakes, and cookies for the lunch to be served after the performance. My classroom had now become part stage, part seating for the audience, and part lunch room. It was filled with the noise of busy women bustling about and chatting as they enjoyed making their contribution to the occasion.

At the appointed time, the members of the audience took their seats. They sat in anticipation of seeing their children act the roles of the characters involved in the familiar Christmas story. When the pageant began, the faces of the audience revealed their shared feeling of proud parenthood as they watched their children perform.

Anne had arranged a surprise for the actors and the audience. She had persuaded John Ban Gillis, the finest violin player in our community, to come and play Christmas music. So, while the students were performing the pageant, he played Silent Night softly in the background. To the moving strains of this music, the actors in the pageant captured the mood of the Christmas story, and the members of the audience were in awe of the special beauty the music brought to the performance. They greeted both the pageant and the music with enthusiastic applause. After the pageant, the rest of the class, who had served as stage hands, joined the members of the pageant and the audience to sing the traditional Christmas carols to the accompaniment of the violin. The parents were touched by the opportunity to participate. After the concert, they stayed around to chat and have lunch, and then, with a feeling of satisfaction, they headed for home. On this cold but moonlit winter night, it was a beautiful sight to see and hear the horses and sleighs moving so gracefully away in the crisp white snow.

Anne and I were the last to go. We had been very busy; so we took our time and enjoyed the opportunity to chat over a cup of tea. We felt good about our contribution to making the Christmas season more enjoyable in our community.

I suggested that the violin music made this year's concert extra special.

"I didn't know John Ban played the violin so well," I said. "How did you get him to play?"

Anne's reply was, "He offered to do it in memory of Father."

We looked at each other as tears came to our eyes.

As I pulled myself together, I commented, "It was a good cause."

Anne nodded in approval.

"Ah, Christmas. How will we get through it without Father?" I asked myself.

I was soon to learn that Father's passing helped to enhance the spirit of Christmas in our community. Our loyal neighbours made it their mission to help us to enjoy Christmas.

John, our closest neighbour, reflected this spirit when he said to his wife, "Mary, we'll do everything we can to bring Christmas joy to Margaret and her family."

And his efforts began the week before Christmas with the butchering of a steer for Mother so she would have meat to make her Christmas sausages. On the day the butchering was to be done, and just as John was arriving, Mother went out to the barn with two buckets.

"John," she asked, "Would you kindly save the blood from the animal so that we can make blood puddings?"

I made sure that I did not go near the barn until the poor animal was dead. I wanted no part of the initial act in the butchering process. I knew I would collapse with the animal when they knocked it out with a mallet to the forehead. This was supposed to be a humane practise, but I did not see it that way. I once witnessed this spectacle at a neighbour's house when I was a little girl. I vividly remember every gory detail. First, the animal was led to the scene of the slaughter and its head was held motionless by ropes. Then the farmer picked up a mallet, pulled it back, and swung it at the animal's head with full force. As the animal slumped to the ground, I was so upset that I vomited. I vowed that I would never be present at the butchering of an animal again.

John and his son slit the throat of the animal and collected its blood in the buckets Mother provided. They then gutted the animal and removed the intestines, tongue, liver, heart, stomach and kidneys before they skinned it. Nothing went to waste. Handling this carcass made our homestead a beehive of activity. Catherine and Anne and I helped Mother to lug the intestines and the stomach to the stream that meanders through our property where Mother put them in a container that would let the water run through them.

After the intestines were thoroughly cleaned in the cold, clear water, we took them to the kitchen where Grandma was busy making blood puddings. She was waiting to get the cleaned intestines to use as casings for the puddings. We found her busily stirring a big pot of blood mixed with meal and spices, which was slowly cooking on the back of the stove.

"I am making them just the way my mother made them when I was a little girl in the Highlands," she informed us.

She took advantage of the occasion to remind us that when Highlanders were hungry toward the end of the winter, they sometimes bled their animals to make blood puddings to provide nourishment to keep them alive. This story made Anne and me look at each other with disgust as Grandma went about her business.

As she added spices to the pot, we smiled as we listened to her talking to herself. "No, I think it needs a touch more. No, still a bit more. Ah yes, now that is just right."

Grandma next busied herself with cutting up some of the best pieces of meat to mix with spices and meal to be used to make a delicious sausage known as *isbean*.

"Come on, girls, pitch in," she said.

We were only too glad to help her. We cut and we chopped and as the task neared completion, Grandma, with a glint in her eye, commented, "Won't it be great to have this fine food to serve friends who come to visit over Christmas."

Grandma loved company, for it gave her an opportunity to share her stories of the past and to learn of the news of the community.

The cold winter weather enabled us to keep some roasts, steaks, and stew meat frozen in the shed for several months. The fresh meat froze quickly and remained frozen until we took it in to thaw.

John later butchered a pig for Mother. I watched her take the pig's head to harvest some meat from it to be combined with the meat she had saved from the cow's head to make a dish called potted head, another delicacy to the Highland Scots.

As she finished preparing the dish, I heard her say, "This will be such a treat."

John had a smoke house where he stoked the fire with wood from an old apple tree to cure some of the bacon for us. Ah, how I looked forward to some of that delectable bacon smelling of apple wood, frying slowly in a thick black pan on the back of the stove, to be eaten with warm bannock, topped with strawberry preserves, and good hot tea on a leisurely Sunday morning.

In addition to having an ample supply of meat, we were also well supplied with vegetables. Our root cellar was overflowing with potatoes, turnips, carrots, parsnips, cabbage, onions, and beets from our garden, which we had helped Mother harvest in the fall.

Mother and Catherine made a trip to town to buy the spices, dried fruit, and nuts Grandma needed to make Christmas cakes. When they returned, Grandma went to work laying out all the ingredients she needed. This was one of her finest hours. She moved around the kitchen as if she were ten years younger. We made our contribution to the task by chopping up the dried fruit and nuts and suet for her. Then she went to work meting out the right amount of each ingredient, which she knew by sight and feel, mixing all of the ingredients together, and then putting the batter into big black pans, and the pans into the oven to bake.

As she used her apron to wipe the flour from her hands, and with a far away look in her eye, she turned to us and said, "You know, we had nothing this good back in the Highlands."

When the baking time was about up, she stuck a straw in the middle of each cake, and then we heard her predictable reactions. "No, it is not quite done," or "Ah, that is just about perfect."

At the right time, she removed these delicious confections from the oven, and their tantalizing smell permeated the house. There is no question that Grandma had the touch of a fine cook. Pleased with the results of her efforts, she exclaimed, "There is nothing better than the simple pleasure of a good hot cup of tea and a piece of delicious fruitcake shared with a friend."

For all of us, the crowning glory of the Christmas season was midnight mass. Every family in the community hitched their horses to their riding sleighs or bobsleds and headed for church. It was a cold, clear Christmas eve with the light of the stars and the moon creating a blue cast on the snow. In keeping with the spirit of the season, the air was still and a peacefulness had descended over the land. The silence of the night was broken only by the sound of the horses' hoofs in the crisp snow and the jingle of the bells on the shafts of the sleighs ringing to the rhythm of the horses' hoofs. The joyousness of the occasion was reflected in the exchange of greetings and pleasantries between and among our neighbours as they moved into the church. The traditional Gaelic greeting, *Ciamar a tha sibh,* Gaelic for how are you, was heard repeated joyously over and over again.

Our little log church was lighted only by candles, which gave a festive glow reflecting the spirit of the occasion. While we waited for the service to begin, John Angus MacQuarrie started singing the traditional Christmas hymns in his beautiful tenor voice, and the rest of us joined in the singing. We then joined with the priest in celebrating the mass that commemorates the birth of Christ and provides us with a poignant reminder of the love and mercy of God. Because it was such a beautiful night, we all lingered outside the church after mass, enjoying the pleasure of being together. Then we climbed into our sleighs and headed for home.

When we got home, I stirred up the fire in the kitchen stove; Mother made some tea, and Grandma prepared a plate of goodies for us to sample. We sat around the fire and ate quietly as we basked in the full enjoyment of being together. Father's death had taught us not to take life's simple pleasures for granted.

On Christmas morning, Mother had the plumpest chicken from her flock plucked, cleaned, and ready to be stuffed. Grandma had boiled potatoes which she mashed and combined with bread, butter, onion, and spices to make stuffing.

As she sampled the stuffing, I heard her say, "Now that is going to be really good."

She filled the cavity of the chicken with this aromatic condiment and placed the roast pan in the oven where the bird slowly turned to a golden brown. Then she chopped the giblet to be combined with the juices from the bird to make giblet gravy. The smell of the delectable bird permeated the house and made us ravenously hungry. With the delicious meat and stuffing, we had boiled parsnips drizzled with butter, which taste so sweet with chicken, and fluffy mashed potatoes covered with gravy.

We had just settled down to eat when we heard a rap at the door. It was Maggie John Allan, a homeless woman, who made her living going from house to house offering her services in exchange for food and lodging. Her forlorn look and her sad smile would touch any heart.

When Mother opened the door, Maggie said, "It's just me, the ole hag."

Laughing, Mother replied, "Now Maggie, you know you are not that bad. Come on in. You are just in time for dinner."

I'm sure this is what Maggie had in mind, for she seemed to know exactly when we were going to eat.

"Set another place at the table," Mother told me.

We felt good about sharing our meal with someone who would otherwise not have a Christmas dinner.

A few minutes later, we heard another rap at the door, and this time it was Roddie Jim Angus, who was the only homeless man in our community and who made his living in much the same way as Maggie.

As he stood in the doorway, with his shoulders stooped, his head down and his eyes cast on the ground, Mother said, "Well if it isn't himself. Roddy, don't just stand there; come on in and have dinner with us."

And once more I heard, "Mary, set another place at the table."

I'm sure arriving at our place in time for dinner was a plan worked out between the two of them, and it worked.

In a private moment out of the earshot of our guests, Grandma, in her best philosophical fashion, reflected the thoughts of all of us when she said, "Remember girls, sharing this meal with someone less fortunate than ourselves reflects the true meaning of Christmas."

We invited Maggie and Roddie to stay the night. After dinner, we lit a fire in the fireplace in the parlour and we spent the rest of the day sitting around the fire enjoying a chance to relax.

Maggie and Roddie were friends, likely brought together by sharing the same lot in life. They were the only two homeless people in our community and looking after them became a community project. Regardless of how cramped the quarters in the homes were, people managed to find room for them. When you consider that several generations of a family usually lived in each home and that its space and resources were utilized to the limit, this was quite an added responsibility. Both Maggie and Roddy's parents were dead and their siblings had moved elsewhere, leaving them to fend for themselves. They survived by going from house to house offering to do some work in exchange for their keep. Even if people did not need their help, they would take them in and find something for them to do.

Maggie was the sharper of the two and she had learned a coy way of requesting work.

She would come to the door, tip her head to the side, and with a shy smile say, "I am here to help ye."

How could anyone be so cold-hearted as to say no.

Maggie was a middle-aged woman who looked old beyond her years. Her weather-beaten face showed the consequences of spending too much time out of doors. Her smile revealed a mouth full of decayed teeth. Her lean body was swaddled in layers of clothing she had picked up as she went from house to house. And yet there was a sweet innocence in her face that gave her a certain attractiveness.

Most of the time Maggie was a lively expressive individual, but there were times when she had dark moments. When she knew these spells were coming on, she would withdraw from everyone until they had passed. At these times, she wanted to be alone. She clearly suffered from occasional bouts of mental disease. In these spells, she was tortured by the perceived presence of evil spirits that taunted her. People who had a chance to observe her in this condition noted that the torment of these mythical creatures prompted strange talk and gestures and occasional outbursts of kicking and screaming.

Because of the preponderance of people with the same last name in the community, the residents often assigned nicknames to differentiate them from one another. Because of Maggie's flights from reality she was given the nickname, Maggie in the Sky. She did not much like this name, and so in deference to her wishes, people simply called her Maggie. In some ways, her vulnerability was a strength, for it moved people to have compassion for her.

Maggie went through a trauma in her teen years that left its mark on her. Our neighbour, Mary, has sad recollections of what had happened to Maggie. Mary was walking down the road one day when she heard a noise coming from the ditch. It sounded like someone moaning. She turned to find Maggie, alone, abandoned, afraid, and in terrible pain, giving birth to a child.

When Maggie saw Mary, she raised her hand as she pleaded, "Please help me."

Mary jumped into the ditch and got down on her hands and knees to help Maggie. She repeatedly told Maggie to push until she saw the baby's head appear, and then she helped to extract the rest of the body of the baby from Maggie's womb. Maggie survived the birth in these adverse conditions, but the baby did not.

Mary asked Maggie if she would let her look after the body of the baby, and trembling and with tears in her eyes, she agreed on one condition: "No one is ever to know this happened. My parents would kill me if they knew," she said.

Mary was filled with pity for this poor little girl. She assured her that, under the cover of darkness, she would take a shovel to the graveyard and bury the baby's body in her father's grave.

She thought to herself, "No one should ever have to go through this experience unloved and alone."

Maggie had no one to turn to, not even her mother or grandmother. Maggie confided that she was terrified of what these women might do to her if they found out she was pregnant; so she wore layers of loose clothing to hide her condition.

What should have been a joyous event in Maggie's life was a terrifying experience from which she never fully recovered. It was shortly thereafter that she began to have mental problems. Mary MacLean kept Maggie's terrifying experience a secret until others found Maggie in one of these spells.

Roddie did not have Maggie's social graces. He was a man of few words; in fact, he was quiet to the point of being sullen. He kept his head down and only spoke when he was spoken to. His large awkward body, his slumped shoulders, his expressionless face, his hesitant responses created the impression that he was slow. His whole countenance exuded a terrible sense of inadequacy which, according to Grandma, arose from a childhood filled with rejection. Grandma suspected that his problems could be traced to his being born out of wedlock. Mother recalled how Roddy's mother, Mary Anne, had disappeared from the community for a number of months prior to his birth. Her parents did not want people to know she was pregnant. Being born out of wedlock was a terrible disgrace in our community, as it was in other communities. To help to mask "the shame," as it was called, his mother's family took him in, pretending he was a relative, to raise as their own, but they never really accepted him. To them he was an outsider who was tolerated for the sake of the reputation of his family. He was given neither the love nor the encouragement needed to develop confidence in himself. And hence when his grandparents and mother died, and their children moved away, without giving any thought to what was to become of him, he was not prepared to cope on his own. Lacking both competence and confidence, he became a beggar who went from door to door looking for his keep.

He would simply come to the door, rap, lower his head and ask in a low voice, "Can I come in?"

Everybody knew what he wanted.

Maggie befriended Roddy when she realized that they shared the same lot in life. Their livelihood was totally dependent on the good will of the people who answered the door. Maggie was by far the smarter of the two. She had the sly cunning of a fox and she used this ability to sustain both of them. She kept tabs on every home in the community. She watched to see when families were butchering because she knew they would have fresh meat. She kept an eye on who was carrying a big salmon from the shore, for she knew there would be more than enough poached salmon to go around. She knew who the best cooks in the community were, and she had a good nose for determining when they were doing some extra good cooking or baking. She was particularly sensitive to the smell of blueberry pie wafting from the windows of homes during the blueberry season, for this was her favourite dessert. And, of course, all this information was put to good use in determining the right time to hit a home to exchange some work for her keep.

When the time was right, Maggie would say to Roddie, "I think we best pay them a visit."

Maggie shared with Roddie the useful information she gained from sizing up the homes in the community because she knew Roddie needed her help. She was the leader and he was the follower. By working together they managed to survive.

That evening, Mother told Maggie that she was welcome to sleep on a cot in the hallway. Mother opened the door to let some heat from the fire in the parlour into the hallway and she put an extra quilt on the cot. Because we had no more sleeping accommodations in the house, Mother told Roddie that he could use our sleeping quarters in the barn. In one corner of the hay mow, there was a bunk Father had built. Hay formed the mattress, which was covered with woollen bats, and there were a couple of blankets for warmth. The heat from the bodies of the animals kept the chill down, and the mow was reasonably comfortable. Because it was an unusually cold night, we heated some large stones for Roddy to put at his feet. Before I went to bed, I decided to go to the barn to see if Roddy was all right, and what did I find. There on the bunk were he and Maggie making out. They were so preoccupied with each other that they never noticed me; so I quietly closed the barn door and went back to the house.

I smiled as I thought to myself, "Now I think I know what is meant by 'a roll in the hay!'"

Boxing Day kicked off a round of social gatherings in our community, and our house was chosen for the first ceilidh. It started in the early afternoon.

As Grandma looked down the road and saw some of the guests coming, she exclaimed, "This is great. I love a house full of happy people."

A rap at the door, and there were our neighbours, John Dan and Mary MacLean. Soon another rap, and there were John Ban and Ann Gillis. A third rap, and there were Roy Ronald and Mary MacDonald. A little later, John Angus and Jenny MacQuarrie arrived. John brought a gillick, which the men slowly consumed with deep satisfaction. A few drinks and John was ready to sing, and we gladly joined in singing the traditional Christmas songs. When we tired of singing, we settled down to talk, and the sound of agreeable chatter filled the room. Each family has its own highs and lows over the course of the year, and our conversation embodied our reflections on both. In the early evening, we invited our guests to feast on the fine food Grandma had prepared especially for the holiday season, from her tasty blood puddings and isbean to her delicious Christmas cake. And with some variations on this routine, we passed the days until New Year's Eve very agreeably.

New Year's Eve was a very special occasion. On that night, we gathered in the largest home in the community, that of John Angus and Jenny MacQuarrie. As was customary on New Year's Eve, the men raised their glasses to the freedom we enjoy in the New World.

Then, in a nostalgic vein, the men launched into stories about what happened to their families in the Highlands during and after the 1745 Rebellion. These dark memories, like sores that will not heal, seemed to be burned into the minds of generations of Highlanders. John took the lead in storytelling. In a rather morose mood, he recalled how his great grandfather was cut down in a hail of bullets on Drumossie Moor in 1746. He told of how the friends of this man, who stood beside him in battle, vividly remembered the sight of his blood-soaked body as he lay listless on the ground. Apparently the first redcoat who came along pierced his body with a sword to make sure he was dead.

"And if that wasn't bad enough," John said, "the redcoats chased his brother to his cottage where he locked himself safely inside, or so he thought. So what did those miserable creatures do? They burned his cottage to the ground; that is exactly what they did."

Others followed with graphic details of the rape of women, the brutal killing of their children, and the hanging, drawing, and quartering of Highlanders who were believed to be leaders of the insurrection.

And the teller of each story ended with the exclamation, "May those redcoats burn in hell."

All the men responded by exclaiming in unison, "Hear, hear."

These horrendous stories prompted John Ban Gillis to intervene. "All right, all right," he said, "It is time to put those horror stories from the past behind us." Then he got out his violin and extended an invitation, "Come now, let us dance and enjoy ourselves."

And with that invitation he put his bow to his violin, and to the music he played we danced until we were too tired to dance any longer. Then we shared a midnight meal and headed for home, exhausted but happy.

On the way home, I said to Anne, "Can you just imagine how Father would have enjoyed this gathering."

She smiled and nodded her head in agreement.

21

The harsh reality of winter brought a keener realization of how hard it was to carry on without Father. While I was busy at school, Mother and Anne and Catherine braved the biting cold to do the barn work. Each day, they let the animals out to go to the brook for water. On very cold days, Anne trudged through the snow following the trail made by the animals, carrying an axe to cut a hole in the ice so they could drink.

As she made her way back to the barn, she thought to herself, "If Father were here, I wouldn't have to do this. Oh, there are so many ways I miss him."

While the livestock were at water, Catherine and Mother cleaned the stables.

As Catherine forked manure out the window of the shed, her thoughts were in the same vein as Anne's, as she too remarked, "I wouldn't have to do this if Father were here."

Mother simply responded with an affirming "Aye" as she moved to fill the cows' stalls with fresh hay.

Each morning and evening, Mother milked our three cows, fed some of the milk to the calves that were bawling and straining on their halters to be fed, and took the rest of it into the house for our own personal consumption and to be turned into dairy products to be sold in the town store.

While Mother and Anne and Catherine were doing their evening barn chores, Grandma prepared supper. In the bitter winter weather she thought it to be important to have an extra good hot meal ready for them when they came in. On these cold days, they especially appreciated her cooking. The barn work made them ravenously hungry. On this particular evening, I drooled as I saw her take a golden brown roast of beef from the oven, surrounded by vegetables caramelized in its juices. She had a knack for cooking the meat to perfection. It was medium done with just a touch of pink in the middle.

As Mother stood warming herself in front of the fire, after she came in from the barn, she exclaimed, "That smells so good."

While we ate, we shared the news of the day. Grandma looked forward to these conversations. To make our conversations last longer, she often put a fresh pot of tea on the stove to steep and cut a slice of her delicious fruitcake for each of us.

Mother and Grandma and my sisters then spent most of their evenings knitting and quilting in front of the fire. They sang softly while they worked, and this provided the backdrop against which I spent my time at the kitchen table, correcting and preparing for the next school day. For hours we worked on separately but together, and even though few words were spoken, I could feel the strong bond that existed between us.

On one of these winter evenings, when Catherine was sure that Mother and Grandma had gone to bed, she turned to me and said in a low voice, "Mary, I have something to tell you. I'm going to Boston to work."

Taken by surprise, I exclaimed, "You are what? Am I hearing you right?"

"Yes you are," she said. "I've been thinking about it for a long time. I'm an adult now and I want to get out and earn my own living. You earn your own keep; so why can't I? I want to spread my wings. Grandma keeps reminding us that her parents came to the New World in pursuit of their dream of a better life. Well, I have the same dream, but much as I love my family, I want to pursue it elsewhere. I don't want to get married right now. I want to get out on my own and experience what life is like. I see no future here for me. I know other girls from the area who made the move and I hear they love their work."

It took a while for my surprise to subside, and then I said to her in an earnest fashion, "Catherine, are you sure you really want to do this?"

To which she replied, "Yes, Mary, I am." Again she emphasized, "I need to get out on my own. If I don't make the move, I'll never forgive myself."

I nodded as I took all of this in.

Then Catherine continued, "As soon as possible, I plan to leave for Boston. Now, don't get me wrong; I dearly love my family. While I am away earning my own living, I will save some money to send to Mother."

"Are you going to discuss your plans with Mother?" I asked.

"Of course I am," she replied. "This is not something that came off the top of my head. I have mulled this idea over and over in my mind. I know what to do and how to do it. And my friend, Agnes, in Boston has offered to help me find work."

Catherine had obviously spent considerable time planning the move. In retrospect, her plan should not have surprised me. She always had a certain independent spirit. She had great energy and an even greater interest in new things. She really did need to expand her horizons.

The next day, Catherine sat with Mother and Grandma and repeated the story she had told me the night before.

At first Mother was shocked. "Catherine, dear, this will break up our family," she said, with an expression of grave concern on her face.

"No, Mother, it won't," Cathrine replied. "I may be away, but my heart will always be here with you and I will keep in touch. And," she added, "I will come home as often as I can."

Mother was silent for some time and then she said, "Very well, I can see that your mind is made up. It would be selfish of me to stand in your way. You may go with my blessing, but on one condition. My girl, you are green. You have never been out of Antigonish before, and I worry about you travelling to 'the Boston States' on your own. What do you know about dealing with strangers. Because of that, I do not want you to go until Mary can accompany you, and she can stay with you until you get settled."

Mother's idea took me by surprise. I had never even thought about going to Boston.

Then Mother continued. "You can travel when the school year is over and Mary is free for the summer. Right, Mary?"

Even though I was totally unprepared for this overture, under the circumstances I felt an obligation to answer. "Yes."

The proposed timing for our travel prompted me to ask, "And who will do the summer harvesting?"

"Don't worry about that," Mother replied. "I know the neighbours will help."

That evening, while Mother and Grandma were sitting by the fire, I heard Grandma say to Mother, "You know, Catherine's move to Boston is not such a big deal when you consider that when I was a little girl, I travelled here all the way from not just another country but another continent. And the trip did not take a few days; it took weeks."

Mother looked at her as she replied, "Yes, but you had your parents with you."

For the remainder of the winter and spring, Catherine talked of nothing but her move to Boston. Her imagination was filled with ideas about the trip and life in the city.

Over and over I heard her say,

"Can you imagine the two of us travelling on a big steamer?"

"Think of all the new people we'll meet."

"I can just see the two of us walking around the city, gazing at the beautiful sights it has to offer."

"I see myself working in a beautiful house with fine furniture."

"I see us shopping in stores with a large choice of fine household linens and furniture and clothes."

"Think of how grand it will be to have my own money."

"Just think of how independent I will be."

"And think of the beautiful things I can buy for Mother and Grandma."

And on and on she talked, sometimes whirling around the floor in the sheer joy these thoughts evoked. That girl has a very active imagination. Every time she talked, she added to the story. I listened to this monologue every night. She did not want to hear my reaction to what she had to say. She just wanted to dream. So out of respect, I kept quiet.

22

The winter flew by, and fantasy quickly changed to reality. By the end of June, 1901, Catherine and I had both packed our bags and we were ready to go. True to her word, on the first Saturday in July, Mother drove us to the train station in Antigonish town. There Mother hugged Catherine as she cried. Catherine was not as independent as she thought. As we moved toward the train, Catherine, with tears streaming down her cheeks, kept looking back at Mother. Mother looked at us wistfully, and I knew how much she was going to miss Catherine. And Catherine was beginning to realize how much she was going to miss her. From the train station in Antigonish to the train station in Halifax, she did not utter a word. The enormity of her decision was beginning to sink in.

When we got off the train in Halifax, Catherine and I walked a short distance along the harbour to the boat that was to take us to Boston. As Catherine walked aboard the boat, her mood quickly changed from sadness to excitement. Her desire for adventure was starting to be fulfilled.

She took great interest in observing the other passengers. Most of them were young women like herself, and she assumed that they too were heading to "the Boston States" to work.

When she saw some of them looking at her, her gregarious side came to the fore, and with a gleam in her eye, she said, "I'm going over there and meet some of those girls."

As she moved toward them, one of the girls who looked like a mere child stood up.

Catherine extended her hand as she said, "Hi, I'm Catherine Laughie Lody MacDonald from Arisaig,"

The young lady replied, "I'm Anne Angus Mor MacDonald from Mabou."

Catherine then said, "I assume you are going to Boston?"

"Yes, I have friends there," Anne replied, "and I am going to get a job as a domestic, just like them."

"But you look so young to be on your own," Catherine exclaimed.

"I know, but I have to find a way to pay for my keep," Anne said. "There are fourteen children in our family, more than our parents can look after. My parents told me that they can no longer afford to keep me; so you see, I had no choice but to get out and try to make a living on my own."

"Are you scared?" Catherine asked.

"I'm scared to death," she replied. "But I'll meet some of the girls from home who are working in Boston and I think they will help me."

Catherine ended the conversation by wishing her well and by expressing the hope that they would meet again. Catherine came back to where I was sitting and filled me in on the story of the girl from Mabou.

She ended her story with this comment, "Can you imagine how scary it would be to have your parents tell you to go? Our parents would never do that."

"But they did not have fourteen mouths to feed," I replied.

We sat in silence for a while and soon both of us fell asleep.

The next evening, as we watched the boat approach the dock in Boston harbour, we gazed in awe at the city: the high buildings dotting its skyline, large majestic churches, impressive statues and monuments, its parks, and close to the shore, a number of large dingy houses built close together near the docks.

As Catherine looked at these houses, she observed, "I heard that it is in these houses close to the shore that men who come here looking for work live. Maybe this is where our uncles stayed after they arrived."

When the boat docked, we walked down the plank to find Catherine's friend ,Agnes, waiting for us. Agnes was excited to see Catherine.

She threw her arms around her and hugged her while she exclaimed, "I am so happy to see you, girl."

Then she straightened up and said, "I'll help you with your luggage, and while we are walking to my place, you can fill me in on the news from home."

The two of them walked slowly and nattered on for almost an hour. They were so engrossed in conversation that they ceased to notice I was there. I really did not mind, for I knew Catherine needed time with her good friend.

When the news from home and from away was exhausted, Agnes suggested it was time to talk about work. She turned to Catherine and said, "I have some great news for you. There is a wealthy family in Cambridge who are looking for a cook. I know the lady of the house and I told her you were coming. So we'll just go right over there in the morning."

Agnes rented a large room with an adjoining kitchenette and bath in a private home, and Catherine and I spent our first night in Boston with her. Agnes had originally worked as a domestic, but she left that work to take a job as a clerk in a large, ladies clothing store. It was not customary for women to live on their own, but Agnes broke with tradition, because she wanted to be more independent.

The next morning, Agnes decided we would take the train to Cambridge. After we got off the train, we had not walked very far before Agnes stopped and said, "There it is."

Catherine and I stood in awe, for it was no ordinary house. It was a mansion, and as such, it was quite a contrast to the simple, practical plank houses that dotted the landscape back home.

When we arrived at the entrance, Catherine stopped, took a deep breath, and pulled the knocker. On that cue, Agnes departed while I stayed with Catherine to be of support to her. A refined lady answered and invited us in. We introduced ourselves. Her name was Jean MacNeil. To set the record straight, I immediately explained that I was not looking for a job but was here to help my sister, Catherine, get settled in Boston. She nodded to indicate that she understood. After we had exchanged pleasantries, she took us on a tour of the house.

She looked at Catherine as she said, "I want to give you a first-hand view of the place before we talk about work."

We were impressed with its beauty and its comfort. Huge rooms with every amenity. An elegant fireplace in each room. Beautiful decor. Fine furniture. And it was as practical as it was beautiful, for it had indoor plumbing.

The lady of the house turned to Catherine and inquired, "Do you like it?"

Catherine replied, "It is beautiful; I've never seen a house like this in my life."

Mrs MacNeil looked pleased and then she said, "Then maybe you would like to come to work for me. I need a cook. Do you think you would be interested?"

In her exuberance, Catherine blurted, "Yes, yes I am."

"Excellent," Mrs MacNeil exclaimed.

Catherine was so anxious to get work that she asserted her interest in the job without asking any questions about the conditions of employment. Fortunately for her, that did not turn out to be a mistake, for Mrs. MacNeil proceeded immediately to outline the terms of employment. She told her that her pay would start at thirty dollars a month and that there would be regular annual pay raises. Her work day was to begin at seven in the morning and end at seven-thirty in the evening, and she was to have one day a week off and one month during the summer when the family were away at the shore. She also told her that she would be able to go out between lunch and dinner on days when the preparation of food was not time consuming.

Then she gave Catherine a warm smile as she said, "Don't worry, I'll look after you." These words of assurance were followed by the question, "You will take the job, won't you?"

Being impulsive, Catherine replied without hesitation, "I would love to have the job."

"Good," Mrs MacNeil said approvingly. "You can move in today and start work tomorrow morning. Mary can stay here with you until you get settled."

Mrs MacNeil then asked us to accompany her to the room she had designated for Catherine. It was a bright, cheerful room with a bay window overlooking the tree-lined front yard. To our delight, there was a bathroom next door. Catherine looked at me in amazement, and I could tell she felt rather grand about the idea of having her very own room. She certainly did not have that back home. After the guided tour of the second floor of the house, Catherine thanked Mrs. MacNeil and assured her that she would get her belongings and return immediately.

As we walked to get the train, I could sense a mixture of fear and exhilaration wafting over Catherine.

She turned to me and said, "I was too embarrassed to say anything, but I don't know how to use the facilities in that bathroom."

I replied, "Don't worry. We'll ask Agnes to show us how to use them again."

Then Catherine looked at me and asked pleadingly, "How in the name of God am I going to learn to cook the kind of food those people want?"

The brave adventurer was beginning to have doubts, and so I tried to be reassuring. "You'll be all right," I said. "I believe you have learned everything you need to know from watching and working with Mother and Grandma in the kitchen. You also know how to read and that gives you the advantage of being able to use cook books. Not all the domestics from the East have that advantage."

When we got back to Agnes' place, Catherine shared her misgivings with Agnes. The first thing she said was, "How am I going to learn to cook for that family?"

Agnes relieved her anxiety with an earnest offer to help in any way she could.

"Don't forget that I too was once a domestic," she reminded her.

Catherine was anxious to accept all the help she could get. Agnes had lots of cook books, which she was willing to share with her.

She pulled out the best ones and passed them to her with these words, "These books have recipes for the food people here like. Believe me, there is a great similarity between what they like and what we ate at home. That will make it easier for you."

Then Agnes added, "I am going to show you how to set and serve a table and how to greet your employees and their guests. That well may be harder for you than the cooking. Because you know how to read so well, you will have no trouble following the recipes in the cookbooks. Pity the poor domestics who come here not knowing how to read."

She gave Catherine all the tips she had promised, and Catherine was all ears and eyes. Agnes was a fine actress, and we were both amused by her show-and-tell performance. She put on her apron and proceeded to put a place setting on the table. She described where each dish and piece of cutlery was to be placed. She then took out the dishes in which the food was to be served and put them in their proper places. While pretending to serve the dishes, she talked to each of the diners. She did all of this with such ease. It was second nature to her now, and that was comforting for Catherine.

Catherine laughed as she said, "I have one more thing to ask before I go. As you probably know, I never saw indoor plumbing before I stayed here with you and while I think I know how to use it, I want to be sure. So how about another lesson?"

With that Agnes took us into the washroom where she again demonstrated the use of the hot and cold water taps and the flush on the toilet while she said, "That is all there is to it."

With a deep sense of appreciation Catherine said to Agnes, "I don't know what I would do without you. I can just imagine how scary it would be to come here alone and have no one to show me the ropes. Thank you from the bottom of my heart."

We then gathered our belongings and headed for the train for our trip back to Catherine's new abode.

Mrs. MacNeil met us at the door and once again showed us to Catherine's room where she left us alone. Catherine was truly excited about her new room. Oh how she delighted in its brightness, its spaciousness, its delicate beauty. She was so exuberant that she spontaneously broke into a little dance. She was in the habit of dancing when she was happy.

As she whirled around the room, I put out my hand to stop her as I cautioned, "Remember the lady of the house doesn't know you, and if she sees you dancing like that, she won't know what to make of you."

"Oh, all right, all right," Catherine said, as she stopped and headed for the hallway.

When we came downstairs, Mrs. MacNeil took some time to show us where all the kitchen appliances, utensils, and supplies were. Then she described the kinds of food she and her family liked to eat at each meal and how they liked to have them prepared. And most reassuring of all, she told Catherine to feel free to ask her anything she needed to know about her new job.

"You know, I know a thing or two about running a kitchen," she said. "We saw poorer days, and there was a time when I did all my own cooking."

These words made Catherine feel a special kinship with her. She sensed that they were going to get along well together.

The next morning, I got up at five o'clock when Catherine did, so I could give her a hand in the kitchen. There was no need to get up this early, but Catherine was anxious and could not sleep. By seven, the orange juice was squeezed, the smell of coffee brewing on the back of the stove wafted through the house, the eggs were scrambled, and the bacon was cooked to a golden brown. The smell of the breakfast food was enough to make anyone hungry. Shortly after seven, Catherine's new family came down stairs to the table. Looking as if they were half asleep, they ate their breakfast in silence.

At the end of the meal, the man of the house, Mike, exclaimed, "That was first rate."

And sleepy as they were, the other members of the family nodded in agreement. I could tell how pleased Catherine was. She had passed her first test.

The next challenge was lunch. And this was easy because the only person at home for lunch was Mrs. MacNeil. For her, Catherine heated some soup that had been prepared before she arrived and made a chicken sandwich. Mrs. MacNeil announced that she was going to eat her lunch in the kitchen with us, and that from henceforth we were to call her Jean.

"I look forward to enjoying your company," she said.

We sat opposite each other at the kitchen table and began to chat. Jean wanted to know all about our lives in Arisaig. Catherine was pleased at how well they were getting along.

Catherine's final challenge of the day was dinner. She asked Jean what the family would like for dinner. Jean decided that the best way to help Catherine was by providing her with a menu. Her first dinner was to include roast beef, mashed potatoes, carrots and peas, and some cake that Jean had baked. Fortunately, these were all familiar foodstuffs. Catherine had helped Grandma prepare these foods many times and she thought of her as she went about getting dinner ready. She roasted a fine prime rib to medium done, just the way Grandma did. She mashed the potatoes and made them extra creamy by adding some cream and soft cheese. She boiled the vegetables and then drizzled them with butter. She made a chocolate sauce for the cake and kept it warm on the back of the stove.

Catherine smiled as she looked at me and said, "Grandma would be proud. She taught me well."

Then we both set the table to make it look as attractive as possible. Our relationship could be described as that of a chef and her assistant.

When the family arrived, Catherine sliced the roast beef and arranged it on a platter. She then lit the candles to add some ambiance, and when the family was seated, we carried the steaming bowls of vegetables and gravy and the platter of meat to the table. The family ate with obvious satisfaction. Jean asked Catherine how she learned to cook roast beef like that. And Catherine just smiled as she thought again of the lessons she had learned from her grandmother. The two children particularly liked the warm chocolate sauce on the cake. When Catherine asked if there was anything more she could get for them, they shook their heads to indicate that the answer was no.

Jean then thanked her for a good dinner and then added, "Catherine, I think you are going to be a gem."

"Yes," Catherine thought to herself. "I made it through day one."

Together Catherine and I cleared the dishes from the dining room and washed them, and with those acts our work was done. Now we had time to sit at the the kitchen table and really enjoyed our own dinners. Because it had been such a busy day, we were both glad to return to the quietness of Catherine's room.

As soon as Catherine closed the door, she exclaimed, "I think they like me."

And I replied, "I think they like you too."

Then Catherine pulled down the covers, crawled into bed and fell fast asleep. And this was basically her routine for every working day. As I worked with her day after day, I often thought of how much more suited I was to the classroom than the kitchen.

Catherine and I both looked forward to her first day off. We could hardly wait to get "downtown" to see first hand what the city had to offer. When Saturday came, we were so excited. Agnes too had a day off, and so we arranged to meet her at an identifiable spot in center city. First we headed for Macy's Department store and we explored every part of it. It was quite a change from the general store in the town nearest home, Antigonish. We were in awe of the massive array of fashionable clothing and toiletries and perfumes on the first floor. And equally in awe of the beautiful furniture, fine dish wear, and linens on the second floor. Neither of us had ever seen anything like it.

Catherine bumped my elbow and exclaimed quietly, "Can you believe this."

Catherine had a little money left from what Mother had given her for the trip and so she offered to buy lunch for Agnes and me at Macy's lunch counter. I could see that she was really enjoying herself. She sat proudly on a stool at the lunch counter and ordered a toasted cheese sandwich and tea for each of us. It made her feel grand to be waited on, now that she waited on others for a living. We really luxuriated in the experience, for this was also the first time either of us had eaten out. We lingered at the lunch counter, like ladies of leisure, talking and laughing and watching the other customers.

Feeling refreshed, we then set out for Filene's Bargain Basement. This store certainly lived up to its reputation. The array of merchandise and its good quality were impressive. The clothes available in the bargain basement were the talk of working girls in Boston. Believe me, there was nothing in our lives to prepare us for this adventure. I couldn't believe the commotion. We had never before thought of shopping as a competitive activity. Women were jostling one another for attractive items of clothing and, then and there, in the middle of the aisle, without any regard for modesty, they would strip to try them on.

With a sly grin on her face, Catherine remarked in a low voice, "Some of those bodies should never be exposed. Those women have no shame."

Agnes enjoyed watching us go through this experience for the first time. Much as we enjoyed it, a few minutes in the midst of the me-lee was all we could take. The noise, the heat and the confusion were too much for us and we decided to pull out. Catherine told me that she would come back at a later date, when the store was less crowded, and buy some clothes for the women at home.

"Of course, I have to get paid before I can think of buying anything," she said in a matter of fact way.

Now that we were tired of shopping, Agnes decided that we should do some sight-seeing. We walked around to get a closer look at the beautiful churches, fine mansions, and impressive historical monuments that we had observed from the boat before it docked. When we had seen the highlights of the area, and when our feet would not carry us any farther, we decided to go home. We thanked Agnes for our guided tour and then headed for the train. Never in our lives had we had a day like this and we returned to our abode still in awe of all we had seen.

Once we were back in our room, I was surprised to see Catherine become somewhat melancholy.

In a soulful voice, she pined, "There is nothing in this world I want more than to sit in front of a blazing fire in our Arisaig home with a good strong cup of tea and share the adventures of the day with Mother and Grandma and Anne."

I knew where she was coming from. In my mind's eye, I could see how the women at home would look at each other as we told them of our first venture into center city. Her reflections reminded me that we are a family who share our joys and our sorrows, and that is what makes the good times even more enjoyable and the bad times more bearable. Our lifestyle may be modest, but in many ways we are rich.

Catherine's mind and my mind were on the same page when she turned to me and said, "We are very lucky to have the kind of family we have."

I smiled in acquiescence.

Then a serious look came on Catherine's face. This provided a cue as to what she was thinking.

Her independent streak came to the fore, as she turned to me and said, "I am now very comfortable in my new home and I think I can get along just fine on my own. I want you to feel free to go back to to Arisaig."

That was my cue to go home. Much as I enjoyed the experience, it left me firmly convinced that Arisaig was the place for me and that teaching was what I wanted to do. So the next morning, Catherine and Agnes accompanied me to the boat; we said our good-byes, and I was happy to sail for home.

Sitting alone on the boat back to Halifax gave me lots of time to think. My experiences in Boston, brief as they were, moved me to reflect on the quality of my life. I realized that if I stayed in Boston, I would have access to more amenities than I ever would at home and more opportunities to make money. But there is more to the quality of life than amenities and money. The strength of the bond between my grandmother, my mother, my sisters and me is a source of personal wellbeing. Missing them the way I did strengthened my realization that I would never want to break that bond. And what is more, while some Bostonians have the luxury of living in mansions, I doubt if many of them have the opportunity I have to be influenced daily by the beauty of the sea and the land. Living close to nature is a source of continuous spiritual wellbeing. It brings peace to my soul. The Americans may have more material goods, but I believe I am the one who is truly rich.

23

Deep in her heart Anne sensed she had a calling, a voice within urging her to pursue a religious vocation. But she didn't quite know how to broach the subject with her family. During the two years since her father's death, she had worked side by side with her mother and grandmother and she did not want to part from them. She too had a strong bond with these women. Because of these circumstances she tried to put the idea of a religious vocation out of her mind. But putting the idea out of her mind didn't work. It was as persistent as an itch.

"I have no choice but to do something about this," she thought to herself. "I'll broach the subject with Mary and see how she reacts. Then I can figure out how to put it to Mother and Grandma." While Anne was walking with me along the ocean one evening in early July, she decided to face the issue head on. So she abruptly turned to me, and in her quiet gentle voice, said, "Mary, I have something very important to tell you. I have decided I want to join the Sisters of St. Martha. Each of us has a dream of what we want to be. That is my dream."

Taken by surprise, I exclaimed, "You ... you want to be a nun."

"Yes, Mary, I am dead serious."

"How long have you been thinking about this?"

"For a couple of years. Remember when Father MacDonald read the letter from Bishop Cameron inviting young women from the diocese to consider joining the order. That's when I really began to think seriously about my vocation."

"Are you sure that is what you want?"

"Yes, I am."

"I really don't know what to say."

At this point, I stopped for a moment to collect my thoughts and then I continued our conversation.

"If you really think this is what you want to do, you need to talk to Mother."

"But I am scared. Mother will think that I am selfish for wanting to abandon my responsibility to our home."

"You know Mother better than that. She will understand. Talk to your mother."

"But I don't think I am ready for that."

"Then when will you be ready?"

"I don't know."

As I reflected on Anne's aspirations, I began to realize how much they made sense. Anne was a warm loving soul who sees goodness in everyone. I suspect this is the way nuns look at people. But, at the same time, I realized that Anne was also a woman of the world. While she was quiet, she loved to mingle with people of all ages and she took a great interest in their lives. Her inner sensitivity was also reflected in her love of music and art. We had no musical instruments in our house; so she expressed herself in song and she sang beautifully. With only a pencil and paper, she could produce impressive etchings of the local landscape. Her aesthetic sense even extended to her feet. At the local ceilidhs no one danced with more grace and charm than Anne. Her grace and charm were enhanced by her beauty, particularly her fine facial features. Put all these qualities together and you can see why the young men of the community were attracted to her.

Anne also had a stubborn streak. If she wanted to do something, there was no discouraging her.

I remember when she decided to work little Jimmy into the Christmas pageant, I warned, "You can't do that; he is too young."

She dismissed me with a look that said, "Just watch me."

And, sure enough, she charmed the little fellow into doing exactly what she wanted. When you thought of her in terms of those qualities, I think she could make her way in any walk of life.

A few days passed, and Anne made no overture to talk with Mother. She was anxious. She was not at ease with the idea of discussing the subject with her, or with anyone else. She mulled the situation over and over in her mind. It wasn't that her mother would object to her aspirations, but with the death of Father and Catherine's move to Boston, she felt guilty about not continuing to carry her share of the load. Sensing her discomfort, I again pleaded with her to talk to her mother. Again she ignored me.

After this uneasiness had plagued Anne for several weeks, she decided that she had no choice but to do something about it. At this point, she felt that the only way to alleviate her anxiety was to deal with the problem head on.

That evening, Ann found her mother alone in the kitchen and she figured that this was as good a time as any to talk with her.

As she fidgeted from one foot to the other, she said hesitatingly, "Mother, I have something important I want to discuss with you."

"Well lass, I see something is bothering you. You know you can tell me," Mother replied.

And then Anne summoned the courage to speak up. As she looked her mother in the eyes, she said slowly and deliberately, "Mother, I want to join the Sisters of St. Martha. I have been thinking about this matter for a long time, and it is something I really want to do."

Mother was taken by surprise and for a moment she said nothing. And then she heaved a sigh, which reflected her reservations about Anne's aspirations.

It did not take her long to realize that she had no reason to be concerned because Anne was such a sensible girl, and to Anne's surprise and delight, she took both of her hands and said, "Anne, if that is what you really want to do, then do it. You have my blessing."

Anne threw her arms around her mother and hugged her, and then she said, "It is such a relief to hear those words from you. You have no idea how much it means to me. It is such a load off my mind to know you understand. You are a good mother."

Then Mother added, "Don't worry about us. Grandma and Mary and I will get along just fine."

Mother was a good one at planning and she quickly figured out what needed to be done to help Anne achieve her goal. The first thing she and Anne decided to do was to go to the convent of the Sisters of St. Martha and meet the sister in charge to find out how a young woman goes about entering their congregation.

So the following Monday, Mother and Anne and I drove into town to the Motherhouse, which was located on the campus of St. Francis Xavier College, so that Anne could see the sister in charge of new recruits. When we arrived at the convent, Anne did not say a word. With fear and trepidation she walked up the steps to the front door. She turned around and looked at us. Then she turned back, took a deep breath, and knocked on the door. She was greeted by a young novice who invited her to come in. When she requested to see the sister in charge of the novitiate, she immediately called Sister Remegius. Sister Remegius, mistress of novices, invited Anne into a small sitting room where they could talk. She put Anne at ease by asking her to tell her a little bit about herself and her family. After they had talked for a while, she told Anne that she thought she knew what had brought her here.

This was the opening Anne needed to talk about her desire to enter the congregation. "This is something I have wanted ever since I heard about your congregation. It is an idea I cannot get out of my mind," she informed her.

Sister Remegius told Anne how much her interest in joining the order pleased her. Then she went on to describe how religious formation is nurtured in the novitiate. Toward the end of their conversation, she gave Anne an application form and told her that if she could get a recommendation from her pastor, there was a good chance she would be accepted into the novitiate.

"I have a good feeling about you," she said. "Our little conversation will take the place of the interview normally required for admission. You take a couple of weeks to think about our program. That will give me time to get a recommendation from your pastor and to review your application."

These were the words Anne wanted to hear. She thanked Sister Remegius, and looking very pleased, returned to meet us.

As soon as Anne got home, she went to the Glebe House to see her pastor, Father James MacDonald. With hesitation, she rapped on the door.

Father MacDonald opened the door and welcomed her with these kind words, "Ah lass, what brings you here today. Do come and sit and tell me what is on your mind."

Anne got directly to the point of her visit. She started by saying, "Father, I need your help."

As he looked at her attentively, she told him of her aspirations, and he was both surprised and pleased. He particularly wanted to know how she arrived at her decision. Her story of how this plan occupied her mind and heart assured him that her decision was arrived at through serious reflection. Furthermore, he could tell that she had arrived at her decision without any pressure from her family. Being a member of the clergy or a religious congregation was such a source of prestige for Highland families that sometimes it was hard to tell if the candidate was joining to fulfil his or her wishes or those of the parents. After Father MacDonald and Anne had finished discussing religious life, he assured her that he would support her application.

Two weeks passed, and Anne's resolve remained firm. She spent a couple of evenings filling in the application form Sister Remegius had given her. The application form was lengthy, but she had no trouble filling it in, until she came to the final question: Why do you want to be a sister? This question stopped her in her tracks. In her mind and heart she knew she wanted to be a sister, but she wasn't able to articulate the reasons why. She threw down her pen in frustration.

Perplexed, she called to me for help. "Mary, what am I going to say about why I want to enter the congregation?" she asked.

Being a teacher, I answered her question with another question, "Can you tell me why you want to be a sister?"

"Of course I can," she said. "You know why."

"No I don't," I replied. "You tell me."

Ann stopped for a moment to think and then she said, "I want to be a sister, because I feel an inner urge to do so. The reason lies deep inside me, in my spirit, in my soul. I cannot say it well in words because it is something I feel in my heart."

I raised my hand and said, "Stop right there. Now write down just what you told me."

"What did I say?" Anne asked with a laugh.

I repeated her words verbatim as she wrote them down.

"Do you think that is enough?" Anne asked.

"I am quite sure it is," I assured her.

With my encouragement, Anne completed the form and gave it to the mail driver the next day. I was right. Shortly thereafter, Anne received a letter from the mistress of novices indicating that she had been accepted as a postulant, the first stage in preparing to be a sister. She did not use words to express how pleased she was. She did not have to; you could see it in her face.

The last Sunday in September was the day that marked a turning point in Anne's life. Before she left for the convent, she decided that she had to say goodbye to her life-long friend. Hughie. They had been friends from the first day they entered school. She knew that on Sunday morning she would find him down by the ocean, which he loved so much. So off she went to meet him. She sensed this would be an awkward situation.

When he saw her coming, he exclaimed, "What a beautiful day for a walk. I'm so glad you came."

She looked at him seriously, as she said, "That's not why I came."

He turned to her and asked, "Is there something wrong?"

"No, no," she replied. "I have something to tell you. We have been friends for so long that I thought I should tell you personally. Today I leave to join the Sisters of St. Martha."

Taken by surprise, Hughie asked, "Will I ever see you again?"

She put her arms around him and hugged him, as she said, "I sure hope so."

Then, with tears in her eyes, she turned and walked away. Hughie just stood in silence as he watched her depart.

When she got back to the house, she turned to Grandma and the two of them held each other and cried, and through her tears, Grandma said, "Anne, you have been with us so long; I am sure going to miss you."

Then Anne said, "Yes, and this is really something for a member of a family that has strong pagan roots."

And the two of them roared out laughing.

Then Grandma pulled back, looked at Anne, and with these words put her vocation in perspective: "You know, Anne, your decision to pursue your vocation does my heart good. Several centuries ago, the dreaded Penal Laws outlawed the practise of our faith in the Highlands. The religious persecution suffered by our people, instead of lessening their fervour, served to deepen their faith and that of generations to come. You are a shining example of the strong faith of the Highlanders and of this family. I am very proud of you."

Ann smiled as she again hugged Grandma and quickly left the house. Mother and I drove her to the convent. She turned and said goodbye to us at the entrance. This was a sad moment, for as we hugged and cried, we sensed that Anne was gone from us for good.

With tears in her eyes, Mother held both of Anne's hands and asked, "When will we see you again?"

"I'll let you know, Mother," was Anne's less than reassuring reply.

It is never easy to leave the family you love. With her heart bursting at the thought of leaving her mother, Anne raced up the steps to the convent. Knowing how traumatic this moment was for her, Sister Remegius, mistress of novices, accompanied by Sister Mary Jean, made sure they were at the door to welcome her to her new life.

Sister Remegius, in a warm and inviting manner, said, "Welcome to your new home. We are so happy that you have come. I want you to meet Sister Mary Jean. She is to be your spiritual adviser and she will do everything she can to ease your way into your new life."

Sister Mary Jean immediately took Anne to the common room where she met other young women who were entering the congregation. She introduced Anne to the postulants and then left them alone for a while to give them a chance to start to get to know one another. Being naturally gregarious, Anne loved every minute of the informal social gathering. She had never met so many women of her own age and it wasn't long before she began to bask in the warmth of their friendship. Having been so isolated in her pursuit of her vocation, she felt particularly good about being with others who were like-minded. She no longer had to put up with people asking questions that pried into her life. She grew particularly tired of hearing people ask, "You're not married yet?" as if there were something wrong with her.

Sister Mary Jean returned and accompanied Anne to her little room with its cot, wooden chair, small bureau, and a closet. The only embellishment on the walls was a crucifix above the foot of the cot. This was to be a constant reminder of the central message of Christianity. To outsiders, this room might look austere, but it was what Anne expected and it soon became her home. While Anne was putting the few belongings she had brought away, Sister Mary Jean remained to talk, and they soon began to get to know each other. Anne quickly found out that they had a lot in common. Sister Mary Jean too had lived on a farm, and their upbringings were very similar. She shared with Anne the concerns she had before she entered the order.

"I had no one to talk to," she said, "no one who would understand my aspirations. It was a very lonely journey to my decision."

Anne appreciated the opportunity to share her concerns about leaving her family. She talked of her guilt about leaving her mother and grandmother alone to look after the farm. She was relieved to find that Sister Mary Jean understood her situation.

"These uncertainties are inevitable when you are uprooted from your way of life. If your presence counts for something in your family, your departure is bound to leave a void. You see, in that way it is a good thing," she told Anne.

She promised to guide Anne through the trials of being a postulant. She also promised to be her friend.

"I will be there for you in good times and in bad," she assured her.

She then explained what the purpose of this first period of formation is. "You will be a postulant for six months, and this part of your program will enable you to determine if the religious life is for you," she said. "At the end of that period, you will be interviewed by our general superior and members of her council to assess how well you are adapting to religious life."

Anne's six month trial period as a postulant had begun. The rest of the afternoon passed quickly, and before supper, she joined the other postulants and novices in the chapel for prayer. After supper, it was time for recreation. Ann was delighted to join some of her new friends for a game called basketball in the college gym. Ann had never seen a basketball before, but it did not take her long to get the hang of the game. The physical activity left her covered with sweat and panting for breath. She was so exhausted by the time she got back to her room that she quickly fell into a deep sleep. It seemed that she had not been in bed very long before the bell rang indicating it was time to get up. She groaned when she saw that it was five o'clock, the usual time for the sisters to rise. With sleep still in her eyes, she bathed and made her way to the chapel to join the other sisters for morning prayers and meditation, followed by mass at 6:30.

When she arrived for breakfast at seven o'clock, she remarked to the sister next to her. "I feel as if I've been up all night."

The sister's only comment was, "Get used to it."

And they both laughed.

Each new postulant was assigned some duties. Anne's job was to help in the kitchen twice a day—one hour from eight to nine, and another hour after noon. She quickly learned to help the sister in charge of the kitchen do whatever needed to be done, sometimes washing dishes, sometimes paring vegetables, and occasionally doing what she loved to do best, cooking.

As she chatted with the other sisters in the kitchen while they worked, Anne remarked, "This is just like working side by side with Grandma in our kitchen in Arisaig. And if you knew my grandmother, you would know that is a compliment."

The physical activity associated with work in the kitchen was a welcome change from prayer, meditation, and study. It brought balance to her life. It wasn't long before she had an opportunity to produce some of the good food her mother and grandmother had taught her to cook.

Each day, Anne and the other postulants found themselves immersed in spiritual activities. From nine o'clock until noon they spent time in class studying scripture, the sacraments, religious vows, and other subjects that provided direction for their way of life. They engaged in one-half hour of spiritual reading in the afternoon, followed by another half hour of adoration and prayer, including the rosary. Wisely the congregation worked some diversity into their daily routine. From three to four they broke for activities to cultivate their interests: Some dabbled in the arts;

some played an instrument; some read; some engaged in knitting and sewing. For the first time, Anne had access to paints and paint brushes and she couldn't wait to see what these colours would do for her art work. Then the postulants went back to their studies for one hour before supper at five o'clock. After supper they looked forward to one hour of recreation. By 8:30, they were happy to crawl into bed. And this became Anne's routine for the entire six months of her novitiate.

While to outsiders this program to nurture spiritual life might seem boring, to Anne it was fulfilling because it evoked a spiritual response that was central to her being. It did much to uplift her mind, her heart and her spirit. From the beginning, she knew that it was exactly what she wanted. She was happy. She learned to love the silence of the chapel for the invitation it provided to explore the depths of her soul. She found great comfort in sharing the details of her spiritual journey with Sister Mary Jean.

Her obvious sense of fulfilment moved Sister Jean to comment, "It would almost seem you were born to pursue this way of life."

The hour of recreation the postulants had each evening helped them to develop well-rounded lives. Anne's favourite form of recreation was skating. She could not wait for winter to come so that the rink would have a sheet of ice. And to her delight, winter came early that year. In the second week in November, the sisters got to use the rink. Anne loved to don her skates, put her scarves around her head and neck, and whirl around the outdoor rink. The cold crisp air and the fast graceful movements were truly exhilarating.

As she skated, she thought to herself, "I love every aspect of my life. I don't care what people say; I really do belong here."

Anne often recollected that no one had ever encouraged her to be a sister, much less told her about that way of life. And yet somehow she knew that this life was exactly what she wanted.

At these times, she thought to herself, "That must be what the sisters mean by a calling to a religious vocation, that mysterious little voice that speaks to us from within."

Anne had one regret that left a wrenching ache in her heart, and that was separation from her family. The special bond that existed with them had been undermined. Anne knew there was a price to be paid for achievement in every walk of life and sadly this was hers.

Anne's six months as a postulant passed very quickly and she soon found herself before Sister Consolata, the superior, and her council for an interview to determine if she was acceptable to the congregation and if religious life was what she really wanted.

The purpose of the interview prompted this body to pose just one very basic question, "Why do you want to be a sister?"

This time Anne was ready for this question. Ever since Mary's questioning, she was keenly aware of her need to be able to articulate her reasons for wanting to enter the novitiate.

Her reply was slow and reflective. "I have thought a great deal about this question and I have come to realize that there was no external pressure influencing me," she said. "I never heard our parish priest mention the subject except when he read a letter from Bishop Cameron encouraging young women to think about a vocation. Even though our family consisted of three girls, our parents never raised the subject. Nor did any of my friends express any interest in this walk of life. In fact, some of them thought my choice to be quite odd. One even suggested that I was too big-feeling to marry one of the Arisaig boys." At this point her interrogators laughed.

Then Anne continued with her answer. "The fact of the matter is that I liked the Arisaig boys of my age a lot. And I smile every time I think of how much I loved to dance with them. But I wanted to walk a different path in life. Before coming here, I had never even seen a sister, but somehow I knew I wanted to be one."

Then she concluded, "In spite of a complete lack of external influence, there was something inside urging me to do this. I felt it deep in my heart, in my soul, and I still do. That may sound pretty simple, but it is the reason I am here."

Anne's thoughtful and sincere response gave both the superior and her council a strong sense that she belonged in the congregation, and without any hesitation, they informed her that she was accepted as a novice, the next step in the formation of a candidate for the congregation. The members of the council offered her their congratulations and she thanked them. This rather formal exchange masked the joy that leaped in her heart. Her acceptance meant the world and all to her. She hastened to find Sister Mary Jean to tell her the good news.

It was reassuring for her to know that her mentor, Sister Mary Jean, the woman who had been such a good navigator, would also be in charge of her formation as a novice. She was to continue with the religious studies and religious formation she had started as a postulant. For the first time, she was to get to wear the uniform of a novice, a little black dress with a while collar and a net veil for her head. She was well on the road to becoming a Sister of St. Martha.

24

The subject I enjoy teaching the most is history. I suspect my love for this subject may be attributed to Grandma's storytelling. It was she who made me realize how important it is to remember our past. Thoughts of her homeland and her early years in Nova Scotia preoccupy her mind. As I have said so many times, I owe such a great debt of gratitude to that woman. To make something of yourself, you need someone to show you the way. For me Grandma is that person. Ever since I became a teacher, she often asked if I was teaching anything about the Highland Scots.

"Over the years I have spent a great deal of time telling you what life was like for the Highland pioneers and their families before and after they came to Nova Scotia. It would be a shame for their story to be lost," she recently reminded me.

And then, with reverence for the past resonating in her voice, she repeated the words that I have come to know and love, "Mary, it is so important to remember."

I repeatedly told Grandma that this topic was not part of the school program. And her usual reaction was, "Well dear, I think it is up to you to do something about that. Remember, the history of the Highlands touches all of us."

Of course, Grandma was right, but it would take me a while to figure out how to do what she had suggested. I examined the school curriculum to see if it would be of any help. It simply confirmed what I already knew, that British history is the core of the school history program. As a result of giving considerable thought to how I could use that emphasis to my advantage, I began to realize that Highland history could be taught as a part of British history. The inclusion of British history in the school program in five different grade levels, no doubt, is meant to rub our noses in our colonial status, even though that was becoming a thing of the past. A more common view is that it is meant to bore us to death. The rebel in me made me take more than a little satisfaction in planning to use the subject for purposes other than those intended by the educators who drew up the school program. Furthermore, the pervasiveness of British history in the school program gave me ample opportunity to instruct across grade levels.

Making this subject interesting proved to be a challenge. Sadly, the treatment of British history in the school textbooks went from encyclopedic accounts of one monarch after another to one war after another—and there seemed to be so many of each. The history of the Highlands was dismissed in a few sentences. The point the texts emphasized were that the British brought political unity and economic improvement to the Highlands—just exactly what you would expect from an Englishman! The treatment of these points only reflected the point of view of the English. There was nothing to indicate any understanding of the aspirations of the Highlanders or their traditional way of life. And, worst of all, there was no consideration of a central concern of the Highlanders, the reasons why they did not want to be under the thumb of the British. Therefore, these accounts of Highland history did not reflect differing points of view nor did they arouse controversies that were screaming to be addressed. There was nothing inspiring in them. What could I do to bring some life to the subject? How could I help my students to connect with it?

With these concerns in mind, I started to look for an appropriate topic under which to teach Highland history. As I thumbed through the history text, I came across a reference to the Act of Union of 1707 between England and Scotland, and I said to myself, "Ah ha, there it is."

The fact that England and Scotland were now united politically gave me a reason, or some would say, an excuse, to expand the coverage of the history of the Highlands in British history. This certainly was not something that those who wrote the British textbooks or those who supervised our instructional program had in mind, but so much the worse for them.

I felt my students could learn a great deal about the history of the homeland of the Highland pioneers by exploring the reasons why they came to Nova Scotia. And, furthermore, this approach would bring a better balance to the treatment of British history than that found in the history texts.

When I announced my plans to the students, they gave me a questioning look. To them this was something very different from anything they had done previously. To provide a setting for this topic, I used maps to show the students where Scotland is, where the Highlands are within Scotland, where England is, and where these countries are in relation to Nova Scotia. I then took out a large-scale map of the Highlands and pointed out the areas from which the people of Arisaig came. Most of them came from the west coast of Inverness-shire, a lesser number from the islands of Eigg and Rhum in the inner Hebrides and a few from South Uist in the outer Hebredes.

"You mean that the people who settled in Arisaig are a part of history," asked one student, with a look of mild surprise.

"Yes they are," I replied, "and we shall soon find out why."

To enhance the reality of the situation, I took my students to the Arisaig graveyard to look at the grave markers. Sure enough, at my request, they quickly located the grave sites of relatives who were buried there and then they began to note the information the tombstones contained about their relatives: their places of birth, their dates of birth and death, whether each was single or married, and if married, the names of their children and their dates of birth and death. Then I asked them to look for the same information on the other grave markers. They were surprised to find that many of their grandparents were born about the same time and in the same part of the Highlands. This gave rise to the question of why so many of them left that area.

The curiosity of my students was aroused by this exercise. For the first time, they saw these grave markers as more than grave markers. They were learning to extract information from them as an original historical source. This exercise also reinforced the map work I had done with them. And most important of all, seeing the relationship between what they were learning in history class and the history of their own families made this information personally meaningful to them.

I was delighted when one of my brighter students summed up the value of this exercise in these words, "We are learning how history touches our lives. Now that's quite a change from what we usually learn in history class."

The map work and our examination of the grave markers provided a setting for further treatment of this topic. At the beginning of the next class, to keep my students focused, I put the question under examination on the blackboard. Why did the Highland Scots come to Arisaig? They were to discuss this question with their parents and grandparents. This approach made them look forward even more to continuing to study this topic. They went home buzzing with curiosity about their assignment. They had never thought of their own families as having a history, much less being a source of history. The only source of history they knew was history texts, and the encyclopedic coverage of past events in these dry books turned them against the subject. The exercise I proposed was designed to do something about this problem. My students went forward with a renewed interest in history. I figured I could help by filling in some of the gaps in their story and that I would have a captive audience for this exercise. I was beginning to feel very optimistic about this venture.

I began the next history class by telling my students that, through this exercise of learning why their families came to Arisaig, they were learning history firsthand as opposed to learning history from the text. To elaborate this point, I said, "Your relatives who came here as pioneers were eyewitnesses or knew eyewitnesses to the events that drove them from their homeland. They had relatives—parents, grandparents, aunts, uncles—who either lived through these events or learned about them from others who had. Such people are the sources from which history is made. Without information from these sources, the history books could not have been written."

This idea was intriguing to them. They had never before thought about where the information in their texts came from.

Once again, I put the question we were exploring on the board to keep the discussion focused.

Then I asked, "Who would like to begin?" Many hands went up.

"Alex John Ban, would you start?" I asked.

Alex told the story of how his parents came here to gain religious freedom. Their Catholic church in South Uist, the place his people came from, was burned by the British soldiers and their parish priest disappeared. The people were shocked to hear the rumour that the redcoats found him and put him in jail. It was against the law for priests to say mass; it was against the law for people to attend mass.

Alex said that, according to his Grandfather, "It was indeed a sad day for our people when practising their faith turned them into criminals."

Alex then went on to elaborate further the price the clergy and laity paid for practising their faith. He said, "Priests who were caught saying mass would be put in jail or sent out of the country. One landowner even made threats to try to force Catholics into the Kirk. He used his yellow cane to try to drive them into his church, and as he did, he barked, 'Either sign this paper renouncing your faith or you will lose your land.' My grandfather said those were pretty tough words for people who were landless tenants."

Alex's story told us that he was descended from pioneers who originally came to P.E.I. to avoid joining the Kirk, which they called "the religion of the yellow stick," and then moved on to Arisaig.

Then I asked, "Did your people tell you anything about why your Catholic relatives were being persecuted like this?"

Alex then resumed his story. "My grandfather said, 'After the Battle of Culloden in 1746, Catholic Highlanders were punished for their loyalty to Bonnie Prince Charlie. They supported the prince because they felt that if he got on the throne, he would restore their freedom to practise their faith. The prince lost the battle, and religious persecution got worse.'"

"That is quite a story, Alex," I said.

Roddy Big Allen then raised his hand, and I asked him to tell us what he had learned.

His was the story of how ashamed his grandfather and grandmother felt when they were not allowed to be married in the church because the practise of their religion had been outlawed. They refused to have the ceremony performed in the Kirk; so they had no choice but to live in common law.

"'Can you imagine how ashamed they were to have to "shack up?"' my father said. He summed up the price they paid for supporting the prince in these words: 'Being denied the practise of their faith was a terrible form of persecution; being denied the use of their native tongue was unnatural.'"

I smiled for I knew the origin of the familiar words this young man was repeating.

I then asked if anyone else had learn anything more about the relationship between religion and their relatives' decision to come to Nova Scotia.

Mary Anne Donald Malcolm put up her hand, and when I asked her to respond, she expressed the view that not all families came to Nova Scotia because of religion. Her father told her that religion was not a concern for many families in Pictou County. "He said, 'I met many people in Pictou County who came for other reasons.'"

I affirmed the accuracy of what her father had said by telling my students that there are religious differences between the settlers in Pictou County and the settlers in Arisaig.

I said, "The reason why so many of your people talk about religion as a reason for their forebears' departure from the Highlands is that all the settlers here in Arisaig are Roman Catholic, whereas most of the settlers in Pictou County are not."

At this point, I decided to ask a different but related question. "What do your grandparents remember about how they and their forbears felt about these attacks on their religion?"

Many hands went up. And these were the responses they put forth:

"Afraid. They were scared to death that when the redcoats finished destroying the churches and chasing out the priests, they would then come for the parishioners."

"Sad, because they did not have a church to go to. Sad, because they missed being able to attend mass."

"Defiant. My grandfather boasted that, no matter how hard the soldiers tried to stamp out his religion, they could never take it from him. 'I will carry it in my heart and in my soul, and they cannot reach it there.' Honest to God, those were his words."

These responses prompted me to ask how the Highlanders who did not have a church or a parish priest worshipped.

Ronald Hugh Martin responded by telling of how Highland families who did not have religious services prayed the rosary and the following litanies, and of how they continued this practise here in Nova Scotia.

"Even now the members of my family kneel and say the rosary and the litanies every evening," he said.

At this point, I intervened to reinforce the importance of this knowledge of how people reacted to the persecution of their faith in understanding the decision of large numbers of Catholic Highlanders to come to eastern Nova Scotia.

Then I reminded the students of what Mary Anne Donald Malcolm had said, that factors other than religion influenced many Highlanders to come to Nova Scotia. I asked them to discuss this matter with their parents and grandparents at the supper table.

When I raised the topic the next day, the hands went up. The students obviously continued to enjoy this form of homework.

James John Ban was anxious to talk about how the persecution of the Highland Scots by the British turned the Highland Scots against them. He told of how his grandfather never forgave the redcoats for what they did to his grandfather Angus in the Battle of Culloden. "According to Grandpa, 'Angus was so badly wounded that he could not drag himself off the field after the battle was over. A redcoat appeared, and as his grandfather begged for mercy, the redcoat responded by driving his sword through him.'"

A collective shudder went through the class. And then James continued by telling his grandmother's story of how the violence against the Highland Scots affected her family.

"'It wasn't enough to put a licking on our men,' she said. 'After the battle, the British soldiers locked my grandfather, Hughie, in his home and set fire to it. His poor wife, Annie, stood outside the door of their burning home and looked on helplessly while Hughie screamed as he burned to death. One of the redcoats smashed her mouth with his musket to make her stop crying. This kind of treatment terrified the Highland people, and many decided that it was time to start thinking about getting out.'"

This answer reminded me of the words of my own grandfather, "I was beginning to feel like a stranger in my own land."

Then Roddie Red Alex became very anxious to talk. When I asked him to respond, he recalled his grandfather's story of how the violence against the Scots continued long after the battle was over.

"The redcoats were turned lose on the surrounding countryside. No one was safe. Our people were hunted just like animals," he said.

Then Angus Laughie Mor made the point that the Highlanders were punished in other ways. He recalled his father's stories of attacks on their culture. He said his father told him that, after the uprising was over, Highlanders were not allowed to wear their plaids or their kilts or to play their their bagpipes.

"His exact words were, 'Can you imagine a bonnie laddie without his kilt or his pipes?'"

Again, I knew exactly where this story came from.

"And it was not just that," Ronnie Donald Miller interjected. He repeated his mother's story of how teachers forbade their students to use the Gaelic language.

"'Their teachers were English and they made fun of the Gaelic. They said that my relatives who spoke it were backward. They even called them savages. They wanted to turn the Highlanders into Englishmen, indeed they did,' my mother said."

To pull these points together, I related all these restrictions to the objective of the British rulers to undermine the language, religion, music, and garb that were basic to the Highland folk culture.

On the following day, Angus Ban Gillis changed the direction of our discussion when he raised his hand to suggest that one of the reasons the Highlanders left had nothing to do with the English. He said that, for his great grandfather, the final straw was realizing that his lot of land was too small to support his family.

"'Either we get out or we will starve,' he said."

His grandfather then told of how he became very worried when he heard rumours circulating in the community that the land he and his neighbours occupied was to be turned into a sheep pasture.

"My grandfather turned to his son and said, 'Laddie, how would you like to make a trip across that big ocean that separates us from the land of plenty in the New World?'"

I asked Angus when his people left the Highlands. He told me that when Arisaig was sold in 1813, his people left for Pictou.

Angus Laughie Mor then raised his hand to contradict what Angus Ban had said. According to his father's story, the British rulers had plenty to do with the problems the people had with the land.

He said, "These problems can be traced back to their decision to end the clan system, which was the way the Highlanders held land for centuries. When they got rid of the clan system, the chiefs became landlords who got control of most of the land, and many of them forced their tenants off the land. That is why my people came here. They were driven out by the clearances."

I ended this discussion by telling my students that all their contributions were excellent.

The next day, I took some time to sum up what my students had accomplished and to tell them how proud I was of them.

"Your families have retained a great deal of the history of their homeland," I said. "And you went after this information in the same way historians do. You are beginning to develop a sense of how history is made. Instead of reading what historians have to say, you did what they do. You talked to witnesses to past events or to people who had heard these accounts first hand from witnesses."

My students were intrigued, and their pride in what they had done showed in their faces. Because they were now beginning to realize the importance of history in helping them to understand their lives, they began to see history in a new light. This approach added an element of realism to the study of events of the past that one does not get from reading a history text.

The change in the attitude of my pupils toward the subject was summed up in one of their comments, "It is only now I realize how much history tells us about our people."

This exercise also had an impact on me. It deepened my appreciation of the educative value of the ceilidhs where storytellers in the Highland communities narrated the history of the Highlands to keep that story alive. It was quite evident that their stories had more impact on the minds of the settlers than all the history courses taught in the schools. Come to think of it, my grandmother was an outstanding example of that influence.

I didn't know if the people in charge of the school curriculum would approve of the way I treated this topic, but I really didn't care. The textbooks gave only the British side of the story. The Highland heritage of these students demanded that attention also be paid to the Highland Scots' side of the story. Furthermore, I don't think the bureaucrats who were assigned to oversee what we teach were prepared to harness their horses and get into their wagons and ride over the mountain to see what I was doing.

After my students thoughtful reaction to the history of the events that drove their people from their homeland, I felt particularly good as I headed out for my afternoon walk. The sun was warm, the air was refreshing, and as is usually the case in the fall, the maples were crimson and gold. This time of year, the countryside was truly spectacular. The visual feast slowed my walk so that I could take it all in.

For me those walks are more than a change of pace; they are a spiritual journey. It is first and foremost to these walks along the shore that I look to replenish my soul. The blueness of the sky on a fine day, the redness of the sun as it sets over the Arisaig shore, with its magnificent reflection on the water, and the soothing sound of the waves lapping on the shore —these are the sights and sounds that nourish the human spirit. Here I was in the midst of some of the creator's masterworks, and this never ceased to arouse a sense of awe that sunk deep into my soul.

This view is not meant to dismiss the spiritual value of my religious experience. I love the sense of mystery aroused by the celebration of mass. Moving as this liturgical ritual is, it cannot compare with the spirituality my walks in the countryside evoke. The beauty and tranquillity of the physical landscape are unrivalled in their ability to evoke peace and awe in my inner landscape.

Grandma told me that this response has its roots in the worship of nature, which was part of our pagan past. She said that the missionaries who brought Christianity to the Highlands let Christian and pagan beliefs exist side by side.

"If they saw no contradiction, why should I?" she concluded.

Satisfied with this reprieve from reality, I headed for home and the first thing I did was to tell Grandma how I had spent the last two weeks teaching Highland history. As she listened to the details of this venture, I could see that she was filled with pride. She looked at me with a broad smile of approval.

She then approached and took both of my hands as she said, "Mary, you are my soul mate."

That was quite a compliment, coming as it did from the master storyteller in our family.

A week after I had finished teaching Highland history, the chairman of the trustees of the Arisaig school district came to my class to see me, and I was worried.

"I hear you have been teaching Highland history," he said.

Hesitatingly, I said "Yes."

At that point, my heart sank. I feared there had been complaints about what I had done. He then asked why I taught Highland history, and in response I gave him the same reasons I had previously given my students.

As I looked directly at him to gauge some sense of where he was coming from, he looked at me approvingly and said, "Good for you. The trustees heard about what you had done and they asked me to come and thank you. They said that it was about time that the school taught something about the students' heritage ... And one of them added, 'A fine bonnie lass she is. I am very proud of her,'" he said, as he laughed.

I thanked him for his kind words, and with enthusiasm, I added, "I am so pleased that you understand what I was trying to do."

But I was also very, very relieved. A negative response to what I had done could have cost me my job.

25

Another fall had passed, and all too soon, the three women of our household found themselves once again busy preparing for Christmas, but this time without Anne, without Catherine, and without Father. We keenly felt their absence. We went about the Christmas rituals, but without much enthusiasm. At times I noticed tears in the eyes of Mother and Grandma. I also noted that they were quieter than usual.

I overheard Grandma say, "I just don't have the Christmas spirit this year."

They were particularly worried about Catherine—alone and so far away. On Christmas eve, we received a box and a letter from her, and this lightened their mood—and mine. Her letter read:

Dear Mother, Grandma, and Mary:

Here I am facing Christmas away from home. If you asked if I am lonely, I would say yes, but I am even more excited. Mrs. MacNeil and I have just completed decorating the house, and I must say it is truly beautiful. We have evergreen boughs and wreaths, decorated with red berries and gold ribbons, tastefully hung throughout the downstairs, inside and out. Candles are carefully placed around our large living room, and the light of the candles combines with the light from the fireplace to create a warm glow throughout the room.

On my days off, I go downtown. And I wish you could see the outside and inside of the stores. The decorations on Macy's department store extend for a block. The way the evergreens are arranged around shimmering glass ornaments in the windows is a delight to behold. And the counters are loaded with goodies: the very best clothing, finery, perfumes, nuts, and candies. On Saturday, choral groups and musicians perform the traditional Christmas carols near the lunch area in the store. I often take advantage of the free samples of the candies, cakes, and cookies the store provides. The sights, the smells, the tastes, and the sounds of Christmas are a feast for the senses.

I finally got the courage to go to Filene's Bargain Basement to compete with the mass of women who haunt that store to buy some blouses, sweaters, shawls, and gloves that you cannot get at home. That is what is in your package.

Christmas will find me busy in the kitchen. Christmas preparation starts here even earlier than at home. Mrs. MacNeil has already given me instructions on how to prepare the table and cook and present the food for Christmas dinner. You would think the queen was coming! It is indeed going to be an exquisite meal: two ducks stuffed with a savoury potato dressing, to be roasted to a golden brown, tart cranberry sauce, fluffy mashed potatoes, candied sweet potatoes, and sweet parsnips drizzled with butter. All this will be washed down with a good white wine served in their finest crystal. The meal will end with a steamed fruit pudding served with a hot rum sauce. I have never even tasted rum and here I will be cooking with it! While I am responsible for serving the meal, Mrs. MacNeil has asked that I also sit and have dinner with the family. I will be proud to share their table.

At this time of year, I think of you so often. When I look at all the things people have here, I realize that we did not have much, but at the same time, we lived well. We knew how to use what we had to make us comfortable. And most important of all, we had each other. In those ways we were rich. I'll miss sharing Christmas with you. And, above all, I'll miss sharing it with Father.

With love,

Catherine

On the one hand, we were delighted to receive Catherine's letter, and for the moment it raised our spirits. But it also served as a further reminder of her absence, and an even greater absence. Above all, we continued to miss Father: his good nature, his calm reassurance, the twinkle in his eye, and his warm smile. Christmas heightened our sense of loss. While we knew we would have occasions to see Catherine and Anne again, we also knew that we would not get to share Christmas with them. So we had our reasons to be sad. And the tears quietly running down Mother's cheeks reflected the feelings of the three of us.

"Oh come now," I said, "It's Christmas eve. Let's put these gloomy thoughts behind us. I think we should try on some of the clothes Catherine sent us."

The three of us got into the act. Mother put on a fine pair of leather gloves and gracefully moved her hands to illustrate their beauty as she exclaimed, "Pretty good for hands that have been digging in the dirt for forty years."

I put on a lovely sweater and sashayed around the room to display its fine qualities.

"Just the proper thing for a teacher," I remarked.

Grandma put her beautiful shawl with its delicate satin trim over her shoulders and swayed back and forth to make her fashion statement.

"Just the thing for an old lady," she asserted with a laugh.

Indeed, our little fashion show was the occasion for more than one laugh and it did a great deal to raise our spirits. We were now in a festive mood, and it carried right through Christmas day.

To our surprise, another letter arrived from Catherine shortly after Christmas. This was a sure indication that Catherine too was lonely. Christmas away from home, particularly for the first time, can be so hard. From her letter we were relieved to learn that she too had found a way to counteract her loneliness. And this is how it read.

Dear Mother, Grandma and Mary:

After I came home last night, I was just bursting to talk with you. So I decided on the next best thing, a letter.

On Tuesday past, Agnes and I made our way to the Down East Club, a place where people from home gather, and I was just overcome with a sense of belonging. As soon as I walked in, I was made to feel at home. All the other Down Easterners came and introduced themselves, and we shared information about our families and happenings back home. I was surprised to find that some of them still speak the Gaelic. When you are far away from home, the sound of the Gaelic is so heart warming—even though for our family it was not the first language. I was surprised to learn that some of our people could speak no language other than Gaelic when they first came here. I don't know how they managed on the job. This gathering provided a great chance to learn what the other young people from the East are doing in Boston. I don't think any of the women have jobs that are better than mine.

Suddenly, everyone stopped talking as a man appeared with a fiddle, and then, just like we did at the ceilidhs in Arisaig, we danced the night away to the jigs and reels he played so well. He reminded me of John Ban Gillis. I danced until my feet got sore.

Even though I was meeting these people for the first time, I felt I was one of them. We have so much in common. It is nice to know I have a place to go where I can feel the warmth and cheer of home.

With love,

Catherine

After I had read Catherine's letter aloud, I added, "And it is nice to know she has a place to go to keep her from being lonely. I can just sense the warmth with which she would introduce herself to everyone at that gathering."

News that Catherine had found a way to relieve her loneliness raised the spirits of Grandma and Mother.

"Now we can get on with enjoying the rest of the Christmas season," Grandma announced.

The New Year's Eve ceilidh was held at the home of John Ban Boyd. I was engaged in lively conversation with the neighbouring women, who were preparing lunch, when John Jim Joe MacDonald came over and asked me to dance. While I had seen him at other ceilidhs, I never had the opportunity to meet him. On this, our very first encounter, I was quite taken with him. He was long and lean and light on his feet. He exuded kindness and warmth and we hit it off. As we danced, I noticed some of the neighbouring women giving me the eye. They don't miss much. In a close-knit community like ours, you do not have much privacy, and being a very private person, I found that awkward. However, that feeling of awkwardness did not prevent me from having a good time. At the end of the ceilidh, John walked me home. Walking hand in hand, we were very comfortable together. Because I had spent so much time in a school for girls, I never had a boyfriend. I found this new experience exhilarating.

When I resumed my walks in the winter snow after New Year's, John sometimes joined me. I must say that we enjoyed each other's company. We were both the same age and we had much in common. Like myself, he was the only child at home. He had three brothers working elsewhere. His mother was a widow, and he was honouring his father's dying request for him to stay home and look after her and the farm. Maybe it was all this responsibility that made him so thoughtful.

As John and I grew used to walking together along the shore and through the woods, we took great joy in sharing our love of the beauty of nature. For us this enduring beauty never lost its magic. We shared that special ability to observe it with a fresh eye each day and never cease to find something at which to marvel. We had only to look at each other to know what each of us was thinking. That was a common bond that drew us closer. This response may indeed reflect the appreciation of the beauty of the rural landscape that is so deeply ingrained in the Highland Scots. There is something of the soul of the artist in each and every one of us.

The common bond that developed between John and me enabled us to share our innermost thoughts and feelings. To put it simply, our relationship felt good. John told me repeatedly how much he enjoyed my company.

He would often look at me with a glint in his eye and say, "I like being with you."

And I would reply, "And I with you."

Then I suddenly realized why I felt so comfortable with him. In many ways, he was like my father. I found this discovery very intriguing. This must have been what drew me to him in the first place. It pleased me to think that this was the basis of my attraction to him.

While I was enjoying our relationship so much, Grandma and Mother were expressing concerns when they thought I could not hear them.

I overheard Mother say, "I am worried about Mary's friendship with John. He is very fine, and so is his mother, but his brothers, well, they are something else. Thugs I'd call them. Those boys caused a lot of trouble in our community before they left. I think they got out because they sensed that they had gone too far and the people of the community were about to run them out. I don't think Mary would have any idea of how to deal with such people. Their father was a terrible drunk, what we would call a mean drunk. He was pretty rambunctious, and no doubt, that left its mark on the boys."

Grandma agreed with her concerns and expressed the hope that I would never find myself in a position of having to have anything to do with them.

I didn't quite know how to take this exchange. I didn't even know those fellows. I decided, perhaps naively, that I never intended to have anything to do with them, and thus they should not be a problem for me. Nevertheless, this matter stayed in the back of my mind.

The next time John and I walked, he mentioned how often he thought about the death of his father. I took advantage of the opportunity to ask him what happened.

A very serious look came over John's face; he breathed a deep sigh, and then he began. "It was an accident. I'll never forget that horrible moment; it still haunts my mind. The two of us were cutting firewood and we were making great progress. Then my father made one slip. A powerful swing of the axe missed the log and got him right in the thigh. He bled all over the place."

At this point, John began to cry. These painful memories were too much for him. I put my arm around him, and then he pulled himself together and resumed his story.

"I was surprised by how calm I was when I swung into action," he said. "I tore off my shirt and wrapped it around Father's leg to see if it would stop the bleeding. It didn't work. So I tore off my scarf and wrapped it around the wound. That didn't work. The bleeding continued. Then I feared the worst, that the axe hit an artery. I wanted to run for help, but in my heart of hearts I knew it would do no good. I decided it would be better to stay with him. All I could do was to hold his hand and pray. And through the silence in the woods, you could hear my prayers rising to God. It wasn't long before Father blacked out. As I watched the blood drain from his body, I became physically ill. My head was whirling; I vomited; I felt guilty."

These horrible memories caused John to stop again. He breathed a deep sigh and then he continued. "A ton of questions rushed through my mind. How could I have prevented the accident? How am I going to get Father home? How am I going to tell Mother? And many others. When I was sure he was dead, I attempted to pull myself together and I headed for home.

"As I entered the kitchen, Mother said with alarm, 'John, you are pale as a ghost. What's wrong?'

"I could not look at her as I told her the terrible truth. She put her arms around me and sobbed as she shook her head in disbelief. As I comforted her, I assured her that I promised my father that I would stay home and look after her. And that promise I have kept and I will continue to keep."

I took both of John's hands and for a moment we stood in silence. Then I commented, "We have even more in common than I thought."

John did not say anything. Remembering and retelling that tragic event left him drained.

I broke the silence with this remark, "Events like that sure leave their mark on us."

He just nodded, and we walked on in silence.

The next time we were together, we talked about the impact of his father's death on his mother.

John digressed from the topic to say, "Mary, there was something about Father's death I did not tell you: He was drunk when he died. That is probably the reason why the axe slipped. The truth is that my feelings were not all remorse. They were part remorse and part rage. I must admit, even though I am ashamed of it, that when I was certain my father was dead, I kicked him, as I said, 'You son of a bitch, you even had to die drunk.'"

As John looked at me to see what my reaction was, he asked with a tinge of anxiety in his voice, "Does that make me a bad man?"

"No, no, I think I understand," I replied. "You were simply venting your frustration. I'm sure the drinking made your father a hard man to put up with. And to have him die the way he lived made the circumstances of his death so much harder for you and your mother to bear."

"Telling you about this very private part of my life eases my mind. It means so much to me to know you understand; to know you care," John said, as he heaved another sigh of relief.

Then he smiled as he said, "Now that I have that off my chest, we can talk about how Mother is getting along. I must say she is doing just fine. I hate to admit it, but I believe that in some ways she is better off without Father. She is a strong woman who is used to fending for herself."

John then surprised me with this request, "I would really like you to meet her. Will you have supper with us on Friday evening? I'll come for you."

Without any hesitation I replied, "I'd love that."

And then I thought of the "thugs." The idea of changing my decision flashed through my mind, but I did not want to disappoint John.

John arrived promptly at four on Friday afternoon with his riding sleigh and trotter. He helped me into the sleigh and we took off through the snow. The horse pranced, the sleigh bells jingled, the runners of the sleigh skimmed over the snow, and we laughed all the way to John's place. The ride was exhilarating.

When we arrived at John's house, his mother, a big matronly woman with an outgoing personality, greeted me with a warm hug and made me feel at home. Knowing we were coming for dinner, she drew from the oven a beautiful roast of beef with potatoes, onions, carrots, and parsnips baked to a golden brown in the juices from the roast. The aroma of the roast made us ravenously hungry, and we sat down to enjoy this wonderful feast.

After dinner, we were in a mellow mood as we sat and relaxed in front of a roaring fire in the fireplace. Our conversation eventually wandered back to the old country, as Highland settlers' conversations usually do, and this drift in the conversation moved John's mother to recall the story of her great grandfather's experience in the Battle of Culloden.

"John Angus Mor had both of his legs broken by grapeshot and he was left on the battlefield to die," she said. "When the redcoats came round to finish him off, he pretended to be dead. They poked him with their muskets and not finding any sign of life, they decided to move on. With sheer grit, he was able to use his hands to drag his body to the nearest hut. He wasn't there long when other redcoats came round to check the dwelling, and they too poked him with their muskets. Again he pretended to be dead and again he fooled the soldiers, and they moved on. Eventually he did recover, and even though he was crippled, he managed to live a fairly normal life. However, recurring memories of the dead bodies soaked in blood on the battlefield haunted him. 'So many young lives lost,' his children remembered him saying over and over again. Our people have endured so much suffering," she concluded.

This story made my ears prick up, for it reminded me once more of the strong tendency of Highland families to retain memories of their past. For this we must credit the local bards who make it their mission to keep the history of Highland families alive—just as the bards did back in the Highlands. This made me think again of what effective history teachers these bards are. As I said before, classroom history teachers could learn a thing or two from them. I certainly did.

We exchanged stories about the old county until midnight, and then I decided it was time for John to take me home.

Just as we were about to leave, there was a thump on the kitchen door. We looked at each other, not knowing what to expect. Then John hesitatingly opened the door, and in walked his brother, James, with an unsteady step. He was obviously drunk.

"What are you doing here?" he asked me with a menacing look on his face.

John intervened to say, "That is none of your business."

James took a swing at John and missed. He fell flat on his face on the floor. John dragged him to the couch and left him there and then drove me home without saying a word. Sensing the tension in the air, I decided it was not the time to ask questions about the brother. I was beginning to get a sense of what John and his mother had to put up with. I was also beginning to appreciate what Grandma and Mother had to say about the brothers and their reservations about my association with that family. Clearly the father's drinking and rambunctiousness had rubbed off on James. Thinking about this incident made me toss and turn all night.

The next day, when I shared the story of the antics of John's brother with Grandma, I was shocked to learn that this young man, and also John, the one I loved, were the grandsons of the man who tried to run Grandma's parents off their farm, the very farm on which we now live. I could now understand why Mother and Grandma had reservations about any association I may have with the family. The people of our community have a crude saying for the repetition of bad behaviour from one generation to the next, "The lamb is like the ram."

26

An important part of Anne's formation as a novice involved service to others. When this period of her formation was about to begin, Sister Mary Jean Sister met with her to discuss the additional responsibilities she was to assume. She informed Anne that she was to take on the domestic work associated with looking after the rooms of ten senior students at St. Francis Xavier College. This entailed making their beds, dusting, mopping, and taking away their bedding, towels, and clothing to be cleaned and repaired.

Anne objected, "But I will be doing much the same work as my sister who is a domestic in Boston. I didn't come here to be a maid."

Sister Mary Jean responded gently, "Now stop and think about it for a moment and you will realize that you will carry out this assignment in the special sense in which a sister does her work. By that I mean the spiritual focus of all our activities. Working with these students will provide a great opportunity to provide some wise counsel. And, most important of all, you have to remember that ours is a life of service to others."

Anne raised her hand as she said, "Forgive me. My reaction was selfish. What you say is true."

Sister Mary Jean ended their conversation by reminding Anne how her free labour and that of the other sisters helped to keep tuition low so that more students could attend college.

"That is a good cause," she said. "It is a great contribution to the education of young people. It also helps to bring a woman's touch to an otherwise all-male institution. Believe me, that is sorely needed. You have no idea how bad living conditions were before the sisters came. The students' rooms were dusty, dingy, sometimes downright dirty. The students' clothes went unwashed. The food was coarse.

I was here when the sisters arrived and I was able to see first hand the delight of the students in the beautiful food the sisters cooked and in the improved cleanliness of their surroundings. It did my heart good to overhear a student in the dining hall say, 'Now this place is more like home. And it is not just the good food; it's the kindness and gentleness with which it is served. The sisters have become our mothers away from home.'"

Even though Anne's studies and her domestic duties kept her very busy, she continued to look forward to chapel where she would sit in silence and put all her cares out of her mind by contemplating the life of the spirit. This was her route to inner peace and happiness. Her religious vocation was a source of great fulfilment.

Anne's move into domestic duties gave her an opportunity to get to know the ten students whom she was assigned to serve. She soon learned to enjoy it. It wasn't long before the students to whom she was assigned sensed they could confide in her and they began to share with her stories of their lives, as well as their problems with their studies, with their finances, and sometimes even with their girlfriends. As they got to know her better, they looked forward to sharing their joys with her: the new friends they had made, their success in sports, their summer job opportunities. Anne learned to listen, and hard as it was, she tried not to judge. Her calm demeanour, her warmth, and her sincerity made her words of encouragement very special to them. As she got to know them well, she sometimes offered carefully chosen words of advice.

Anne had grown to understand that these students were truly good people. It was some time before she learned that most of them were heading for the seminary to study for the priesthood. Very few young people went to university and these students, realizing that university attendance is a very special privilege, felt a strong sense of responsibility to contribute to society. Most of them would later do this by ministering to their parishioners.

Through their daily give and take, Anne grew very close to the students. It didn't hurt that she was the same age as most of them. Truth be told, she loved working with them. But at the same time, she tried to remember that her relationship with them was guided by the idea that she was one with them, not one of them. She thought this kind of relationship made it easier for them to trust her and to seek her counsel.

The students soon learned to confide in Anne so much that they even shared their humour with her. In their lighter moments they took delight in telling her about the latest prank, a new joke, or some goof that made one or more of them look comical or stupid.

She smiled to herself as she recalled one of them asking, "Sister, do you know the name of Mary Magdalene's theme song?" When she shook her head in the negative, he provided the answer, "Don't Get Around Much Anymore!"

And through this informal give and take, she managed to become a confidante and a counsellor for these young people. She thought that they made her a better person and she hoped she had the same effect on them. And this is basically how she fulfilled the service part of her life in the novitiate.

However, there was one student with whom she had a problem. His name was Bill MacNeil and he was very shy. Anne found that he was the last of the students to confide in her. As he grew comfortable with her, he took every opportunity to slip around to where she was working to seek her counsel. She didn't help by misreading the situation. She felt that because of his shyness, he needed her attention more than the other students, and so she spent more time with him. Then she began to notice that he went out of his way to find every opportunity to be with her. Then and there she knew she had a problem. She sensed he was developing feelings for her.

"Oh Lord, what am I going to do?" she thought to herself.

What was she to do? First, she figured that if she tried to avoid him, he might get the message. That didn't work. He reacted by trying harder to see her and he was getting very ingenious at finding ways to do so. As soon as she started to make the beds, he was there helping her. He gathered the piles of laundry and carried them to the laundry. In humour, she said to him one day, "Bill, if you keep up this work, you are going to put me out of my job."

He just smiled and kept working. She continued to ponder what she was to do. She certainly did not want the other novices to know about her problem. What would they think? She feared that some might look askance at her. Others with a good sense of humour might laugh. And worst of all, there might even be one or two straight-laced characters who thought she had encouraged him. Just the thought of these reactions made her feel embarrassed. The problem was starting to get out of hand. She had to do something and she had to do it fast. Worrying about what to do kept her awake at night. She prayed for the inner strength to do the right thing. Then she decided she had no choice but to act and that the best thing to do was to face the problem head on. She braced herself for this undesirable moment.

The next time Bill came to look for her, she told him they had to talk. He was obviously pleased. This was one more chance for him to spend time with her. There was no one else around, and so she began. She moved about dusting to settle her nerves. She started by telling Bill that she did not want to hurt him by what she had to say.

Then in a gentle manner she tried to make her point. "Bill, I'm afraid that your relationship with me might be interpreted as inappropriate," she suggested. "I don't know if you realize it, but I think you are looking for a girlfriend. Your friendship with me cannot be of that kind," she said in a kindly fashion.

Bill was obviously embarrassed and he raised his hand to stop her from talking.

He said, "Sister, I am so embarrassed. I like you so much I didn't realize what was happening. I don't have any close friends. I was lonely, and you were the only one who was really nice to me."

Anne was amazed by how forthright he was. She could see tears starting to come into his eyes.

"Sister, I will stop it," he promised.

He obviously felt bad. She needed to do something to soften the blow.

So she spoke kindly to him. "Bill, don't be embarrassed. We know what happened. The other students do not. Starting now, our relationship will get back on the right foot. We can still be friends, just like the other students are my friends. Agreed."

And he nodded his head.

Then, to end their conversation, she said with a smile, "Bill, get out of here before someone sees you."

Again he nodded, and with a shy smile, he turned and walked away. And with that Sister Anne breathed a sigh of relief, looked to the sky, and said, "Thank you, Lord."

Anne decided to confide in Sister Mary Jean, and because she was her personal counsellor, she told her the whole story. Being very wise, Sister Mary Jean had an excellent idea about how to help Bill.

She said, "You know, Anne, what this problem indicates is that Bill needs a friend. Why don't you try to help him form a relationship with one of the other students. I would suggest that one of the easiest ways to do this is to find some task on which they have to work together. You know better than most that it is what we have in common that draws us together."

Anne thanked her, for she was very appreciative of her insight. "Why couldn't I think of that?" she said with a wry smile.

As Anne's life as a novice moved forward, the seriousness of her calling began to weigh heavily on her mind. Mind you, when she entered the convent, she understood that she was making a commitment for life, but she did not think a great deal about it until now.

"Yes, I am really, really here for life," she said to herself over and over again. "I'll forever be bound by the vows of poverty, chastity, and obedience. That means that I'll never have any possessions beyond the bare necessities of life. Of course, I never had much. I shall never marry. I'll always be in a position of doing the bidding of my superiors. The routine of my daily life will be laid on until the day I die."

The magnitude of this commitment was now a preoccupation. Again and again she asked herself, "Am I ready to embrace this way of life for the rest of my days?"

As Anne continued to ponder this questions, she came to realize that she was already living the lifestyle of a member of the congregation and finding it highly agreeable. This helped her to put her doubts to rest, and their resolution was timely, for all too quickly her life as a novice was coming to an end.

After three years of formation, Anne was to be reviewed as a candidate for the vows. She was called before the superior of the order and her council, and they posed just one question, a question that is at the heart of the life of a novice, "What did you get out of this opportunity to reflect seriously on your calling?"

Her entire experience in the novitiate prepared her to address this question and she did so with ease. And this is the gist of her answer: She told of how her experience taught her to give priority to the life of the spirit and how her prayer and meditation deepened her consciousness of her relationship with God.

Then she summed up by saying, "This love of God has to be manifested in my love for my fellow human beings, and it guides my relationship with the people I work with. I am a much better person for it."

Next she met with Bishop Cameron who asked her the same question. This time she felt more sure of her ability to respond and she talked with ease, giving basically the same answer she had provided in the previous interview.

After she had shared her ideas with the bishop, he then posed an additional question, "What could you achieve as a sister that you would not achieve as a lay person?"

Having to confront the seriousness of her calling also prepared her to answer this question. She stopped for a moment to think about how to phrase her response and then she answered slowly and carefully.

"Being cut off from family and friends, I can devote my life solely to the service of God and my fellow human beings. My study of scripture reinforces my understanding that this service arises out of the central message of Christianity, which is to love God and to show this love through love for my fellow human beings. Before I deal with any human problem, I now ask myself this question: What would Jesus do in this situation? Lay people too can do this. But, as I see it, being removed from the distractions of the world will help to sharpen my attention to this mission."

Her thoughtful response impressed the bishop, and he terminated their interview by telling her that he was very pleased with the progress of her spiritual development.

What she said must have impressed all of her interrogators, for when the interviews were over, the superior, Sister Consolata, came to see her and immediately informed her that she would be admitted to the ranks of the Sisters of St. Martha.

She took both of her hands and with a warm smile she said, "You give us every indication that you are ready to devote your life to our congregation. You are now one of us. Congratulations."

So on the sixth of June, 1905, all the sisters who were candidates for the vows formally made their profession. For the first time, each of them wore the full habit of the Sisters of St. Martha, the long flowing black dress, the white band around their black headdress, the crucifix, and the ring. This ceremony is to a sister what the marriage ceremony is to a couple. Each makes a commitment for life. And in both cases it is the most important and most joyous day of their lives. The profession ceremony was incorporated into a high mass celebrated by Bishop Cameron in which the liturgy was interrupted after the homily to allow each candidate to come to the altar rail and pronounce individually her allegiance to the vows of poverty, chastity, and obedience. For each of them this is her formal commitment to her chosen walk in life. This is what Anne wanted from life and she felt a deep sense of fulfilment. The fact that there was to be a final profession in three years was of little concern to her, for she knew she had made her choice.

Grandma, Mother, and I drove into town to be present for the ceremony. After the mass was completed, Anne raced outside the chapel to share with us the joy of her celebration. Opportunities for us to be with her were now rare and we savoured every moment we had together.

Anne said what we were all thinking, "I just wish Father could be here to share this moment with us."

Before we parted, Mother asked, "And what do you do now?"

Anne told us that she had not yet discussed this matter with the superior of the order, but when she did, she would let us know.

September first was one of the days designated for visits to St. Martha's Convent, and Mother and I decided to go to visit Anne, who was now known as Sister Anne Marie. We preferred to call her Sister Anne. Because Grandma did not feel well, she decided to remain at home. When we arrived at the convent, we were ushered into the parlour to wait for Sister Anne. We never got used to the austere environment, where the only ornamentation was a crucifix on the wall and the only furniture consisted of hard straight chairs. But the room brightened up when Sister

Anne arrived in a joyful mood, and she immediately threw her arms around us. She quickly disappeared into the kitchen and returned with tea and sandwiches, which were much appreciated after our long ride. While we ate, we filled her in on the news from home and the community, which was of great interest to her now that she was cut off from both.

Sister Anne was in a talkative mood and she regaled us with stories of making hay on the university farm in July.

"There I was, if you can imagine, in my long black dress, with my pitch fork in my hand, covered with sweat as I lifted one fork full of hay after another onto the hay wagon. This job was tough on a girl who is more used to lifting paint brushes," she exclaimed with a laugh. "Our only break from the hard work came when the horses pulled the full load of hay into the barn. I did not want to mow the hay. My experience in hay making at home taught me what a hot, sweaty, dusty job that is; so I hastened to offer to drive the horse that pulled the pitching machine that carried the hay into the mow. I made sure I talked nice to the horse so that he would not lunge forward and land me on my face on the ground."

At this point we all burst out laughing. The thought of dainty little Anne in her long robe doing the heavy dirty work involved in making hay was so ridiculous.

"Don't laugh too much," Sister Anne cautioned. "The food raised on the university farm is the reason why we eat so well."

At the first pause in the conversation, she announced, "Now I have some news for you. After a sister takes her vows, she is given a mission. I had shared my interest in becoming a nurse with our Superior, Sister Consolata, over a year ago, and to help me prepare for the study of nursing she arranged for another sister to tutor me in biology and mathematics, subjects that provide background for course work in nursing. I got my needed academic background this way because Sister Consolata thought I was too old to go back to high school. As a result of our deliberations, she informed me that I am to leave tomorrow for St. Joseph's Hospital in Glace Bay, where I will train to be a nurse. This is the only hospital in our diocese that trains nurses, and therefore, if I want to be a nurse, I have no choice but to go there."

"But," Mother interjected, "you will be moving even farther away from home."

"I know, Mother," she replied, "but I will stay in touch. And when I finish my nursing program, I might even get stationed here in Antigonish. The sisters are talking about building a new hospital in our community next year. We need a place where doctors can treat people who are seriously ill and where they can do surgery."

Sister Anne left the next day for Glace Bay, and we did not see her again for three years.

During that time, I often heard Grandma ask, "I wonder how our little Sister Anne goes about learning to be a nurse?"

There is no end to that woman's interest in learning.

27

After Sister Anne had finished training, she returned to Antigonish. She invited me to spend a day in the convent with her before she assumed her nursing assignment. It felt so good to be together again. We exchanged fond memories of our childhood and of our preparation for our respective professions. We both recalled special memories of how we worked together to put on the school Christmas concert in the winter following Father's death.

As we talked, I learned a great deal about her experiences in the nursing school at St. Joseph's Hospital in Glace Bay. From our conversation, I was able to piece together the story of her life in training to be a nursing sister:

In early September, she and Sister Liza boarded a train for Glace Bay. Neither of them had ever been out of Antigonish; so they were excited about the trip. When they got to the Strait of Canso, they left the train to cross on the ferry. Their excitement quickly turned to anxiety. As the boat lurched up and down in the choppy water, they held on to the rails of the ferry so hard that their knuckles turned white. They were both dizzy and sick to their stomachs. It was such a relief for them to get off the boat and walk on solid ground to get to the train. They changed trains in Sydney for the rest of the trip to Glace Bay. Being used to the cleanliness and beauty of the countryside, they were not ready for what they saw along the way into the industrial area. As the train moved closer to Glace Bay, they passed row upon row of dingy, dark miners' houses built side by side along muddy roads adjacent to the mine sites. The coal dust that rained down on the mining communities turned the environment into a dark, sooty mess. They were anxious to leave this depressing scene and take refuge in St. Joseph's Convent for the night.

The very next morning, Sister Anne was assigned a room in St. Joseph's Hospital where she was to live, study, worship, and work for the next three years. The first person she met was Sister Ignatius, the head of the nursing program, who instructed her in the requirements of the program and its responsibilities.

"Would you believe that we had a twelve hour day: eight hours of work and four hours of instruction each day, for six days a week," Sister Anne exclaimed.

Sister Anne was not given any time to settle into her new environment. As soon as she was acquainted with the requirements of the nursing program, she was put to work. She was disappointed that a great deal of the work part of her program was domestic labour. She was instructed in how to make a hospital bed, but she did not need any instruction in sweeping, mopping, dusting, scrubbing floors, and arranging furniture.

Sister Anne laughed as she said, "While I was down on my hands and knees scrubbing a particularly dirty room, I thought to myself, 'Think of the fuss I used to make when Mother asked me to do that kind of work at home.'"

She later heard her sentiments echoed by a lay nurse in training who muttered while she worked, "I didn't come here to be a damn maid."

She was soon to learn that there was a reason for the domestic labour the nurses in training provided: It helped to keep hospital costs low and thereby enable more people to afford health care.

By twelve noon she had enough of housekeeping and was glad to escape to the classroom for four hours of instruction. Then, after supper, she returned to the hospital floor and did four more hours of work. The part of the work she enjoyed the most was getting to know patients, listening to their concerns and helping to make them comfortable.

Sister Anne worked alongside a qualified nurse who showed her the ropes. She very patiently taught her how to determine a patient's vital signs, how to administer prescribed drugs, and how to get a sense of changes in a patient's condition..

"Basically" she said, "I learned to nurse by nursing."

Being a novice in the field of nursing, she was often asked to revert to the sisterly role of sitting and praying with patients who were very sick.

"I'll never forget how moved I was by my first opportunity to sit with a dying patient," she recalled. "As I held her hand and prayed with her, I saw her body and her face relax, and as she passed away, she seemed to be at peace."

Sister Ignatius asked Sister Anne to accompany her while she reported the news of the patient's death to her family. She wanted her to learn how to deal with this very difficult experience. The father was disappointed that the family did not get to the hospital earlier. When he heard the news, he slumped into a chair and put his head in his hands. The children included five little girls between the ages of three and seven. Sister Ignatius sat with the father to give him a chance to express his grief. As tears ran down his cheeks, in a pained voice he talked of how much he was going to miss his beautiful wife. When the little girls saw their father crying, they too began to cry as they clung to him. Sister Anne took the little girls aside and talked softly to them. As soon as the children stopped crying, their father pulled himself together to take the children home.

As he left the hospital, he said, "Sister, this has to be the hardest day of my life."

After they had left, Sister Ignatius and Sister Anne just looked at each other and shook their heads. They had no words to express what they were feeling. Sister Anne had never before seen a person die; so this experience had a deep impact on her.

"It drained me," Sister Anne later recalled. "And it was just a taste of things to come. Comforting the dying and their immediate families became a regular occurrence."

She confided that, "Too often the suffering and the sorrow that accompanied the death of a loved one left me overwhelmed, depleted, and exhausted. I never got used to watching people die, even though it was almost a daily experience in my line of work. I remember how often I fled to the privacy of the linen closet to cry my eyes out. But, at the same time, consoling the dying and their families was also a great source of satisfaction to the extent I knew that I could be of some comfort to them."

I was fascinated by Sister Anne's story of the relationship between the local mines and the hospital. The mines had a large impact on the kinds of medical problems the nursing sisters faced. Before St. Joseph's Hospital opened in 1902, all medical treatment was done in the home. The kitchen table was the operating theatre; so you can imagine that sanitation left much to be desired.

Mine accidents were common. "I'll never forget my first experience with a mine accident," Sister Anne was moved to tell me. "The first time I heard the hooting of the whistle announcing the occurrence of an explosion in the local mine, I ran to the window to see what was happening, and that sight will linger in my mind forever. It was a real bad explosion. In my mind's eye, I can still see the anguish on the faces of the miners' wives who, upon hearing the whistle, rushed frantically to the pit head to learn the fate of their men. Twenty men were killed; more were injured. It was not long before the rescue squad began to bring out the miners' bodies. I saw the bodies of the dead miners, or parts of them, being put on wagons to be taken to their homes. Rescue men on foot rushed the injured miners to the hospital on stretchers. These men had broken limbs, crushed chests, and internal injuries. It was now time to stop watching and to swing into action. I was appalled to see first hand the condition of the injured men. There was blood everywhere. Men were moaning; men were weeping; men were cursing. One young lad of about twelve years of age was calling for his mother. I had never seen anything like that in my life and I found I was getting sick to my stomach. I kept saying to myself, 'Be strong; be strong.'"

I was so fascinated by what Sister Anne had to say that I did not interrupt her story. Revisiting the emotion wrought by this event caused Sister Anne to pause in our conversation. As soon as she pulled herself together, she continued with her story.

"The experienced nurses attended to the injured miners immediately. While they were working on the one who was most seriously injured, he passed away. His wife and daughter were waiting anxiously in the hallway. Sister Ignatius asked me to take them to the sitting room. I picked up their three-year-old daughter and from the tears in her eyes I knew she had some sense of what had happened. I held her close and whispered soothing words in her ear. I wanted to give her mother a chance to talk.

"The mother had a grey pallor; deep lines of worry furrowed her brow; her eyes were watery. The woman's whole countenance reflected her sense of loss and despair. And then her words poured forth, 'Poor Willie, how I am going to miss him. What will become of us without him. He was a tower of strength. There is no one to look after us now.'

"Suddenly a terrible thought flashed across her mind, and she blurted, 'Lord have mercy; now that Willie is dead, the mining company will put us out of our house, and we will be homeless.'

"And with that awful thought she began to sob bitterly. The woman was not exaggerating. The company would not let her stay in a company house if she had no one working in the mines. While the sight of a lonely widow walking away from her home, pushing a baby carriage, with the rest of her children by her side, was not uncommon, it never ceased to provoke outrage. If there is no justice, can there at least be some mercy on those poor suffering souls," Sister Anne said with anguish in her voice.

All Sister Anne could do was to tell the widow that the sisters would try to help. She told me she assured her that the sisters in the convent would bring food and clothing and that they would somehow make sure that she had a roof over her head. She also assured her that she would remain in touch so that she would have someone to talk to.

With those reassurances, the widow began to pull herself together. "Well," she sighed, "I guess I had better go home and prepare for Willie's funeral."

Anne held her hand for a moment, and then the widow and her daughter turned and walked away.

When things quietened down, Sister Anne said that she breathed a sigh of relief as she thought to herself, "This has to be the most emotionally exhausting day of my life since Father's death."

Her story brought tears to my eyes. I had no idea of the turmoil learning to nurse in a mining community brought to the lives of the young women who served people in distress.

Even more moving was the story Sister Anne told of her delayed reaction to this trauma. At the end of her shift, she headed for the chapel to have a few words with God. There was no one in the chapel; so she was able to speak loudly and sternly to Him.

She was in no mood to kneel; instead, with a severe look on her face, she stood and pointed her finger toward the altar as she addressed God. "What are you doing?" she asked in a scolding voice. "How could you bring so much suffering to these poor helpless people? Haven't they been through enough? Where is your mercy?"

And then she said, "I suddenly realized that I was scolding God and I stopped, overcome with horror at the thought of what I had done. With the release of my pent-up anger, I fell on my knees in the nearest pew and I beseeched God to forgive me, and then I cried—for the fatherless family and for myself. I looked up to see Dr. Angus MacDonald smiling down on me. He was on duty during the disaster, and after things quietened down, he too came to the chapel to soothe his soul.

"I asked him, 'Did you see everything?'

"And he replied gently, 'Yes I did.'

"Then I said. 'I am so embarrassed.'

"He interjected, 'Don't be. We are all vulnerable in times of horrific crises, and we need to have an outlet for our emotions.'

"Then he said kindly, 'And I'll tell you something else; it doesn't get any better. Sister, you do not have to be alone at times like this. I want you to know that when you are hurting, you can come and talk with me. We all need someone to talk to.'"

Then Sister Anne observed, "His understanding of my anguish was a great source of comfort. While I had the sisters to turn to in times of trauma, it was also helpful to hear the reaction of a lay person. It was reassuring to learn that people who are stronger than us suffer from the same kind of distress."

Sister Anne's story prompted me to say, "From what you say, I think that was a great lesson in human empathy."

Then I asked her if she ever took the good doctor up on his offer.

She told me that she did several times after similar traumatic accidents or deaths.

"I would go to the chapel and find him there," she said. "Then we would sit in a pew and talk. Learning that he came to the chapel because he reacted to these events in much the same way I did continued to be reassuring because I had previously thought that my emotional reaction was a sign of weakness. Then I knew that if it was all right for a doctor to react this way, then it was all right for me. Such trying times made me think of what Grandma used to say, 'God will provide.' And sure enough, in my time of extreme distress the good doctor appeared to look after me."

As I listened to Sister Anne's story, I realized how little our family knew about the anxiety and stress that accompanied her vocation. Fortunately for Sister Anne, she was a strong person, even stronger than we realized. She had learned how to survive.

In response to tragedy Sister Anne had developed good coping mechanisms. She told of how she learned to relieved her stress by visiting the children's ward in the evening. At that time things were usually quiet on the floors of the hospital, and this gave her an opportunity to sneak away for a while.

"I remember well my first visit after the accident," she said. "The little eyes that honed in on me as I approached showed that the children were dying for attention. They beamed with delight at my offer of a story, a song, or a game. I needed their attention as much as they needed mine. After they grew tired and settled in for the night, I picked up the smallest child who snuggled close as I rocked him to sleep. I guess God responded to my sense of outrage with this message. This is where you go to heal when your heart is heavy and your soul is sore. And then I knew more about why I wanted to become a nursing sister."

Sister Anne's story made me realize that we had one thing in common in our professional careers: We both found children to be a great source of consolation.

Sister Anne went on to tell me that, as she gained more experience, the sister in charge of nursing education felt she was ready for night duty. Sister Anne was not so sure.

"Little did I know what I was in for," she said.

She then told of the problems she faced on night duty. At night, there was no doctor on duty, and only one certified nurse. On most nights an eerie quietness permeated the place, and Sister Anne fought hard to keep herself awake. This routine was occasionally broken by terrible traumas. On one particularly rough night, a stretcher containing an acutely sick mother was brought into admissions, followed by her drunken, loud-mouthed husband and two very frightened children. The head nurse called the doctor on duty to come, but knowing the lady's condition, he decided she was too far gone for him to be of any help. That left Sister Anne and the night nurse alone to attend to the mother as best they could, but there was nothing they could do. At midnight the woman died. Her husband at first was overcome with sorrow, which was quickly followed by rage.

He turned on the night nurse. "You bitch, you killed my wife. You'll pay for this," he roared.

And then he began to throw furniture. In the midst of his ranting and raving, Sister Anne ran and called the police who appeared quickly. Every effort on their part to calm him failed. He swung to hit one of the police and missed. Before the police could restrain him, he lunged at the night nurse, missed again, and fell to the floor.

When he saw the policeman and the nurses standing over him as he lay on the floor, he shouted, "What the Christ are you looking at?"

As they quickly moved back, one of the police put the man in handcuffs and took him away.

The father's antics upset the children terribly. The night nurse and Sister Anne were left with two distraught children, a boy and a girl. They were inconsolable. Children should never have to see their mother die under these circumstances. The nurses continued efforts to comfort the children did not work. Because they could not be away from the patients for long, Sister Anne called the convent for help. Two sisters got out of bed and arrived shortly. They too did their best to try to comfort the children. They talked quietly to them until they calmed down and then took them to the convent to spend the night.

Sister Anne said she asked her colleague, "What will become of these children? They have lost their mother, and I don't think their father can be trusted with them?"

"I really don't know," was her less than reassuring reply.

Sister Anne told me that, as she was in the habit of doing after every trauma, she went to the chapel where she got on her knees and beseeched God to give her the strength to carry on.

I was amazed to hear her exclaim, "For all my exhortations to God, my stress, my worry, my fear and my fatigue, I love my work."

She talked further of how the nurses did their best to heal the bodies and the spirits of the sick and of how much the patients appreciated it. Through their work they got to know and to understand most of the people in the community. The demands of nursing in a mining community developed in the nurses the physical and emotional strength to face the ordeals that accompany their profession.

The people of the mining community knew the sisters were there for them and many of those who had been in hospital kept in touch. Children who had been their patients sometimes appeared at their kitchen door when they were hungry. And they seemed to enjoy the attention as much as the food. Sitting at the kitchen table with the children provided the sisters with an opportunity to support and sometimes counsel them while at the same time enjoying their company.

"If we did nothing more than make them feel welcome and warm, we had done something for them," Sister Anne suggested.

She told me that these experiences deepened her realization that this is what her vocation was about—demonstrating her love of God by helping her fellow human beings.

"We were doing God's work," she said.

She summed up her outlook on her training for her chosen profession in these words: "Yes, I missed the cleanliness and beauty and peacefulness of our homestead in Arisaig, and even more I missed your companionship and that of Mother and Grandma, but the reward of helping suffering human beings in a coal town made up for all of that."

That was quite a story Sister Anne had to tell, and later I assumed the role of storyteller in relating these events to Grandma. She listened to every word I had to say with undivided attention.

Her final reaction was, "Mary, I had no idea our little Anne had to go through so much. It does my heart good to know what a strong girl she is. I went through a lot in my life, but I think she has gone through even more. I am very proud of her."

28

The acrid smell of pipe smoke greeted me as I came in the door from school on a cold winter day in the second term. I wiggled my nose in response to the pungent smell of tobacco as I looked at Grandma. She looked away and made no comment. Mother was busily occupied at the stove putting the finishing touches on supper.

"Who left the smell of tobacco in our house, Mother?" I asked.

"Oh," she replied, "James Ronald A. dropped in for a visit."

Well, that was interesting. James was the bard in our community, and people loved him. When he was not eloquently spinning a tale at a ceilidh, he was doing likewise in the home of some receptive Scot. Because he was such a skilled storyteller, he was welcome in every home, particularly during the long winter months when the seasonal work for the men was finished and they had time on their hands. With a dram of whiskey in his hand, he wiled away many an hour in front of a blazing fire on a cold winter day, spinning yarns for the menfolk.

James also had quite a reputation for being a lady's man. He was given to bestowing attention on the single women of our community. Combined with his silver tongue, he had a quick wit and a natural charm, which enabled him to carry off this gesture graciously. In fact, women were flattered by his attention. He had never visited our home when Father was alive, and so I was suspicious of his reasons for starting to come at this time. With the death of Father, Mother had once more joined the ranks of the single women and thereby became a candidate for his attention.

The one thing for which James did not seem to have a propensity was work. He was a man of about fifty years of age who still lived at home with his mother.

He was a free spirit. Mundane affairs relating to the everyday world of work were not of much interest to him. It was well known that often while his mother was out doing the barn work, he would be napping on the couch. He was a welsher, but you could not dislike him.

After Mother went out to the barn to finish her chores, I looked questioningly at Grandma and asked, "What was he doing here?"

She gave me a knowing look, as she replied, "Oh, he has been here quite a few times of late. He comes in the afternoon and he and Margaret have a good long chat over a hot cup of tea. He is very charming, you know."

I just raised my eyebrows and thought to myself, "If you say so." Then I asked, "And how long has this been going on?"

"For the last three or four weeks," she said. "He's here almost every day. Didn't you know that?"

"No, I didn't know that," I replied with some aggravation in my voice. "No doubt he comes while I am in school so as not to arouse my suspicions. He knows that I would see right through him."

I really didn't know what to make of the situation. On the one hand, it was nice of him to come and spend some time with Mother to help fill the void created by Father's death. On the other hand, I wondered if he saw our place as a good thing and if he was looking to his own welfare after his mother, a woman of more than seventy years of age and in poor health, passed on.

I was peeved. Then I thought to myself, "I know it is really none of my business. If he is good company for Mother and makes her happy, I have no objection. After all, the loss of Father put a big gap in her life, and he is helping to fill that gap. Now that Catherine and Anne are away, she could do with some additional companionship. And there is an added advantage. Since Mother started seeing James, she has spruced up her appearance. She let herself get a little dowdy looking after Father died. I suppose you would have to expect that of a woman who is going through a period of mourning. Now she has taken to putting her hair up in an attractive bun and to wearing her good dresses more frequently. This combined with her attention to improved posture has once more turned her into an attractive woman who looks younger than her years."

And in this manner I debated the pros and cons of the affair, as I tried to talk myself into coming to terms with it.

A few weeks later, I learned that Mother and James had taken to going for walks along the footpath through the woods.

This prompted Grandma to raise her eyebrows and say, "I think they may be getting serious."

Now this for me was a matter of concern. So long as James was an agreeable companion, I could accept that. But if he was beginning to pursue Mother, I had a problem. I thought again of his history with his own mother. While she was busy working her fingers to the bone on the farm, he was off storytelling, dancing, singing, and ingratiating himself to the ladies, and when he was not doing that, napping on the couch. His mother would soon not be able to provide for his keep. Very uncharitably, I again wondered if he saw my mother as his next meal ticket.

Well, regardless of what I thought, the relationship continued. James began to accompany Mother to the local ceilidhs. When he was not occupied with storytelling or singing, he was very attentive to her. When the fiddle music began, he would take her out on the floor to dance. He danced so beautifully that you could not help but notice. Tongues began to wag.

Mary Alex Dan from the next farm exclaimed, "Aye, your mother has a new man."

I gave her a withering look. I felt like telling her to hold her tongue, but I made myself withhold that biting comment. While James and Mother whirled around the floor, the women gave each other the eye. Again I bit my tongue and pretended I didn't notice. As I overheard the gossip, I noted that the opinions of the women on the affair were mixed. There were those who thought it was nice of James to provide Mother with some companionship. Then there were others who were concerned for my mother because they thought he was a gold digger. They were going through the same debate as I was. Some of them were even worried enough to seek me out and express their concerns to me. I tried to remain neutral, but in the end that proved to be impossible. The gossip in the community only added to my misgivings.

I could tell that Grandma was anxious. She shared her concern with me. "You know, Mary, I put up with that kind of relationship throughout my married life and I do not want to see Margaret make the same mistake."

I understood where she was coming from and I nodded in agreement.

"Unfortunately there is nothing much we can do about it, is there?" I added. "It is not our place to meddle. I am counting on Mother's usual ability to make good judgements."

"Let's hope," was Grandma's only response.

I tried to put this affair out of my mind. I continued to tell myself that mother's good judgement would carry the day. I was doing pretty well until one Friday afternoon when I was walking home from school earlier than usual, I saw the two of them walking arm in arm. That stopped me in my tracks.

"Well I'll be damned," I thought to myself. My less charitable side came to the fore. "That lecherous creature. He knows that if he moves into our house, Mother will look after him in the manner to which he has become accustomed. He is nothing but a damn freeloader."

These were pretty strong words, even if they were thought rather than spoken. Then, for the umpteenth time, I tried to tell myself that I had to put my anger aside and look at the other side of the story. I realized that what I thought really did not matter. After all, Mother was an adult, and as such, she was free to live her own life. I had no choice but to respect her decision, whatever that might be. And this realization made me bite my lip in anger. The truth of the matter is that I did not want that fellow anywhere near my mother or our home.

I raced into the house and I said to Grandma, "Do you see what is going on?"

She just looked at me and nodded her head.

As time passed, we were getting used to seeing Mother and James together. We were beginning to convince ourselves that our concerns were misplaced and that nothing would come of their relationship. How wrong we were. Just when our guard was down, the lightning bolt hit. At dinner that evening, Mother looked at us with a beaming smile as she announced that James had asked her to marry him. I was speechless. The announcement floored me.

"What did you say?" I asked, with a worried look on my face.

Mother, pretending not to notice, went on. "Oh, I told him that I need some time to think. You know, he is such a lovely, attentive, thoughtful man."

"Yes," I thought, "when he has something to gain from it. Where was his thoughtfulness when he was lying on the couch while his mother was doing the barn work."

"Is something bothering you?" Mother asked.

I guess she could read my thoughts in the expression on my face and I was embarrassed. She always had a keen ability to see right through me.

My cowardly reply was, "No, no, nothing."

I couldn't wait for Mother to go to the barn so Grandma and I could talk.

When she went out, I said to Grandma, "They sure fooled us. I never thought it would come to this. What do you make of it?" I asked.

To which she replied, "I don't know. I know that James is filling a void in her life. But, as I said before, once they get married, I fear he will become a burden to her. He is the nicest person, but while he is personable, charming, and eloquent, he is also shiftless. As I told you before, I lived through that kind of relationship and I would never want your mother to have to go through it. It is worrisome, isn't it."

"Well Grandma," I mused, "If they get married and he moves in here, I can get a little place in the community, and you can come and live with me."

"No, no, I could never think of leaving your mother," she said. "After all, I have been with her all her life. Furthermore, if things do not turn out well, I want to be there for her."

"I know, I know," I replied. "That suggestion was selfish of me. I was only thinking of both of us having an alternative to living in the same house with that fellow."

Well, time passed. We learned nothing more about the relationship. We did not know if Mother was going to agree to James' proposal and we did not ask. We only knew that the relationship continued. And with the passage of time my feelings on this matter did not subside. Every time I saw them together, my blood boiled. However, I did manage to maintain the good sense to keep my mouth shut. At bottom, I respected Mother too much to interfere in her life. I guess I was also steeling myself to the idea of having James around. I made a point of being more cheerful with Mother, partly to make her feel comfortable and partly to make up for the guilt I harboured for my negative feelings about her relationship with James.

I was miffed when Catherine Angus Ronald, one of our neighbours, flippantly asked if I teased Mother about her new man. The manner in which she asked the question reflected a certain amount of disrespect that I did not like. I hoped she would get the message when I told her that I respected Mother too much to even think of doing that.

Then one afternoon, after I had arrived home from school, and Mother and I were having a cup of tea, she said, "I have something to tell you."

I looked her in the eye without saying a word. "Here it is," I thought to myself, as I prepared to cope with whatever she had to say.

Then she carefully stated her case. "I have been thinking about my relationship with James for some time, and for me it has been a source of great joy. I have also had time to think about his proposal and I have come to a decision. I am not going to marry him. While I enjoy his company so much, I just do not see myself in another marriage. One marriage is enough for any woman."

I could not conjure up a comment that would not betray my relief; so I said nothing. Then, after the news had time to sink in, I decided to ask how James took her reply.

She thought for a moment and then she said, "As well as you could expect. James is a dear man and a gentleman, and I was very pleased at how respectful he was of my decision. When we had discussed the matter, he then asked if he could still come and have tea with me now and then. He said he enjoyed my company so much that he did not want to lose it. I think that was pretty decent of him."

I began to feel guilty about my negative attitude toward him, for it was not justified. Now I know that he had genuine feelings for Mother for, even though she rejected his proposal, he still wanted her companionship. And with the end of their affair, another traumatic chapter in our lives came to a close.

29

As winter passed into spring, the days became longer and warmer, the snow melted, and to my great delight, I was able to spend more time out of doors. On the first of May, I decided to forsake my time for preparation after school for a peaceful walk down by the ocean. The eerie quiet of an overcast day was disrupted only by the sound of the waves washing in on the shore and then back out to sea and the cry of the seagulls. I was enjoying the solitude when it was broken by the appearance of John.

"Can I walk with you?" he asked, knowing full well that I would be delighted to have his company.

He was such good company, and I looked forward to our time together. Our walk extended into the early evening. For a while we walked in silence.

Then John abruptly broke the silence when he turned to me and asked, "Mary, will you marry me?"

His question stopped me in my tracks. I wasn't expecting it; I wasn't ready for it. I turned to look at him and he put his arms around me, and neither of us said anything for a moment.

Then I gently pulled away from him and said, "John, your proposal takes me by surprise. I am so honoured, but I really don't know what to say. I need some time to think."

"Take all the time you want; I think you are worth waiting for," he said.

We put the question aside and again walked on in silence. And then we went our separate ways. It took a while for the question to sink in. And think about it I did. My heart and my head were in combat. I found myself caught in the horns of a dilemma. I thought of how much I enjoyed John's company. How thoughtful he was. How well he treated me. How good it felt being with him and being close to him. And most important of all, how much I loved him. Indeed there was much to recommend his proposal. But then I thought of Mother and how dependent she was on my help to maintain the homestead and on my emotional support. I felt I had to be there for her. Grandma was getting to the age where, instead of looking after people, she needed to be looked after, and Mother could not do everything alone.

And of no small consideration was how much I enjoyed my teaching. I think I was born to be a teacher; I loved every minute of it. It may sound selfish, but I had to admit that I would find it very hard to give up my beloved teaching. I knew full well that if I got married, the school trustees would take my job from me. In their eyes, the classroom was no place for a married woman. I have yet to figure out why married women are viewed to be unfit to be teachers. And so I mulled the up side and the down side of John's proposal and I still could not make up my mind. On the one hand, I weighed all the reasons why I could not marry John. On the other hand, I had to face the reality that I loved him and wanted to marry him. Why does life have to be so complicated?

A couple of weeks passed, and concern about the reputation of John's brothers weighed even more heavily on my mind. While they did not live at home, their visits were too frequent for my liking. After seeing James in action—and I understood that the other brothers were equally bad—I now knew that they were not only rowdy boys but also drunks. Living in John's home would put me in the path of destruction, and that very thought made me quiver with fear. Then and there I decided that I could not marry John.

It wasn't long before I began to have second thoughts about my decision. The arguments for marrying him once more raced through my mind. He was so good to me. He was such a delightful person. How could I hurt someone I loved so much? Why should I let fear of his brothers interfere with our lives? And in this manner I continued to agonize about the decision.

After a couple of weeks of indecision, I had to face the reality that I owed John an answer. Reluctantly I decided to tell him that I was not ready to get married at this time. That night I did not sleep a wink. I tossed and turned and, like a cyclop, I kept one eye open to look at the clock. The full moon, sitting in the crook formed by the branches of an old apple tree, shone brightly on my clock, which is on the windowsill in my bedroom, and by its light I was able to tell the time. Mercifully for me, morning finally came, and tired as I was, I was relieved to get up and go to work.

When I went down for breakfast, Mother asked, "Is there something wrong?"

I ignored the question as I thought to myself, "If you only knew."

It was not one of my better days in the classroom, but I got through it. When the school day was over, I was still nervous and fidgety. Because I could not concentrate, I decided to head out for a cold bracing walk on the shore. I needed the healing effect of the ocean air. The beauty and tranquillity of the landscape usually restored peace to my soul.

Just then I turned to see John walking toward me.

"Oh no," I thought, "I am not ready for this."

I could tell by the look on his face that there was something wrong.

He took me by the hand and said, "Mary, I might as well tell you right off; I have some bad news. There is serious trouble at home. Mother is critically ill. I had the doctor out to see her, and he says she had a severe heart attack and will not recover."

I turned to him and with deepest sympathy said, "John, that is just terrible. You cannot look after her alone, and at the same time, look after the farm. What are you going to do?"

"Well I guess that has been decided for me," he replied, with a tinge of bitterness in his voice. "My brothers have been nothing but trouble. James, the one you met when you came for dinner, arrived home to see Mother. Out of the blue, he informed me that he is going to take over the farm. Can you imagine the gall of him? He gave no consideration to the fact that I have spent my life improving the place. Apparently Father's will states that the farm will pass to me on the condition that I am married at the time of Mother's death. If I am not married, any son who is married can take over the farm. I was shocked. I couldn't help but think that Father must have been drunk when he made his will. What difference would my marital status make to my willingness to look after my mother and the farm? The thing that gets me is that when he was dying, it was me he asked to stay home and look after the farm and my mother. He made no such demands on my brothers. How fair is that?" he asked.

That was a rhetorical question; so I did not reply.

Then John continued. "My brother James never before showed any interest in the farm. He's been working in town since he was sixteen. James claims he is married. However, I know nothing of his marriage. I wonder if he has papers to back up his claim. After all the work I put into the damn place, this leaves me out in the cold. It is so unfair. It galls me that Father did not tell me that one of the conditions for taking over the farm is that I be married. He was drunk so often that he may not have remembered that requirement. To think that this happened while we are considering marriage. I have thought long and hard about my situation and I have decided that I have no choice but to get out. And I want to get out of here as quickly as possible. I have friends in Boston who will help me and I am going to go there and get a job."

Then he turned to me and said, "Mary, I am so sorry. I am afraid that this turn of events throws our plans for marriage up in the air. I would not even think of asking you to join me until I get established. Under these circumstances, I think we need to put off our decision regarding marriage for a while."

The news shocked me, and I just stood there in silence. In high school, I had learned that in Greek drama sometimes a conflict is resolved by an external mechanism known as *Deus ex machina,* God out of a machine, and I think that it applied in our case. I felt so sorry for John, but at the same time, I felt relief from the pressure of having to tell him that I was not yet ready to marry him. It was a stroke of fate that different circumstances put each of us in the same position.

I turned to John and said, "I think that your decision is better for both of us at this time."

We then hugged each other and that was the last time John and I walked the shore. I had a terribly empty feeling as I walked away.

The next day, John's brother James met me on the road to school and asked if he could talk to me.

Without waiting for a response, he scowled at me as he threatened, "Stay away from my brother. I'll be watching you. If I see you near him again, bad things are going to happen to you."

It took all the strength I had to give him a defiant look as I turned and walked away. I did not say a word. I was so terrified that I was trembling. No matter how hard I tried, I could not concentrate in school.

"Bad things are going to happen to you." Those words pierced me like a sword. They preoccupied my mind all day.

After school, I did not go for my usual walk. I went straight home. And believe me, I kept an eye for anyone who might be following me. I had never before felt unsafe while walking around Arisaig and now that had changed. I was so unnerved that I couldn't sleep that night. I didn't want to tell John about the threat. It was strange that James delivered the threat when the steps preliminary to marriage in the Catholic church take weeks and thus rule out a quick marriage. But considering the kind of person James is, he may not know too much about his church.

My mind was preoccupied with the distasteful thought of meeting James again. I just hoped that he would not come near me. I could not figure out how to enhance my safety. I usually walked to and from school alone. I also walked along the shore and through the woods alone, except when John kept me company. Either way I was vulnerable. So I decided to be brave—some would say foolish—and walk as I usually did and take my chances. Scared as I was, I didn't want anyone to know, particularly James. As I walked, I continued to have an awful feeling that someone was watching me.

I was quieter than usual and Grandma noticed. "What's wrong, lass?" she asked.

I just smiled and said, "Nothing."

She turned and looked at me, and I was relieved that she did not probe further. I did not want to discuss the matter.

This situation lasted for two weeks and it wore me down. I was nervous, irritable, fidgety and fatigued from want of sleep. I had a hard time going to sleep, and when I did, I had nightmares in which I sensed someone was following me. I often woke with a scream.

I overheard Mother and Grandma talking about me. "Did you hear her last night?" Mother asked.

Grandma replied, "How could I miss it. I wonder what is bothering her. I fear there is something terribly wrong. There is no point in asking her, because I know she won't tell us."

Mercifully, this reign of terror was relieved by the death of John's mother, for this event left James free and clear to take over the farm, and I was no longer a threat to his aspirations. Even though I never wanted to see James again, I had no choice but to go to the wake. Well, wouldn't you know it, the first person at the door was James. As I looked at the sneer on his face, I was again seized by fear. I told myself that this fear was irrational because I was now of no threat to him. So I braced myself, walked past him, and went directly to commiserate with John. John was delighted to see me and as we chatted, he said that he would walk back with me. The deep hurt had not subsided. He was still so upset with the turn of events that once again he talked about them all the way home.

Several times he repeated, "I have no idea what Father was thinking when he made his will."

He concluded with these words, "I now feel like a stranger in my own home."

I concurred with his view of the injustice of the situation. It was hard to say goodbye, but we had one parting moment together that will linger in our memories—maybe our last moment together. For sure we knew this was the last time we would see each other for some time.

John was so angry at the way his brother got control of the farm that he left for Boston the day after his mother was buried. He did not want anything more to do with his family. I was left with the nagging fear that I would never see him again. Distance can destroy a relationship.

In spite of all my indecision about marriage, it would take me a long time to get over John. I missed him terribly and doubted that I would ever meet another man whom I could love so much. I had never felt lonely before, but I felt lonely now. An emptiness filled my soul. As I mulled the situation over in my mind, I felt guilty about not telling John about my decision. On the other hand, circumstances made it unnecessary for me to do so. And, furthermore, because I loved John so much, I was glad to be able to avoid hurting him. He did not need to know. It was ironic that each of us came to the same decision for very different reasons. So with the end of spring, John was gone from the area and from my life, at least for a time.

30

After all the emotional turmoil, I was relieved when spring gave way to summer. I was really looking forward to some time away from school, some time to read, to think, to walk the shore, and to help Mother with the farm work. Above all, I needed time to heal my heart and to ponder my relationship with John. I needed someone to talk to, but it could not be Mother or Grandma.

When I got home, I found I had a note from Catherine. She informed me that her employer, Jean MacNeil, had given her money to come home for the entire month of July, while she and her family were at the shore on vacation. That was good news. I needed my sister; she was the one I could talk to. She would be a great distraction from my emotional pain. There were things I could discuss with her that I could not discuss with Mother or Grandma.

On July the first, Mother and I rode into town to meet Catherine. Mother was absolutely shocked to find her standing on the platform at the railway station surrounded by four men.

"Who are those men?" I asked.

With a broad smile and sparkling eyes, Mother turned to me and stated emphatically, "They are my brothers."

"Oh my God." That was all I could think of to say.

As Mother exclaimed, "I don't believe this," she ran joyously to her brothers and they hugged and cried.

Alex looked at his sister and said, "You have changed so much."

And she replied, "And so have you. What did you expect after all these years?"

And they both burst out laughing.

Then Mother exclaimed, "You have no idea how much joy you are going to bring to your mother."

Catherine and I stood aside to let the siblings enjoy their reunion. I had never met these men and so I decided to move forward to introduce myself. I didn't have to.

Mother intervened to say, "In all the excitement I forgot. This is my lovely daughter, Mary. She is the second coming of your mother."

Because to me these men were strangers, I didn't know how to greet them; so I simply nodded and gave them a warm smile.

After we had exchanged pleasantries, Alex said, "Let's get moving. I can't wait to see Mama."

Ronald, knowing we would not have room for the men in the wagon, arranged for a stagecoach to take them home. Catherine had a large suitcase and several boxes, which the men helped her to load onto the stagecoach.

As I muttered, "This is unbelievable," the three of us crawled into the front seat of the wagon and headed for home, followed by the stagecoach. The first thing I asked Catherine was how she got together with her uncles.

"Believe it or not, it was entirely by accident," she replied. "Ronald and Alex were visiting with their brothers in Boston and decided to go to the Down East Club to see if they would meet anyone from home. I saw these four older men standing on the sidelines of the dance floor, and because there was something familiar about them, I decided to go and introduce myself.

"When I told them who I was, John looked at me curiously as he said, 'Say that again.'

"When he knew he had heard what I said correctly, he exclaimed, 'Look at you. You are my sister's daughter.'

"And each of them hugged me. It was such a touching moment. You can imagine my surprise at finding out who they were. No wonder I thought they looked familiar.

"They kept looking at me, and finally John spoke up and said what they were all thinking, 'You look just like Margaret.'

"When I told them I was coming home at the end of June, then and there they decided they were coming with me. And John added, 'Our return to see Mama is long overdue.'"

And then Catherine shrugged her shoulders as she said, "And here we are. I can just see Grandma's face when we arrive."

We talked and laughed all the way home. As we drove into the yard, Grandma came out to greet us. She looked surprised and puzzled to see the stagecoach following our wagon. And that was nothing compared to her surprise when she saw her sons, who had been gone for so many years, get down from the stagecoach. As she limped toward them, they ran to her and they hugged and cried.

Through her tears, Grandma exclaimed, "I was so afraid I would never see you again. This is the best day of my life."

After dinner, Grandma and her family spent the rest of the evening talking. Catherine and I did all the work so that Grandma and Mother would be free to spend time with the men. You could see the delight in Grandma's eyes as they sat around the kitchen table together. Later we returned to the table with them. Curious as always, Grandma wanted to know everything about the lives of her sons in the States.

The next evening the boys decided to visit old friends in the community. That gave Catherine an opportunity to open the boxes and take out the finery she had bought for us in Boston.

"Wait till you see what I brought you," she said.

She pulled out beautiful summer dresses, blouses, fancy underwear, silk stockings, and fine gloves.

"Try this one on; try that one on," she urged as she raised each piece of clothing, and she went on and on in this vein until we had tried on every last piece of clothing.

After she had pulled the last item from the last box, she exclaimed, "Now you will be the best dressed women in Arisaig,"

And that comment made us burst out laughing, as Mother said, "It won't be hard for these clothes to compete with our homespuns."

I was very impressed by the quality of the products and by Catherine's good taste.

"Where did you get such beautiful clothes?" I asked.

"In the usual place," she replied. "You know that on my days off I go downtown to watch the sales and to scour Filene's Bargain Basement, and I am getting good at it."

This was a fun evening, and I really needed it. I knew Catherine would help me to get my life back on track.

The following evening, after the men had gone out again to visit the neighbours, the four of us lingered at the table with our tea, and the first thing Mother did was to ask Catherine to tell us what she did for pastime when she was not working. And in reply, Catherine elaborated on the information she had provided in her letters, but particularly for Mother, hearing it directly from her made it even more interesting.

"Each week on my day off, I go downtown to window shop and to browse through the big department stores. I never tire of doing that," she said enthusiastically. "You are probably wondering why I go so often. I regard shopping to be a form of recreation. It is a reprieve from being couped up in the house all day. So you see for me the stores are a place to go and shopping gives me something to do. I have never ceased to be amazed at what these stores have to offer. The products they have change frequently. Almost every time I go, I see something I have never seen before. As I told you in my letters, their clothes, their household linens, their house wares, and their furniture are a feast for the eyes. There is nothing like it around here. And then I discovered Filene's Bargain Basement. I have already described the buying frenzy that goes on in that store. The reason for this madness is that among the mass of clothing on sale in the bargain basement, there are some very good products at unbelievable prices. I shop slowly and carefully to make sure that I am selecting what I want and to make sure that each product is of good quality."

Catherine smiled as she said, "That is how I got most of the clothes I brought home in those boxes."

Then Mother asked, "How did you find this store?"

"It was my friend, Agnes, who introduced me to shopping downtown," Catherine replied. "I'll never forget the day we went on our first shopping expedition. I think Mary was with us at the time. Among the variety of stores and the variety of goods, I was like a kid in a candy shop. Agnes has good taste and she served as a very helpful and agreeable guide. And with her help I joined the pilgrimage of Highland women to these stores."

"Now what about your social life?" Mother asked.

I think she was fishing to find out if Catherine had a boyfriend. Catherine did not take the bait. In fact, she was so private that even I did not know if she had a boyfriend.

"Oh," Catherine replied, "the two are related. When I get tired of shopping, I go to a little tea room to get lunch. I vividly remember the first time Agnes and I went there. It was much more comfortable than the lunch counter at Macy's where I took Mary when we first went to Boston. It is small, and intimate, and quiet, and the service is excellent. We just went in and took a table, and a lovely waitress came over and asked what we wanted. We both ordered hot buttered scones with preserves and tea. The waitress was so kind and helpful that we felt very comfortable. She brought our order attractively laid out on a nice plate accompanied by a pot of hot tea, a jar of strawberry preserves, and a small pitcher of cream. I'll never forget how grand I felt as we slowly consumed our delicate pastries and drank our tea. It is so nice to be waited on instead of waiting on somebody else. Now I go there for lunch on every day I have off. It adds a real touch of luxury to my life."

And we all smiled as we shared her joy in the simple pleasures that made her happy.

Catherine also told us she quickly discovered that the tea room was a meeting place for girls from the East.

"On their days off, they flock there to have lunch or tea with their friends and to share the news from home," she said. "Like myself, they like to be waited on for a change. We are all made to feel so welcome. But most of all, we go there because we feel the need to be with our own kind. We always talk about our work. We share ideas about cooking and presenting food and interacting with our employers. We are close because we have so much in common.

"And is that all the social life you have?" Mother asked.

She was still fishing. At this point, Catherine gave her a questioning look. She didn't know whether her mother was being nosey or just enjoyed hearing the details of her life in Boston.

After a pause to think, Catherine reminded her mother that the people in Boston from the East have their own Down East Club to which they try to go once a week.

"But you already know that," Catherine said to make her point. "The atmosphere at the club is wonderful," she exclaimed joyously. "As I have told you before, we talk and we dance and we sing Highland Scottish songs. The stories told by the storytellers are similar to the ones we grew up listening to at home. We are all drawn together by the warmth and cheer of our Highland way of life. I have so much in common with those people that when I am with them, I feel at home."

Mother may not have gotten the information she was looking for, but she thoroughly enjoyed what Catherine had to say.

It meant so much to me to have Catherine home. After the trauma of the past months, it felt good to have someone to talk to. She and I were quickly becoming soul mates. We could share our innermost thoughts, secrets, hopes, and fears. I used to be able to do this with Anne, but since she went to the convent, we live in two different worlds. Sadly, we had lost the common bond we used to share.

Catherine and I decided to stand aside to leave Mother and Grandma to their family. The next evening, while we were having tea on the veranda, I poured out my soul to Catherine with the details of my breakup with John.

She was surprised. "You mean you turned down that wonderful man. I thought you two were inseparable," she exclaimed.

I raised my fingers to my lips to indicate to her to be quieter. This was the first time I had shared my trauma with anyone. I don't think Mother had any idea that John and I were so close and I figured it was better to leave it that way.

In answer to her question, I proceeded to tell Catherine about the dilemma I had faced: how, on the one hand, I dearly loved John, and on the other, how hard it would be to give up my beloved teaching to marry him. Then I explained how this dilemma was resolved by forces beyond our control: the death of John's mother and the passage of the farm to his no-good brother James, leaving John, who had looked after the farm and his mother since he was a boy, out in the cold.

Catherine intervened to ask, "Was that fair?"

"Fairness was not a consideration," I replied. "James knew what John did not know, that marriage was a condition for John to inherit the farm, and he took advantage of the situation. That was a terrible blow to John. So you see, he really had no choice but to get out. I feel so sorry for him—and I miss him so much."

Catherine looked at me as she said, "That must have been so galling. The old saying, 'You can choose your friends but you cannot choose your relatives' is sure appropriate in this case."

I agreed and then I added, "And what is even more galling is that James is nothing but a thug. And a drunk, just like his father before him. When I think of it now, the behaviour of the father and the son must have been a terrible burden for John and his mother. They suffered in silence. John said that when he gets settled in Boston, we can again think of marriage. While I am lonely without him, I think time apart is good for both of us so that we can sort things out."

Catherine then looked at me with grave concern on her face, as she said, "Mary, I had no idea you were going through such turmoil."

"Don't worry; I'll live," I replied with a thin smile.

This was Catherine's first trip back from Boston, and I noticed that she went to considerable lengths to relive the experience of home. I saw her go off by herself to walk along the shore where she used to walk. Other times I saw her walk along our familiar footpaths through the woods and up the hills to the berry patches we frequented. She took great delight in watching the white-tailed deer gracefully dance their way through our fields. It was as if she wanted to renew herself by re-experiencing the sights, the sounds, and the smells of home. It was also a time to revisit sad memories. Sometimes I saw her looking out the front window toward the area where father's body was found. She would stare but never say a word. Once I saw her go to the shore and stand at the spot where father's body had been recovered from the water. A haunting reminder of a sad part of her past. Her sense of loss reminded me of these words from one of Tennyson's poems I had read in high school:

But oh for the touch of a vanished hand

And the sound of a voice that is still.

Another evening, while Catherine and I were sitting alone on the veranda, Catherine turned to me and said, "Mary, now there is something I didn't tell you. You have gone through turmoil, and so have I. Most of my life in Boston has been good, but I went through a very bad patch."

I was surprised. "You didn't mention a word about that in your letters."

"I know," she replied. "The situation was so painful that I did not want to write about it."

Catherine then told of how the problem had started the previous fall when Jean and her family returned from vacation with her nephew, Ralph, for whom she had agreed to provide accommodations while he studied for his business degree at Boston College.

"When she introduced us," Catherine said, "I couldn't help but notice that he was full of himself. I soon learned that he was not to be trusted. The way he profusely thanked me when I waited on him put me off. While I would normally appreciate such thoughtfulness, I sensed there was something phony about the way he did it. It was almost as if he was making fun of me."

I intervened to say, "I hope you called him up short on that."

"No I didn't," Catherine replied. "I felt I was not in a position to do that. And so our conversations continued. "When I was working in the kitchen, he would often come and sit on a stool and talk while I worked. The way he stared at me, almost as if he could see through me, gave me the creeps. I felt as if I were naked in front of him. I sensed that he was paying too much attention to me for all the wrong reasons. I was wary of him."

At this point I asked, "Did Mrs MacNeil notice what was going on?"

"No she didn't," Catherine replied, and again she continued, "Because he made me so nervous, I felt the best thing to do was to keep him talking. He wanted to know all about my life back in Arisaig. And in turn I asked him to tell me about his life in Newport. It was obvious that he lacked for nothing. His people were wealthy; he really did not need to work; nor did he want to work. He made it clear he aspired to a life of leisure—to be the kind of guy he call a playboy. But his father wanted him to go to college so that he would be prepared to carry on the family business."

Her description of Ralph made me feel compelled to interrupt to say, "He was a spoiled brat."

Catherine nodded in agreement and then told of how her uneasiness with him increased.

"I didn't know what to do," she said. "I never wanted to see him again, but I had no choice. Jean continued not to notice, and I didn't say a word. I felt that conveying my suspicions to her might not sound right."

"Yes, now that I think about it, you didn't have much choice," I conceded.

"You are probably right, but let me tell you, I paid a high price for doing nothing," Catherine replied.

"Well," she continued, "the situation got worse rather than better. Sometimes at meals I caught him giving me the eye. Then very abruptly one evening he asked me to go out with him. I was really taken by surprise. I refused because, as I told him, I was a servant in his household and I didn't think Mrs. MacNeil would look kindly on our dating. He shrugged off what I had to say. He said the fact I was a servant should not matter. 'Well I think it does,' I replied. As time went on, my discomfort in his presence increased. And he continued to give me the eye in his evil sort of way. To me he was poison. I began to hate him. I longed for the end of the academic year when he would go home and I would be rid of him."

"Catherine, this put you under terrible stress," I suggested.

Then Catherine began to cry. "You haven't heard the worst of it," she said through her tears. "One evening after the MacNeils went out, he came to the kitchen to talk while I was having dinner. He was unusually charming and personable, in his phony sort of way, but again, I was wary of him. When I finished, he said he was going to his room to study. I breathed a sigh of relief. I was tired; so as soon as I finished my work, I went to my room and went to bed. I was just falling asleep when I heard the room door open. It was Ralph. I was taken by surprise. Before I got up the courage to say anything, he came and sat on my bed. I told him I didn't think he should be in my room. 'Oh,' he said, sarcastically, 'You make too much of the social differences between us. Me, I believe in equality.'"

At this point, the memories moved Catherine to cry so hard she couldn't talk.

When she was able to pull herself together, she continued, "Then he bent over and tried to kiss me. I abruptly pushed him away, but the first thing I knew, he was on top of me. He tried to strip off my night wear. I couldn't believe what was happening to me."

"Oh Catherine, I am so sorry," I exclaimed.

"There is more," Catherine said.

And then these horrible memories brought more tears. I reached for her hand. She held my hand tightly to help her to get the courage to finish her story.

Through her tears she said, "He tried to rape me. That is exactly what he did. But I was able to muster all my strength and push him and kick him in the groin. As he shrieked in pain, I jumped out of bed and screamed at him to get out. He ran to his room."

"Good for you," I exclaimed.

"I was hysterical with fear," Catherine said. "I knew that I had to get out of that place. I packed my belongings in a hurry and as I was racing down the stairs, the MacNeils returned. When Jean saw me crying, she asked what was wrong. Through my sobs I told her that I could not work for her any longer. They were so shocked that they just stood there speechless as I ran out the door and down the street to get a late train that would take me close to Agnes' place."

"Weren't you afraid to be out alone at night?" I asked.

"I was so upset I didn't even think of that," Catherine replied. "Fortunately, I got to Agnes' place safe and sound, and needless to say, she was surprised to see me arrive so late at night.

"'What are you doing out at this hour?' she asked.

"Then she looked at me and when she saw that I was crying, she asked, 'Oh, Oh, what happened? What's wrong?'

"I poured out my soul to her. I told her how afraid I was of Ralph. How afraid I was that he might come after me. I concluded my tale of woe by saying, 'I think I have to go home.'

"Agnes cautioned me to think very carefully about my decision. Then she made a curious remark, 'You know, you can never really go home.'

"I asked, 'What do you mean?'

"Well, she replied, 'It's like this. Once we achieve the degree of independence we now enjoy, we can never go back to being dependent on our families.'

"And our conversation went back and forth all night. I was too nerved up to even try to sleep. The first thing I did in the morning was to call the departure lounge at the port of Boston to get information about the boat schedule for Nova Scotia. The decision to go home grieved me. I had such a good life there in Boston and I resented having to give it up. What Agnes said about not being able to go home lingered in my mind. I began to wonder if I was just running away."

"Were you seriously considering coming home?" I asked.

"At that time I really was, but I changed my mind in the morning," Catherine replied. "When Agnes went to work, I locked the door and in my exhaustion I fell into a deep sleep. After several hours, I was awakened by a knock on the door. I was afraid. I thought it might be Ralph. I did not answer. I remained alert but very quiet. The knocking continued, and I noticed that it was a gentle rather than a persistent knock. So I got brave enough to ask, 'Who is it?'

"'It's me, Jean. Please let me in,' she pleaded.

"I opened the door, and she came in and put her arms around me. She apologized profusely for what happened. She told me that she and her husband tried to talk to Ralph, but they didn't get anywhere with him. However, they figured out what he had done and decided to ship him back to his parents immediately.

"'We will never allow that fellow to stay with us again. I thought he was just a spoiled brat; now I know he is dangerous and I want nothing more to do with him,' she said emphatically.

"Jean told me that he was not doing very well in college and so there was nothing for him to lose academically by going home. She begged me to come back and assured me that this sort of thing would never happen again. I thanked her for being understanding and told her that I would think about her offer. That evening, I discussed the situation with Agnes, and she persuaded me to return to my job."

I continued to be surprised by what Catherine had told me. "I had no idea what you were going through," I said. "I am so glad that you were able to get beyond it, and all on your own at that. I am very impressed."

Thinking of Catherine and Anne and myself, I added, "We never know what the slings and arrows of fortune have in store for us, do we?"

"Now there was another trauma in our family that you did not know about," I told Catherine.

"Good Lord, what else could there be?" Catherine said.

Then I started to tell her about Mother's boyfriend.

"You are not serious," she said laughing.

"Oh yes I am," I said. "James, the bard, befriended her and he began to spend a great deal of time at our place. Then he took to dancing with her at the local ceilidhs, and you should have seen the women give each other the eye. Mother and James were the talk of the community."

"And you didn't tell me a word about this," Catherine exclaimed.

Mary replied, "At the time I was so angry that I thought it better not to discuss the topic. I thought he was a freeloader who saw our home as his next meal ticket. He even went so far as to give mother the ring."

Catherine said, "Noo, this story gets better as it goes along. Obviously, Mother did not accept his marriage proposal. What happened?"

And Mary replied, "Mother had the good sense to say no. She has more commonsense than the two of us put together. I must admit that after they broke up, I felt very guilty about the misgivings I had about both of them."

And we just looked at each other and laughed.

"The things I didn't know," Catherine added, as she shook her head in disbelief.

31

July marked a very important milestone in the life of our family. After Sister Anne had completed her nursing program, she returned to Antigonish to be a nursing sister in the hospital that had recently opened in town. The whole family was invited to a mass to be held in the chapel of St. Francis Xavier College to honour the graduating nursing sisters. The mass was to be followed by a dinner for the graduates and their families.

We were delighted that Catherine was home for the occasion. It was important for our entire family to be there. Even though Grandma was frail, she desperately wanted to attend the ceremony. Her sons expressed concern about her making the trip. Alex said that they were alarmed by how old and frail she looked.

To their expressions of concern, I replied, "You have to remember that your mother is an old lady. You think of her as she was on the day you left, but that was decades ago. She has had a hard life, and time has taken its toll on her. And yet, for a woman of her age, she is truly remarkable."

Then I reminded them, "Grandma has been with us throughout our lives and since she is so close to each of us, it is very important for her to be at the celebration. If she wants to go, she goes. And, furthermore, with her determination, do you really think you could stop her?"

This comment evoked a laugh.

Grandma's sons were due to return to the United States the day after the mass honouring the graduates in nursing. So this was our last night to sit around the table together. The boys decided to have a few drinks, which made them talkative.

In the course of our conversation, we learned a great deal about their lives that they had not included in their letters.

"Is it true that you went back into farming?" I asked Ronald and Hugh.

With an embarrassed look on his face, Ronald replied, "Yes we did. We both have huge ranches on the frontier of Montana. I must admit that we were too ashamed to tell you."

Remembering well the boys feelings about farm work, Mother exclaimed, "It seems strange to me that you went back to farming after complaining so much about farm work here in Arisaig."

Her reaction was greeted with some embarrassment, and they both had sheepish grins on their faces.

Hugh tried to make some sense of what they did by saying, "You have to remember that farming was the only life we knew outside of gold mining."

Ronald then made the point that their ranches were very different from our farm. He told of the thousands of acres of land and the hundreds of beef cattle each of them owned.

With pride shining in his eyes he said, "I just wish you could see our homesteads. Our land extends as far as the eye can see. The western boundary is formed by the Rocky Mountains. As I ride toward the west in the evening, it is awesome to watch the sun going down behind the snow-capped mountains. That has to be one of the most beautiful sights on earth."

Then Hugh told of how they managed their herds with the help of cowboys.

He said, "These men do most of the work involved in looking after the cattle: keeping them from being stolen or roaming away from our land, looking after their feeding and their health, and helping us to bring them to market."

Then he looked at Grandma as he said, "I just wish you could see a cattle drive. When we take the cattle to market, hundreds of them travel together. Sometimes we move as many as four hundred cattle at once. When that many cattle start to run, we can feel the earth moving under their feet."

Grandma just shook her head in disbelief. It was moving to see how much she enjoyed her sons' stories.

Hugh wanted to express some words of reassurance to his mother.

He said, "Mama, I want you to know we make a good living. And believe it or not, it is easier to look after a large herd than a small herd. Because of our hired help, we are able to be away from our ranches for this visit. Things have been going so well for us that, even though we are getting older, we both plan to enlarge our herds. Now we spend our time managing the ranches while the hired hands do the work. If you could see our ranches, you would be very proud of us."

Amazement at the size of their spreads prompted Margaret to suggest, "If your ranches are so large, you can't have many friends or neighbours."

Ronald affirmed what she said. "That's right. The size and location of our ranches keeps us isolated. The nearest town is forty miles away. We don't get there very often. The isolation is probably the reason why we are not married. There aren't too many women around the frontier—except in the saloons! Being very busy helps to keep us from being lonely."

John and Alex then talked about their lives in Boston. John hastened to point out that he and Alex also lived well. He then described their jobs as foremen on the docks.

He said, "Instead of doing back-breaking work, it is our job is to see that it gets done: that we have a full supply of workers for each shift, that the containers get unloaded, that the containers to be shipped out get loaded, that the goods are sent to their destinations."

Mother spoke up, "That sounds like an easy job."

Alex and John laughed.

Then Alex replied, "Yes it does until you learn what it is like to deal with dockworkers. Most are fine men who are breaking their backs to earn a living. And then there are the rest: laggards who pretend to work, thieves who try to steal the company blind, and thugs who would beat you up with little or no provocation. We have to be prepared to deal with those kinds of people every day. When our work gets dangerous, we call the cops."

Ronald commented, "I'll bet some of the cops are as crooked as the thieves."

"It is even worse than that," John replied. "Some of them are actually in cahoots with the thieves. We sit back and watch. We soon learn who is honest and who is not. It is very difficult to deal with crooked cops. If you are too hard on them, they will threaten to beat you or arrest you on trumped-up charges. Over the years, we have been able to establish that we cannot be intimidated. That was not easy. We were tested many times, and believe me, we were scared. If we didn't stand our ground, the low life would have run all over us. Eventually the thugs and the thieves and the crooked cops learned to do their dirty work elsewhere on the docks."

Alex talked of how they learned how things were done on the docks when they first went there looking for work.

"Lord knows, we had plenty of time to learn," he said. "As we stood in line day after day waiting to be picked for work, we saw first hand the ugly side of life on the docks. When John and I were threatened, we stood together, and our size and determination scared off the thugs. We were scared, but we knew better than to look scared."

Grandma wanted to learn more about their wives and children. It turned out that John and Alex had both met their wives at the Down East Club.

John had a twinkle in his eye as he said, "The Down East Club is a great place to meet girls. That is why we used to go there every week."

John then told a bit more about their families. Their wives were friends who came to Boston from Judique and they are still friends.

Then, with with a look of pride on his face, he said, "I already told you that our sons have graduated from Boston College, and we are very proud of them. All four are now businessmen in the city. Some day I hope I can take them home. As you can tell, the lives of both of our families are very similar."

You had only to look at Grandma's face to see how pleased she was to hear of the progress of her boys.

Then, for the rest of the evening, the boys continued sharing stories about their work, their homes, and in the case of Alex and John, their wives and sons. Our delightful gathering only broke up when Grandma announced it was time for all of us to go to bed. I noted that she looked unusually pale and tired.

On the ride over the mountain the next morning to the chapel at St. Francis Xavier College, we could tell that every bone in Grandma's body ached as the wagon moved up and down on the rutted road. We could see the pain in her face, but she did not complain.

When we arrived at the convent, she made this boast: "I am so proud of my granddaughters. Each of you grew up to become an independent woman. You have continued our pioneer tradition of striving to achieve a better life, and each of you in your own way has been successful. And I am so proud of Sister Anne on this day. To think that she is both a member of a religious community and a profession."

She said nothing more, but this thought made her smile of satisfaction linger.

We reached the convent just before the mass was to begin and we were escorted into the chapel. We sat in the back pew and listened to quiet organ music while we waited for the ceremony to begin. At two o'clock, Sister Anne and fifteen other sisters walked down the isle two by two and took their place of honour in the chapel. It was a moving ceremony. Bishop Cameron celebrated mass, and in his homily, he paid tribute to the nursing sisters for their contribution to religious life and to the nursing profession. I kept thinking of how proud Father would be of his daughter if he were here today.

Triumphal organ music played as the sisters came down the isle when the ceremony was over. Sister Anne was so overjoyed to see us that she raced to give each of us a warm hug. We then joined the relatives of the other nursing sisters in the college dining room for a meal to celebrate the occasion.

When the time came to part, Grandma lingered a little longer than the rest of us with Sister Anne. From the tears in her eyes, I could tell she was having a very hard time trying to tear herself away from Sister Anne. When the two finally parted, we noted that Grandma walked very slowly to the front door where we were waiting.

Mother commented, "My, she looks frail today."

Mother and I helped her into the wagon. We drove home in silence, with many thoughts of the day's events running through our minds. As soon as we got there, Grandma informed us that the trip had taken a lot out of her and that she was heading for bed. Because she was weary from the trip and obviously very shaky, Catherine and I helped her up the stairs to her room.

Her frailty prompted Catherine to ask, "I wonder if she is well?"

Several hours passed, and we did not hear her make a sound. When she did not come down for supper, we became concerned, and Mother went up stairs to look in on her.

Mother was disturbed to find that she was conscious but not responding. She came to the top of the stairs and motioned to us to come. We hurried to Grandma's room and hovered around her bed. She did not speak. Her only gesture was to take Mother's extended hand. Then she closed her eyes. We found ourselves suddenly faced with the stark reality that Grandma was dying. And with tears streaming down our cheeks, we all began to pray. It was only a moment before Grandma stopped breathing. She passed away peacefully, surrounded by her entire family. I thought it was a stroke of fate that all her children were with her when she died.

I don't know if anyone is ever prepared for the death of a loved one, but we were totally unprepared for Grandma's death. A strong bond had been rent asunder, and I felt a wrenching ache in my heart. We had lost the woman who was the glue that held together the different generations of our family. I stood in silence as I continued to think of what a terrible loss her passing was.

A flood of memories raced through my mind. I remember how, as a child, this woman held my hand as she opened my eyes to the beauty of the landscape on our frequent walks along the shore. How deeply both of us were in communion with nature. How special that made me feel. I remember how joyously she celebrated each festive occasion with us. I remember how she taught me to cherish learning and how much that influenced my life. I remember how she always had a story from the past to put each family crisis in perspective. I remember how soulfully she narrated the history of our family in the Highlands and here in Nova Scotia.

Farewell Grandma. You taught us well. It is so important to remember.

Teresa MacIsaac

Teresa MacIsaac is fortunate to have grown up in a family of Highland Scottish descent, who perpetuated the traditional Highland way of life. Hers was a family in which stories about their Highland past were told and retold, and in which the traditional household arts remained central to the production of food and clothing. Fond memories of these traditions gave rise to her desire to learn more about her forebears. To this end, she reviewed a large collection of documents pertaining to the Highland tradition. She supplemented information from these sources by conducting interviews with approximately 100 people of Highland descent. Their moving stories, and the heartfelt manner in which they were told, led MacIsaac to believe that a work of literature would be the most effective vehicle for capturing the power and drama of their experiences, the values of the Highland folk culture, and the character of the Highland people.

These sentiments gave rise to HIGHLAND STORYTELLERS. Her research into the Highland tradition also resulted in the publication of a history, entitled A BETTER LIFE: A PORTRAIT OF HIGHLAND WOMEN IN NOVA SCOTIA. In relation to this work, MacIsaac has made a number of television appearances, and one of several presentations on a DVD, entitled HIGHLAND CARAVAN, produced to celebrate the 150th anniversary of the Antigonish Highland Games, the oldest Highland Games in North America.

CPSIA information can be obtained
at www.ICGtesting.com
Printed in the USA
LVOW02s0501241115
463818LV00009B/52/P